EBURY PRESS

OPERATION SUDARSHAN CHAKRA

Born in 1960, Prabhakar Aloka grew up in Bihar. He is a postgraduate from Delhi University. He joined the Indian Police Service in 1986 and was allotted the erstwhile Andhra Pradesh cadre. After a brief stint in the state, he joined the Intelligence Bureau, India's premier intelligence agency with over 125 years of history. In nearly three decades of service in the IB, he was rigorously trained in covert operations. The fiction he writes reflects his extensive experience.

OPERATION
SUDARSHAN CHAKRA

The much-awaited sequel to *OPERATION HAYGREEVA*

PRABHAKAR ALOKA

EBURY
PRESS

An imprint of Penguin Random House

EBURY PRESS

USA | Canada | UK | Ireland | Australia
New Zealand | India | South Africa | China

Ebury Press is part of the Penguin Random House group of companies
whose addresses can be found at global.penguinrandomhouse.com

Published by Penguin Random House India Pvt. Ltd
4th Floor, Capital Tower 1, MG Road,
Gurugram 122 002, Haryana, India

First published in Ebury Press by Penguin Random House India 2022

ISBN 9780143454427

Typeset in Bembo Std by Manipal Technologies Limited, Manipal

www.penguin.co.in

To my wife and children,
For enduring my idiosyncrasies

To my friends,
For exposing me to art, culture and camaraderie

And
To my Labrador pup,
For his unwavering faith in me and his unconditional love

Mission Statement of a Spy

परित्राणाय साधूनां विनाशाय च दुष्कृताम् ।

(To protect the virtuous and to annihilate the wicked)

—*Bhagavad Gita, 4.8*

Prologue

To those looking in from the outside, it might seem to be like any other morning at the residence of Ravi Kumar, the head of the Central Counterterrorism Command, C3, of the Intelligence Bureau (IB). It is 7.30 a.m., and Ravi has just returned from his morning walk. As always, breakfast has been laid out on the dining table along with the morning newspapers. Everything, it would seem, is as it has always been. Except for one not exactly minor detail, the significance of which can be fully grasped only by those who really know Ravi and the inner dynamics of his family. Breakfast has been laid out not by Rita, as she has done every single day for as long as they have been married—except on weekends and public holidays, of course, when it is Ravi's turn—but by the cook, part of an entourage of newly appointed servants. It isn't just that. Rita isn't even going to be eating breakfast with her husband. She lies in the bedroom, confined to her bed, feeling listless and sapped of all energy and zest. There have been moments in between where she has felt better, but for the most part of the last few months, she has been this way.

The doctors diagnosed her with post-traumatic stress disorder, but it is hard to pinpoint what exactly brought it on. The timing certainly wasn't a coincidence. It was soon after they had returned from their vacation in Manali that she had suffered her first breakdown. When they'd embarked on that vacation, it had seemed to them that the Central Bureau of Investigation (CBI) inquiry into the botched-up police operation was a distant nightmare they could forget all about, but upon their return, they had found that the worst was yet to come. With the frenzy surrounding the general election hitting a feverish peak, the death of journalist Jagriti Saha in that police action had been raked up again. And with that, Ravi had found himself yet again at the centre of a political storm, having even been forced to spend a few days in custody. He had come out of it with his name cleared, but he hadn't come out unscathed.

Or at least, Rita hadn't.

She had always believed that the nature of her husband's job, fundamentally concerned with matters of national security, was such that its ambit lay above the murky machinations of partisan politics. In completely discarding this firmly held conviction, the episode had, in effect, shaken the roots of her guarded existence. And although Praja Prabhutva Party had recently swept the elections and its leader Kishan Jadhav, the new prime minister, had taken the unusual step of singling out Ravi for praise and describing him as the unfortunate and most ill-deserving victim of a political witch-hunt, the demons that haunted Rita hadn't been laid to rest.

She now lives in a state of perpetual paranoia, constantly worrying that her husband might be hauled up any moment.

To make matters worse, there is malicious gossip flooding Lutyens's Delhi that she has to contend with. Speculation is rife that the whole thing was orchestrated by Ravi in collusion with Jadhav to give the latter an advantage in the elections, and in return, Ravi would be made chief of the IB, or perhaps even the national security adviser.

The only way she can bring herself to shed these worries is if Ravi were to take voluntary retirement almost five years before the scheduled date. But quitting is the last thing Ravi will consider. Although C3 has for all practical purposes neutralized the Lashkar-e-Hind's (LeH's) operations in India, the fact that its leader Tabrez had managed to escape constantly gnaws on Ravi's mind. Besides, he knows for a fact, from months of interrogation, that there are still sleeper cells across the country waiting to be activated. That being the case, taking early retirement is a thoroughly unacceptable proposition. It isn't the case that Ravi is insensitive to the worries plaguing his wife. He has been affected by her drastic deterioration more than anyone else. It saddens him no end seeing her in her current state. And he has, in fact, taken the unprecedented step—for an officer of his rank and position— of spending most of his time at home, tending to her needs over the last few months.

As a natural consequence of this, the functioning of C3 has been affected. Working from home is something tech executives might successfully pull off, not the head of India's premier counterterrorism agency. Sarita Sanyal, the chief of IB, has been sympathetic to Ravi's travails and has fended off constant attempts by Anil, her second in command, to take over the agency using the pretext of Ravi's lack of attention.

A week ago, Anil had suggested to Sarita that she had to take a clear decision. Either she called Ravi back to work in a full-time capacity, or directed him to go on long leave, effectively ceding his position as head of C3. The latter was not something Sarita was prepared to allow, given that Ravi was hand-picked by her to neutralize the terrorist module involved in the Mumbai train blast and her selection was endorsed by higher-ups, including the prime minister. She had stepped in and ensured that there would be round-the-clock assistance for Rita, so that Ravi could resume his duties full-time. Somewhere deep inside, Rita knew just as well that it could not go on like this. She had tried her best to pull herself up and return to her earlier self. But she just couldn't. Nevertheless, she assured Ravi that she would be able to manage with all the help around the house, and that he could go back to work.

Ravi feels torn inside as he prepares to go back to headquarters for the first time in several months. On the one hand, he is eager to return to the helm and finish the task he had set out to do over a year ago. On the other, he feels a strange sense of guilt—despite her assurances to the contrary—over having to entrust the care of his fragile wife to virtual strangers. It is with mixed emotions churning inside that he bids goodbye to his wife, issues precise instructions to the help—for the tenth time or so—and gets into his waiting car.

* * *

The mood inside Ravi's office is somewhat sombre. While Mihir Kaul, Jose Cherian and Cyrus Bandookwala, young recruits and key members of Ravi's team, are excited to welcome their boss after the long hiatus, they are equally anxious, knowing fully well just how much he has endured in the last few months. It isn't that they have escaped unscathed either. Their losses, as a consequence of the CBI fiasco following the botched up anti-terrorist operation in which Jagriti Saha was killed, have been even graver. Mihir's mother, Janaki Kaul, had succumbed to a lonely death after suffering a second stroke, even as Mihir was in the custody of the CBI. Gehna, the journalist girlfriend of Cyrus, had never managed to shake off the suspicion that her boyfriend had played a role in the killing of her idol Jagriti Saha, and had broken off their engagement. These officers had taken the last few months off to grieve and take stock of their lives. That notwithstanding, they feel deeply troubled by the fact that their boss too has had to bear the brunt. In their minds, he is, after all, somebody immune to the worldly considerations that bother mere mortals.

As he walks into the office, Ravi can immediately sense their anxiety. The uneasy quiet that punctuates the air is of a different order than the one that he is accustomed to. In typical fashion, he breaks the silence, 'Good news is, we're all alive and still have our jobs. Bad news is, there's a lot of work to be done.'

The team nods awkwardly.

'Jose, you're the only one who's been coming to work. Understandably enough, because you're the only one amongst us with no personal life to speak of. How's work on that programme coming along?'

Jose responds with a sheepish grin, 'It's coming along quite well, sir. I have a prototype ready for demonstration, but it will take at least a couple of weeks before it can be deployed.'

'What programme?' Cyrus asks.

'I hope you haven't forgotten the rules, mister jilted Romeo. You will know when you need to know,' Ravi shoots back.

In ordinary circumstances, Cyrus would have taken offence at Ravi taking a casual dig at the heartbreaking failure of his relationship. But this time, he smiles. It is comforting to know that Ravi's sense of humour has remained intact, despite everything.

'I'm sorry sir . . .'

'Don't be sorry. You'll know about the programme soon enough,' Ravi responds, before turning to Mihir. 'I have two words for you—Spa Maid. Let us not forget that she is possibly the senior-most functionary of the Lashkar-e-Hind still out there in this country. We still do not have enough to bring her in, and even if we did, it would achieve little. I want you to re-establish contact with her and cultivate her.'

Mihir nods. If there is one thing that can help take his mind off the tragic death of his mother, it is work.

'And you, Cyrus,' Ravi starts, before pausing to catch his breath. He stubs his cigarette, reaches out for the glass of water on his table and gulps it in one go. Something seems to be off, and Mihir, as always, is the first to notice.

'Is everything all right, sir?'

Clutching at the left side of his chest, Ravi responds in an unnervingly casual tone, 'I'm feeling uneasy.'

For a moment, the others aren't entirely sure if Ravi is simply pulling their leg. It doesn't help when Ravi, sensing the panic in the air, tries to underplay the distress he is in by suggesting to the others that it might just be a bad case of indigestion. Not wanting to take any chances, given how their luck has panned out in recent months, Cyrus picks up the phone and calls up Dr Himwal, the resident medical officer at the headquarters. As they wait for him to arrive, Ravi tries to calm the situation by claiming that he is feeling perfectly all right. But every now and then, his face contorts itself, almost involuntarily, into a particularly unnerving grimace.

Upon arriving, Dr Himwal, a veteran doctor with a distinguished military career behind him—and therefore, enough experience in dealing with patients unwilling to display the full gravity of their discomfort—can tell from one look that something isn't quite right. He checks Ravi's blood pressure and pulse and finds that they are unusually elevated. He reaches into his bag and fishes out a tablet for chest pain. After almost forcefully inserting it into Ravi's mouth, he rushes out of the room and bolts down the corridor towards Sarita's office.

She is in a meeting, and a peon stops him in his tracks. But Dr Himwal has no time to explain and simply barges into the office. From the abrupt urgency of his arrival, Sarita knows immediately that it is a serious matter. He explains to her in one breath that Ravi has most likely suffered a heart attack—possibly multiple heart attacks—and must be urgently taken to a hospital. Sarita rushes out and hastily strides towards Ravi's office before suddenly stopping in her tracks. She turns back and returns to her office. Picking up the phone, she dials Dr Khirsagar, the head of the cardiology department at Ram Manohar Lohia hospital and apprises him of the situation. After quickly conferring with Dr Himwal, Sarita decides it would be best not to wait for an ambulance. Ravi, whose distress is growing by the minute and who is unable to coherently articulate his thoughts, is shifted into Sarita's car and driven to the hospital with two police vehicles leading the way and clearing traffic. By the time they reach the hospital, all arrangements are already in place, and Ravi is immediately taken in for a detailed assessment, personally supervised by Dr Khirsagar.

Sarita and the trio wait outside the examination room with bated breath, each of them uttering silent prayers. After what seems to them like an eternity, the doctor finally emerges, bearing a clutch of reports in his hand.

'There's good news, and there's bad news,' Dr Khirsagar tells them, 'and I'll start with the bad news. Ravi suffered a very serious cardiac event, something that is commonly referred to as a widow-maker heart attack. I don't think I need to explain why it's called that. But to put it plainly, he has developed a near-total blockage in the left main artery.'

'And what's the good news, doctor?' Sarita is quick to ask.

'The good news is that he's been brought here just in time. If we operate immediately, we should be able to reverse the damage and save his life. I've already asked my team to prep him for surgery. It might be a slightly rough road to recovery, but he's going to be all right.'

The group heaves a sigh of relief.

'I wonder why doctors never start with the good news, like Ravi sir does?' Cyrus whispers to Mihir.

'Please go ahead immediately, doctor. Whatever it takes, please proceed without hesitation. I do not have to explain to you just how valuable his life is,' Sarita tells him.

'I understand, you do not have to explain that to me. But as you would imagine, a procedure of this nature entails significant risks and we cannot proceed without having an immediate family member give their consent in writing,' Dr Khirsagar replies, even as he glances at his watch.

'I'm afraid that's a tricky ask, doctor. His wife is incapacitated for the moment, and news of this might severely worsen her condition. It will have to be broken to her very deftly, and right now we don't have the time for it. Please go ahead and operate immediately,' Sarita tells him.

'I'm terribly sorry, but in principle, I cannot, ma'am. It's a legally precarious situation . . .'

'When I ask you to set aside protocol and operate immediately, please rest assured that I'm speaking on behalf of the prime minister himself, no less. I'll take care of everything. Please,' Sarita tells him.

'Very well, then. We'll get started immediately,' Dr Khirsagar tells her, before darting off towards the operating theatre.

As soon as he's gone, Sarita turns towards the others, 'You three . . .'

'Yes, ma'am,' they respond in unison.

'Stay here and keep me posted. I'll have to go over to Ravi's place immediately.'

Rudderless Boat

Despite being based out of Delhi, Mihir had been forced to live separately from his mother and grandmother for several years. It was the only way he could have kept his profession a secret from them. After the brutal assassination of his father, a decorated IB officer, by Kashmiri terrorists, Janki had made Mihir promise that he would not join his father's profession. Mihir had maintained that he was working as a marketing executive in one of the MNCs. When his cover was finally blown, the weight of the revelation had been so severe that his mother succumbed to a fatal stroke. Not long after, his grandmother too had given up on life, passing away quietly in her sleep.

The tragic irony of his fate isn't entirely lost on him.

Every single morning, he is reminded of it when he wakes up in his mother's house, only to realize that his beloved *maauji* and *daad* are no longer with him. But Mihir isn't the sort to wallow too long in these inescapably grim realities of life. He is determined to ensure that even after all that's happened, the choices he has made have been worthwhile. As Ravi had so bluntly reminded them all, the mission that had brought them together was still significantly unfinished. The threat they had staked their lives to neutralize, still loomed large, even if only at a distance.

But now, when Mihir and the others need Ravi's direction and counsel more than ever before, he isn't around. The surgery had gone well, but for Ravi to recuperate fully, the doctors had insisted that it was essential that he rested completely for at least a month. He was still available over the phone, but Sarita had ruled that he was to be contacted only for very critical decisions.

It isn't exactly the case that she trusts the boys to do the right thing. She knows all too well that they still have a long way to go before they can be trusted to independently handle the fast and fluid chaos of the intelligence world. Rather, she trusts the grounding Ravi has given them. At the very least, they can be counted upon to not do the wrong thing.

That's exactly what plays on Mihir's mind, on the flight to Mumbai. Ravi had asked him to reach out to Spa Maid, and he had tried. But her mobile number no longer seemed to be functional, leaving him with no option but to contact her physically. Mihir isn't even sure if she still works at the Grand Meridien hotel. But if she still does, Mihir thinks that it is highly unlikely that she is the woman they seek. For if she really were Rukhsana, she surely would have gone underground after her husband Tabrez had fled the country. But then again, as Ravi had insisted on one of Mihir's visits to the hospital, because they had no real evidence against her, perhaps she'd stayed afloat as a way of affirming her innocence. That made her even more dangerous.

* * *

Tabrez finds himself being chased through the narrow alleys of Mumbai, and then suddenly the jungles of Kerala, before being forced to wade in the Arabian Sea. Wherever he goes, the blurry men trailing him do not seem to give up. To make matters worse, Rukhsana seems to be the one telling the men where to look.

He wakes up with a start. Another nightmare.

He's had these nightmares nearly every night, ever since he fled India and sought refuge in Pakistan. 'Just irrational thoughts,' he tells himself as he gets out of bed and gulps down a glass of water. For as long as he is in Pakistan, he knows that he is safe. But safety isn't quite the same thing as freedom. In India, he was free to do as he pleased. Of course, even then the ISI did watch over his activities closely, but that was from a distance. In Muzaffarabad, which for the indefinite future looks likely to be his home, they hover around at all times. He cannot as much as step out for a walk without having Ghaffar—supposedly his bodyguard turned man Friday, but for all practical purposes, an ISI asset whose task it is to keep tabs—follow him.

Not that Tabrez really minds, however . . .

With the ISI now fully backing him, he knows that he can look to vastly expand the scale of his operations and strike back at India in previously inconceivable ways. But he knows that he will need to be patient. The way he sees it, a reputation now precedes him, and he cannot be floundering his time on minor attacks. Nothing short of a complete destabilization of the Indian state will quench his thirst for vengeance. But before he can even begin to chalk out the plans for something of that magnitude, he knows that he needs to breathe new life into his fledgling organization. Although Iqbal—his most trusted lieutenant—and Rukhsana are both still in India, the Lashkar-e-Hind as it stands today is a mere shadow of what it had been only some months ago. But it doesn't bother Tabrez all that much. He had built the organization from the ground up. Now, he will just have to do it all over again.

And he will do better this time. The more he thinks of it, the more he is convinced that it was only natural that his plans failed the first time around. He had deluded himself into thinking that a small band of jihadis, however dedicated it might have been, could employ conventional strategies of warfare against the might of the Indian state and hope to succeed. It had of course managed to create an atmosphere of fear through attacks on civilians, but that had clearly landed them nowhere. This time around, he is determined to build a more robust network of operatives penetrating deep into Indian society. What exactly this network will look like, and the tasks that it will be expected to carry out in service of his larger goal, is still unclear even to him.

But he knows for a fact that the starting point is still the same—radicalization of the young and impressionable. In a country of India's size, there are hundreds of thousands of them. Even this, however, will necessitate a different approach. Although Tabrez has always encouraged his comrades to look at ways of using the internet and other digital technologies to further their cause, they haven't yet got around to cracking it, and have tended to fall back on the same old methods. Thanks to the ISI, he now has access to the people and resources that would allow him to conceive of new approaches.

Like Abdul Salim Rauf, aka Abu Jihad Al-Brittani, for instance—a British citizen who studied computer science at one of the leading colleges of engineering in Britain, Rauf is just as well versed with the canonical literature of Islam as he is with the ways of modern technology. Moved by the alleged atrocities on Muslims in Bosnia and elsewhere in the world, Rauf had turned to terrorism and had become an important leader in the terrorist hierarchy. Rauf became an invaluable asset for the anti-India operations of the ISI.

From the very first time Tabrez had met Rauf, only a week or so after moving into the safe house in Muzaffarabad, he had found himself completely mesmerized. Rauf was deeply charismatic, always bristling with ideas, and seemed to be able to articulate his thoughts while speaking better than most people could do while writing. His talents were greatly valued, and he was naturally a very well-connected man whose influence extended to the highest rungs of the most notorious Islamist organizations all over the world, including even the Al-Qaeda. Indeed, there are rumours in jihadi circles that Rauf is the blue-eyed boy of Osama bin Laden—the Sheikh.

* * *

As he exits the airport and hails a cab to take him to the Grand Meridien, Mihir reminds himself that his antics at the hotel the last time around surely hadn't gone unnoticed. He had closely interacted with several of the employees, and they were surely bound to remember him. Fortunately, he now has a thick beard and a distinctly older face. In a matter of a few months, he had aged by several years. But even so, he must be careful and cannot linger around for too long. Putting on a round hat and thick sunglasses that block out nearly half his face, he walks into the hotel lobby. After a few moments, he frantically searches his pockets, giving the impression that he's forgotten something. He then sprints back and stops the cab, which is now at the exit gate.

He quickly gets in, and surreptitiously drops his wallet on the floor. He then tells the taxi driver, 'I forgot my wallet in here, sorry. And also, I realized that I have a reservation at the Grand Promenade, and not Grand Meridien. Sorry, I'm really absent-minded.'

This is all just a ruse of course. The few seconds spent inside the lobby had been enough for him to scan the entire space. And he'd spotted her immediately. She is still a receptionist at the hotel.

* * *

At some level, Tabrez is glad that the nightmare woke him up. In just a few hours, he is to meet Rauf for breakfast, and he needs all the time he can get to gather his thoughts. Sunrise is still an hour away, but Ghaffar is already up and about. As is Zubair, the cook, who promptly sets a cup of tea by Tabrez's bedside. As he carefully rolls out his mat on the floor and kneels down to offer the first prayer of the day, Tabrez can't help but think—as he does almost every other day—that it is by all standards a luxurious exile he's being afforded. He has entirely to himself an expansive four-bedroom bungalow, with a well-manicured garden that looks out onto a completely isolated stretch of hillocks and thick vegetation. It is almost like an oasis nestled deep inside a large forest.

When he had fled India, taking a long-winded journey through Nepal into Pakistani territory, he had no doubt that they would help him find his feet. But he hadn't remotely expected to be accorded such lavish treatment. It soon became evident that they viewed him as an extremely important ally and were very impressed by his exploits. And why wouldn't they be? Almost on his own, he had managed to engineer the most-deadly terrorist strikes on Indian soil in over a decade. With active Pakistani support and mentorship, he would be able to achieve so much more. While Tabrez does for the most part enjoy all the luxuries lavished upon him, it does at times make him queasy. Clearly, if they were investing so much in him, they expect great things. What if he failed to deliver? Would they still be as kind, or would he be met with a quiet, anonymous death?

Today, at least, he cannot bring himself to entertain such thoughts and emerges from his prayer with an elevated sense of self-confidence. He picks up his tea and walks to his office in the adjacent room. He turns on the computer and logs into the secure communications platform Rauf has recently set up for him. Two unread messages await him. One from Rukhsana, and the other from Iqbal. In response to a folder of propaganda material Tabrez had recently sent him, Iqbal has written back proposing that the material also be translated into Malayalam, Kannada and Telugu. Tabrez is pleased to see that Iqbal is continuing to take a proactive role. He was always a sharp lad and could be counted upon to come up with such ideas. If they were hoping to reach out to young Muslims across the country, it was essential that they thought beyond just Urdu.

Tabrez then opens the message from Rukhsana:

Something very strange happened today. A guest came into the lobby, looked around, and then acted like he'd forgotten something and ran back outside. He never came back, but somehow, I felt I'd seen him before. I thought about it for quite some time and then I realized. He looked a lot different, but I'm certain it was him. He's finally come back, the 'Businessman', just the way you predicted. I have the messages, the emails, everything. What next?

Yours,

R.

Tabrez smiles to himself. This is exactly what he'd been hoping for. He has to think for only a moment before shooting off a quick, cryptic reply, 'Bewitch him. Everything else will follow.'

* * *

In the driver's seat of a rented car, Mihir stifles a yawn before looking at his watch. It's 6.30 a.m. Time for the day shift to kick in at the Grand Meridien hotel. Time for Spa Maid to report to work. He decides to call. 'Hello, Grand Meridien Hotel,' the same male voice he'd heard all through the night answers. Mihir immediately hangs up.

He gives it another ten minutes, before trying again.

'Good morning, Grand Meridien hotel. How can I help you?'

This time, it's her.

'I'm calling to make a reservation,' Mihir says.

'Sure sir, I can help you with that. Can you please help me with the details?'

'Yes. This is a reservation in the name of Mr Rajinder Talreja, from Santa Cruz,' Mihir responds coolly, hoping she gets the hint. It was the name he'd used the last time around when they'd met at Santa Cruz station.

'Oh, it's you, sir. How have you been?'

'I've been very well, thank you. I've been trying to contact you, but your number doesn't work.'

'Y-yes, sir. I've changed my phone number because I wanted to move away completely from the past . . . if you know what I mean. But I did try contacting you as well. Even your phone number wasn't reachable. H-how can I help you, sir?'

'I'll tell you. But not over the phone. Come outside the hotel, right now, and you'll see a black car. Get in, and then we'll talk.'

'B-but sir, my shift just started. I can't just walk off like that.'

'You do realize that I know a lot that you wouldn't want your parents to know, right?'

Spa Maid lets out a deep sigh, before agreeing. She tells a colleague that she will be back in fifteen minutes and briskly makes her way out of the hotel into Mihir's car.

'Hello, Mr Talreja,' she says, somewhat seductively, even as Mihir turns on the ignition and zips away.

'So, we meet again,' Mihir says cheerily, 'What have you been up to, these days? What's the next city you're looking to bomb?'

Mihir has one eye on the road, and another on the rear-view mirror. He wants to pay close attention to her reactions.

'I don't know what you're talking about, sir. I'm done with all of that.'

'Come on, don't lie to me. I know how addictive violence can be for people of your kind. You can't just be done with it,' Mihir prods on.

Spa Maid grows distraught.

'I swear, sir. I was dragged into it once upon a time through sheer blackmail. But you rescued me, and I will always be grateful for that. But please believe me, I've moved on from all of that. Why would I have continued in the same job, knowing that you'd know where to find me, if I were still involved in that stuff?'

Her confidence intrigues Mihir.

'Okay. Let's just assume for a moment that you are telling the truth. But don't tell me that they've let you get away and haven't made any attempt to contact you. If I could find you, surely, they too would be able to find you.'

She shifts uneasily in her seat. Mihir knows he's onto something here.

'To tell you the truth, they did try, sir. And what I said to you over the phone, about me trying to contact you, is true as well. I can prove it to you.'

Spa Maid pulls out her phone and scrolls through her SMS outbox.

Much to Mihir's surprise, there indeed is a message sent to the discarded number he had used under cover as Rajinder Talreja. The message read: 'Sir, pls help. They r contacting me. I dntknwwt 2 do.'

From the distress apparent on her face, in addition to the SMS, Mihir realizes that she is indeed telling the truth. For a moment, he even feels bad. Bad for her, bad about himself. Here is a vulnerable woman who had reached out to him in her hour of distress, and he had been unable to help. He wants to apologize, but holds back, reminding himself that he cannot do or say anything that might upset the dynamics of their relationship. He has the upper hand, and it must be that way always.

Trying hard to keep a straight face, he finally responds, 'Okay. So how have they tried contacting you? And how many times?'

'All by email . . . I can show you.'

'Where's your laptop?'

'Uhh . . . I don't have one. I just use the desktop at the hotel.'

'You can use mine,' Mihir tells her, pulling up to the side, before retrieving his laptop from the back seat.

She signs into her email ID and moves closer to him, softly brushing against his shoulder. She explains, as she scrolls through the emails, 'They keep reminding me of all the photos and videos they have, and how they can destroy me, unless I choose to help. Then there are these invitations to adult chat forums, all kinds of strange things. I'm too scared to click. What if I get pulled in again? It is divine providence that you've come looking for me. Please, you must help me get away from this once and for all. I'll do anything for you. I want to get away from all of this. I'm sick of this existence, sick of being scared all that time . . .'

Mihir stares at her in silence. At first, he's just processing all the information he's just had to take in. But after a few moments, his attention wanders towards the diamond stud that complements her finely shaped nose, the strangely endearing mole on her cheek, and the single strand of hair curled up over her forehead.

Spa Maid can tell that he's checking her out. She's happy to let him.

Mihir realizes what he's doing, and quickly snaps back into focus. 'I'm so sorry, I just . . . haven't slept all night. Anyway, yes, I can help you. But I'll need you to respond to those emails, get in touch with them, and become part of the group once again. What you will say, what you will do, everything will be decided by me. And don't worry, no harm will come to you. I won't abandon you this time.'

She nods in agreement.

After a few moments of awkward silence, he asks, 'One more thing. I realized that I don't even know your name.'

'Rukmini. Rukmini Jaiswal, sir. A-and yours?'

'You know, already. It's Rajinder Talreja.'

She smiles. A warm smile that fills him with an inexplicable sense of joy.

* * *

Tabrez is in the garden, sitting by himself, when a convoy of three shiny black Pajeros pulls into the compound. Five armed men get down and quickly survey the surroundings, and only after they're convinced that everything is just as it should be, does Rauf step out. Tabrez walks up to the car and greets him with a warm embrace, before escorting him inside. For somebody meeting him for the first time, Rauf might seem completely unremarkable and indistinguishable from the rest of the contingent. Like the others, he sports a long beard and is dressed in the traditional Pakistani attire of kurta pyjama, complete with a skull cap. It is only when one hears him speak that it becomes clear that he is nothing like the others. It isn't just his accent that is markedly British. Even his choice of words carries the peculiar stamp of a thoroughbred Englishman. It is a contrast that only serves to heighten his charisma.

'Tabrez, jolly old chap, how's everything going?' he asks, as they walk into Tabrez's office.

'By Allah's grace, everything's going well, Rauf Miyan. How have you been?' Tabrez responds.

'Let's get straight to work, shall we? I have fifteen minutes to spare. The Sheikh has asked to see me, and I cannot possibly turn him down, can I?'

'Of course not, Miyan,' Tabrez responds, smiling nervously. The mention of the Sheikh fills him with a strange mix of excitement and dread.

'Very well then. Have you figured your way around the platform I set up on your computer recently?'

'Yes, Miyan. So has Iqbal. I've been in regular touch with him. We're going to soon start letting the others also get on to the platform. We've also been slowly reviving our recruitment cell.'

Rauf raises his eyebrows, the mild consternation on his face unmistakable.

'What do you mean by revive?'

'I mean, we're re-establishing contact with some of the preachers who've helped us in the past. Not all of them . . . only those who we're absolutely certain we can trust.'

Rauf shakes his head.

'I'd hoped you'd have learnt your lessons. I'm sure these are people you can trust. Madrasas and maulvis . . . at least the select few who understand that we are truly at war with the infidels and have always been the cornerstone of our recruitment efforts. But it's a very risky method to take at this point if you're serious about building the kind of network you're envisioning. There isn't a single madrasa in India that isn't being closely monitored by the Indian agencies. One whiff of what you're up to, and we'll be back to square one all over again.'

'So, what do you suggest, Rauf Miyan?'

'The internet. It's the only way.'

'But I mean, once we've brought people into the fold, we can add them to the platform and coordinate our operations online. But how do we get them there? The starting point has to be physical in some way or the other, right?'

'Wrong. Youngsters these days spend more time on the internet than on anything else. Naturally, the best way to grab their attention, whether you're hoping to get them to buy a particular brand of junk food or you're hoping to enlist them for a noble cause, is to engage with them online.'

Tabrez listens with rapt attention.

'And how do we go about doing this?'

'Leave all of that to my boys and me. You give us the material, and we'll figure out how to put it out there and build the vast network that you keep talking about. In the meantime, I'd suggest that you start seriously thinking about exactly what you intend to do once that network is in place. There's still a lot of physical work to be done of course, and that's anyway your forte. Knowing you, I'm sure you won't disappoint.'

Tabrez smiles sheepishly.

'What else?' Rauf continues, 'Have you heard from your wife?'

'Yes, Miyan. She has been contacted.'

'Excellent timing . . .'

Rauf looks at his watch and realizes that his time is up.

'Speaking of which, it's time to go. I'll be back soon. We'll get breakfast and talk more. Take good bloody care of yourself until then, yes? And if there's anything at all in the meantime, you know how to reach me.'

'You too, Rauf Miyan. By Allah's grace, we will have a more fruitful meeting next time. Please convey my respects to the Sheikh.'

'Well, once you've proved that you're as good as I believe you are, I'll ensure that you have the opportunity to convey your respects in person. How's that for an incentive?' Rauf chuckles, before getting into the waiting car.

As Tabrez watches the convoy zip through the mountains, he begins to feel the weight of the burden that rests upon his shoulders.

Kamdev's Arrow

Back at the headquarters, Cyrus, Mihir and Jose scan through Spa Maid's email account.

'Everything checks out, Mihir,' Jose tells Mihir, 'the way it's worded, the encryption protocols, it's all consistent with what we know of how these guys operate. This is legit stuff. Also, looked through her antecedents. Her name is Rukmini Jaiswal, at least according to the documents she has used to get this job.'

Mihir asks, 'What more proof do you need?'

'This counts for little. You've been Rajinder Talreja, and ten other people, and each time you've had the documents to prove it,' Cyrus quips.

'This is different. Unlike me, she's not a C3 agent with a Jose Cherian to help her create a new foolproof identity every month.'

'Well, she could be an ISI agent, with a Pakistani hacker helping her out,' Cyrus responds, alarmed by Mihir's strange defensiveness.

'No, she isn't. She's just an innocent girl who was once upon a time trapped in all of this. And she's going back into that trap, just to help us. The least we can do is trust her.'

Cyrus isn't convinced. Nor is Jose, who adds, 'This isn't some childhood friend of yours we're talking about for you to be so sure that she can be so easily trusted. She could potentially be an extremely dangerous woman. I mean, everything adds up until now, but we just don't know enough to be completely sure.'

Mihir realizes that he's beginning to sound irrational. He even feels a tinge of embarrassment and quickly tries to make amends, 'I know, I know. Don't ask me why, but it's just that I am almost fully convinced that she isn't the Rukhsana we're trying to find. It's just a gut feeling I have. I mean, I'm sure if I spent even a few minutes with a founding member of the LeH, I'd be able to tell. And I've spent hours and hours with Rukmini, and she just doesn't seem to be the sort.'

'That precisely is the whole point. Don't forget what Ravi sir has been drilling into our heads from the very beginning—nobody is what they seem to be,' Cyrus snaps back.

Eager to keep things calm, Jose intervenes, 'Okay, we're headed nowhere with this conversation. When you meet her next, I want you to install this software on her laptop. It will give us access to her screen at all times, so we can be completely certain that she isn't playing us.'

'I don't think she has a laptop,' Mihir replies, 'Should I give her a new one?'

Jose shakes his head.

'You could, but she could easily hoodwink us by using this just to show us what we want to see. It might be a very bad idea. Also, are you entirely sure she doesn't have a laptop? How has she been sending and receiving emails all along?'

'On the computer at her workplace, I think. That's why she had to use my laptop to show me these emails.'

Cyrus is flabbergasted.

'What rubbish! See, this is exactly what I'm saying. You're lapping up whatever she's feeding you. Turn up at her house uninvited and search every corner. You can't just assume these things without having sufficient reason and evidence to back it up. Her words mean nothing.'

'Stop trying to sound like Ravi sir, when he's not around. I can't just go in like that. She's a woman, and so . . .'

Anil barges into the room, bringing their argument to a premature end.

'Hello, sir,' the three greet him in unison.

'Hello, boys. Hope you don't mind me coming in uninvited. Just thought I should get a quick update on what you've been up to. So, who is the woman you are referring to?'

The trio exchange puzzled looks. Anil chuckles, 'I know you work for Ravi, but he hasn't been around, in case you haven't noticed. And in his absence, I am the de facto head of C3.'

'Um, sorry sir . . . but we didn't get any official notification,' Mihir responds weakly.

Anil chuckles, 'Oh, screw all the official nonsense. I am senior even to Ravi, so whatever he is cleared for, you can assume I'm cleared too. So, tell me, who is this woman?'

The situation demands Ravi-like tact, and Cyrus rises to the occasion, 'To be completely honest, sir, we were talking about . . . um, this girl Mihir is interested in. She lives with her parents, and um . . . what Mihir was trying to tell you is that because we haven't got any official notification about the new chain of command, and we can't reach Ravi sir, we haven't really been doing much work. We're really sorry, sir.'

Anil throws his hands up, and exclaims, 'That's exactly what I've been saying all along to everybody. We can't just stop playing because our "star player" has been injured. We've got to get on with the game. It's good you told me this. I think I'm going to have a word with the chief, make things official, and then I can give you work to do and stop you from being sidetracked by all this romantic nonsense.'

* * *

Back in Mumbai, Mihir picks up Rukmini from outside Santa Cruz station. It's a Sunday, and she has the entire day off. The drive to his hotel room is spent mostly in awkward silence, punctured only by Mihir's feeble attempts at engaging her in small talk. She can tell that he's trying hard not to stare at her through the rear-view mirror.

They enter his room, and Mihir asks her to sit down. Reaching into his cupboard, he pulls out a package.

'This is for you,' he tells her, 'a brand-new laptop. All the emails that you send, receive, everything will happen through this. That way, we'll know what's happening at all times and can keep you out of trouble. But that's not the only reason why. You've been talking about wanting to find a new career. With this laptop, you can pick up new skills on the internet. Everything and everybody is online these days, you know, not just desperate radicals out to brainwash beau . . . I mean, innocent young women.'

Rukmini beams with joy and draws Mihir into a tight hug. It's the first time he's made physical contact with a woman other than his mother and his grandmother. It fills him with a tumult of mixed emotions. On the one hand, there is an inexplicably visceral sense of reassurance and comfort that he feels in her presence. But at the same time, he can't help but wonder if he is allowing himself to be pulled into a dangerous vortex. He has already gone behind Jose's back by flouting his advice against giving her a new laptop. He can only hope that his instincts are right, and that this will all pay off. And who knows? Perhaps it will pay off in more ways than one.

Rukmini gently pulls away. Tears trickling down her cheeks, she tells him, 'Despite being aware of the horrible things I've done in the past, you've been so kind to me. How can I possibly thank you?'

'We all make mistakes,' Mihir assures her. 'What's important is that you realize you made a mistake and are looking to move on. If anything, I should be apologizing to you for forcing you to deal with all of that again. And I haven't even been truthful to you. I haven't even told you my real name.'

'What is your real name?'

Mihir shrugs in frustration, 'I can't tell you. That's the whole point. My colleagues don't seem to trust you, and if they're right and you end up being . . .'

A grave look clouds Rukmini's face, 'End up being what?'

'A–a double agent.'

Rukmini shakes her head in disbelief. More tears trickle down her cheeks as she looks into his eyes, 'If you don't trust me, then I don't want to do this any more. You can arrest me, or tell my parents, or do whatever. I don't care. I feel so stupid now to have believed that you actually . . .'

'No, no. I do trust you, which is why I'm even telling you all this.'

'Then, why can't you tell me your name?'

Mihir sighs.

'All right, I'll tell you. But you can't ever refer to me by that name. When you call, text or email, you're going to continue sticking to Talreja. Promise?'

Rukmini smiles, 'I promise.'

'Kaul. Mihir Kaul.'

* * *

'I think you should talk to him. What's the worst that can happen?' Cyrus tells an anxious Jose, who can't seem to make up his mind on whether he should reach out to Ravi who is recuperating at home

Jose picks up the phone.

'S-sir, I'm really sorry to be disturbing you, but . . .'

Ravi interrupts, 'In normal circumstances, is it something you would have disturbed me for even at two in the morning?'

'I think so, sir.'

'Is it something that has direct implications for national security?'

Jose remains silent for a few moments.

'I wish it didn't, but possibly yes, sir.'

'Okay, go ahead.'

'Something just doesn't seem right, sir. Mihir's installed a keylogger and a screen recorder on Spa Maid's computer, but there are large gaps in the feed that I'm receiving. It could simply be a glitch, but I have a bad feeling about this. I'm afraid Mihir's got a little too close to her if you know what I mean . . .'

'I don't know why I'm not surprised. What are the possible reasons apart from it being a mere glitch?'

'Only one thing, sir. That they know exactly what we're up to and are showing us what we want to see.'

'And what is it that they want us to see?'

'The coordinates of a dead letter box. We tracked it down to the Nepal border, and Mihir found a message. Something about a shipment of explosives changing hands in Bhawanipur, Kolkata. Very, very specific information, down to the time, spot, and method of handover. A cart-puller, apparently.'

'And all of this adds up with the information she's been voluntarily sharing with Mihir?'

'Yes, sir. She's either been telling him the truth, or the entire thing is a sham.'

'Assuming you're right, and this is all counter-intelligence, why is it that they would want us to stumble on this particular piece of information?'

'Just a false trail.'

'I see. Thanks for the update,' Ravi responds, before abruptly disconnecting.

A befuddled Jose looks at Cyrus, who asks, 'What did he say?'

Jose shrugs his shoulder, 'I see . . . that's all he said.'

'So, what next?'

'I don't know. We just wait, I suppose. Mihir's going to Bhawanipur himself. We'll know soon enough what this is all about.'

Cyrus gets up from his seat, 'I think I should go with Mihir, just . . .'

His phone rings. It is Ravi.

'S-sir?'

'Yes, I'm still alive. Thanks for all the flowers and get-well cards . . .'

'B-but sir, I didn't send any . . .'

'Exactly my point. You seem to be in no hurry to have me feeling better, and back at work.'

Cyrus smiles. Ravi is back in his element.

'Anyway,' Ravi continues, 'This is why I called. I need you to go to Bhawanipur . . .'

'I was thinking of exactly the same thing when you called, sir. I'll go with Mihir.'

'You'll go separately. And Mihir shouldn't know.'

'Y-you mean, I should go spy on Mihir?'

'If that's how you want to look at it, then sure. Let's hope it doesn't come to that, but you might have to save him.'

'I'm sorry . . .'

'It's very unlikely, given the risks involved, but it is possible . . .'

'I'm sorry, sir, but I still don't understand.'

'If she's been playing Mihir the whole time, then there isn't going to be an exchange of explosives. But since they've gone to all this trouble of setting up a dead letter box, and leading Mihir to Bhawanipur at a particular time and date, I'm afraid they might attempt to kidnap him. It's extremely unlikely because they can't possibly expect Mihir to turn up alone, unless he's been singing to her like a canary, but there's still a minute chance. Either that, or we might actually find something. In any case, we'll see.'

* * *

At the Jadu Babu Market in Bhawanipur on a busy Saturday evening, Mihir keeps his eyes wide open for movement around Qureshi Pharmacy. He's looking for a covered cart being pulled by a man in a brown vest and a skull cap. Five hundred metres away, a team of Kolkata's finest police officers remain on standby. As soon as Mihir confirms, they'll swoop in.

It's two minutes to six, the designated time of handover, and Mihir's eyes land on a suspicious character, a bearded sardar who also seems to be restlessly looking at Qureshi Pharmacy. Mihir wonders if he is an intermediary. With one eye still fixed on the suspicious man, Mihir notices the cart pulling in at a distance. Brown vest, skull cap, all boxes ticked. He immediately notifies the police squad, who in less than a minute surround the surprised cart-puller.

The police pull away the cover, revealing several sealed cardboard cartons that are full of branded tins.

'False information,' Anirban Basu, the supervising officer, tells Mihir. 'This is just medical grade potassium permanganate.'

Mihir isn't convinced, 'No, that can't be. Something is amiss. Everything else has turned out to be perfectly accurate. The time, the place, even the colour of his vest.'

'But, this is potassium permanganate. We can't arrest him for transporting that,' Basu responds.

'No, no. I'm telling you. This information has come from a very reliable source. We're missing something here.'

'I'm sorry, but it looks like your source is wrong this time.'

Mihir is angered by the insinuation, 'What are you? A walking laboratory? How can you be sure it's potassium permanganate? Arrest the man, confiscate the supply. Get it tested, and then we'll know.'

Basu, a senior officer due to retire in a year, doesn't take very kindly to Mihir's outburst. 'I have been doing this for longer than you've probably even been alive, and I know what I'm talking about. The only reason I'm going to excuse such utter disregard for decorum and courtesy is because you are Ravi's man. We will get it tested and when the results arrive, I believe that you will owe me an apology.'

Mihir is embarrassed. His unflinching faith in Rukmini has caused him to overstep his boundaries without even realizing it.

'I'm, I'm sorry, Basu Da. I didn't mean to snap like that. It's just . . .'

Mihir's eyes dart away again to the sardar who is paying close attention to everything. He seems to be particularly interested in the contents of the cart. The sardar sees Mihir looking at him and starts walking away briskly. Mihir decides to follow him. The sardar looks behind and realizes that Mihir is after him. He starts sprinting.

A long chase ensues, as the sardar tries desperately to evade Mihir, turning into one busy alley after the other. But Mihir's not one to let go and remains in hot pursuit. Finally, the sardar gives up and raises his arms in surrender. Mihir is triumphant.

'Did you really think you could outrun me?'

The sardar, still breathing heavily, chuckles, 'At the academy, I used to be able to. But now that I've started smoking . . .'

Mihir's jaw drops, as he looks into the man's eyes, 'Cyrus?'

Sudarshan Chakra

'It's your ego that's preventing you from admitting that you've been taken for a ride,' Cyrus yells at Mihir, who is aghast at the insinuations being hurled at him.

They are at a briefing room in the headquarters and there is palpable tension in the air. Even Jose, who is usually the one to smoothen frictions between the ever-quarrelling duo, doesn't hesitate to take sides this time, 'Look, nobody's saying you've willingly erred. Nobody's holding anything against you. All we're saying is that you've made a serious miscalculation. The evidence is overwhelming, and you must admit it right now, so that we can move on from this petty dispute and think about course correction. Every minute we waste is a minute Rukhsana's planning her next move.'

'Stop calling her Rukhsana,' Mihir snaps back. 'You have no proof of that. And this is not a petty dispute. We're talking about branding an innocent girl as the most dangerous woman in this country. Just because we can. We need to be more responsible than that.'

A knock on the door interrupts them. It is Subramaniam, Ravi's secretary. The trio is taken by surprise. They're also worried because they haven't seen Subramaniam ever since Ravi's illness. They wonder if he's bringing news.

'Ravi sir wants to meet you,' he tells them, breaking the suspense.

'At his residence?' Mihir asks.

'No, in his office,' Subramaniam replies.

'Oh, we didn't think he was coming back until next week,' Mihir remarks with a worried look on his face.

'Nor did I,' Subramaniam says. 'In fact, I haven't met him yet. He called me while I was on my way and told me he's back. He also asked me to bring the three of you.'

Mihir's quick to correct any impression that he isn't happy that the boss is back, and says, 'Th-that's great news. We'll be there right away.'

'What's the matter with him?' Subramaniam whispers to Cyrus, as they proceed towards Ravi's office. 'He doesn't seem very pleased to be meeting Ravi sir.'

Cyrus replies, 'That's because he's going to get a royal dressing down.'

Ravi is in his office, gazing at his cigar collection with admiration, when they enter. 'Good morning, gentlemen,' he greets them, still looking intently at his cigars, 'If the three of you would be kind enough to wait outside while I quickly catch up with Subramaniam.'

As the trio exits the room, Ravi asks Subramaniam to sit, but he remains standing. He eyes the cigars with worry, 'I hope you are not going to resume smoking, sir.'

Ravi smiles. 'Not at all, Subramaniam. Not if I want to stay alive, which I most certainly want to, trust me. I was simply admiring these cigars, now my sworn enemies, in the same way one admires an enemy for managing to outsmart you. And these have outsmarted me for almost two decades. I can't but give them credit.'

'I'm very glad to hear that you've finally quit, sir. You look much healthier. If only you would also listen to me and perform that yagna I've been telling you about, you'd be able to permanently overcome all the obstacles that keep coming in your path.'

'Later, Subramaniam, not now,' Ravi replies, repeating a line Subramaniam has heard a thousand times. 'Not when there's so much work to be done.'

'Of course, sir. As you'd expect, Anil sir has been trying his best to . . .'

Ravi has no patience for office politics right now, 'Apart from the fact that Anil has been trying to send me on long leave and take over, what else, Subramaniam? Have you been setting aside my letters as I'd instructed you to?'

'Of course, sir,' Subramaniam responds, before going to a filing cabinet from which he retrieves a stack of letters.

Ravi quickly flips through all of them. One postcard in particular catches his attention.

'And the boys? How's the morale been in my absence?' Ravi asks, as he puts the postcard aside and hands the other letters to Subramaniam for shredding.

'It's best if you asked them yourself, sir,' Subramaniam replies, a hint of hesitation in his tone.

'That means all's not well. Anyway, send them in. But not all at once. I don't want to witness a boxing match on my first day back. Send Jose in first.'

Before Jose can say anything, Ravi rattles off, 'Don't bother enquiring about my health. I'm fine. Don't bother telling me about Mihir. It is none of your business any more. And don't bother telling me about some obscure hack you've mastered in my absence. Something more interesting than any of those things has come up.'

Jose is intrigued as Ravi hands him the postcard and asks him what he thinks of it.

'It's from Monte Carlo,' Jose tells Ravi, pointing at the stamp. Ravi isn't impressed, 'Even Subramaniam's five-year-old grandson would be able to tell me that. What else do you see?'

Jose carefully scans the postcard once again. It reads:

Dear friend,

Getwellsoon. My prayers are with you. When you feel better, please reach out to me. I recently found a new doctor, and he's very good. I'm sure he can treat you better. Just write to me whenever. I've got a new email ID. takshak@photonmail.com

Yours,
Takshak

Jose wears a puzzled look on his face as he thinks aloud, 'It seems like a simple get well soon card, handwritten by some friend of yours. But then again, you wouldn't be asking me if it was just that. Takshak can't possibly be a real name, there's hardly any space between the words get well soon. My immediate guess is that this is a password. But a password to what? The email ID?'

Ravi is pleased. He turns on his computer, and keys in the credentials. The inbox is completely empty, and there are no messages in the sent mail folder either. Jose takes over, and quickly scans through the trash. Nothing there either. Finally, his eyes land on a message in the draft folder. Jose is impressed, 'This is quite ingenious. Sending you a password through physical mail, to an email ID that has material sitting in the draft folder. Even the most sophisticated cyber surveillance systems wouldn't be able to intercept it, simply because it was never sent!'

Ravi's eyes light up as Jose clicks on the message to reveal a set of images—framed paintings on display at a fine-dining restaurant in Monte Carlo.

Jose explains, 'These images are a front. Could have been anything. What we're really looking for is probably hidden somewhere in the metadata. I will run these images through a few algorithms and see what comes up.'

'By all means, go ahead. But if I were you, I'd first examine the images themselves.'

'But these are all quite generic. I mean, they're all very famous paintings, and you can interpret them and find connections in a million different ways and still be correct. And so, it's naturally an unreliable way of sending specific information. My hunch still is that what we're looking for is in the metadata.'

A wry smile plays on Ravi's lips, 'You've read too many spy novels, or so you claim at least. You've never heard of steganography?'

'I most certainly have sir, yes. Concealing secret messages within other messages, or objects. But with all due respect, I think your conception of it is a little outdated. Steganography has evolved rapidly, and now it's all about hiding messages within the metadata of files. I was recently reading a research paper . . .'

'Oh, spare me the lecture. I might be old-fashioned and low-tech, but so is the man who sent this. I'm amazed that you still haven't asked me who Takshak is. Don't ever forget, it's individuals that determine the mode of communication, and not the other way around.'

Jose sighs, 'Wh-who is Takshak?'

'You have an hour to examine these images. Come back and tell me what you find, and then we'll talk about Takshak. On your way out, ask Mihir to come in.'

Mihir's knees tremble slightly as he walks into Ravi's office. Ravi is warm and courteous. Mihir feels a little assured.

'Did you know that historically, particularly in the twentieth century, intelligence agencies all around the world kept a close watch on theatre troupes, and sent in their men to watch as many plays as possible? The best spies traced their origins to a strong background in acting. Quite understandable if you think about it. The mark of a great actor and the mark of a great spy come down to essentially the same thing. It's that extraordinary ability to completely transform into another person and convince the world that they are who they claim to be, that makes a great actor or a great spy.'

Mihir is perplexed, 'I-I didn't know that, sir. But it's fascinating to think about it.'

'You'd also be fascinated to know that your new asset, Rukmini Jaiswal, used to be quite the rage in Mumbai's college theatre circuit.'

Mihir begins to feel a little queasy, 'I-I didn't know that either, sir.'

'I'm surprised, given how much time you've been spending with her.'

Mihir shifts in his seat.

'I-I haven't really enquired about her personal life, sir. I keep it strictly professional.'

'Well, of course. Since you were engaged professionally, I asked Qasim Khan, our most trusted officer under deep cover who is known to you as Examiner, to thoroughly look into her antecedents, and he was the one who told me about her past pursuits in theatre, among other things that a professional like you might not deem too important. So, let's talk about the professional angle. What's the update?'

'As you've probably heard sir, the tip-off turned out to be almost entirely accurate, except for one thing at the end.'

Ravi is stumped, 'One thing at the end? You're making it sound like you were expecting to find a guy in a red vest carrying a consignment of explosives, but as it turned out, it was a man in a blazer carrying a consignment of explosives. Now something like that would qualify as an almost entirely accurate tip-off, except for one thing at the end. In your case, it would be more appropriate to say that the information was completely inaccurate, except for one thing at the start. What does that tell you about your judgement?'

Mihir is puzzled.

Ravi continues, '*Argumentum ad Misericordiam*. A Latin phrase that's used to describe an argument or a position that is basically an appeal to pity, and not reason. Despite warning by your colleagues, you valued pity over logic. It's something law enforcement and intelligence officers must particularly watch out for.'

Mihir shakes his head, 'I'm sorry, sir, but I have no idea what you're trying to say.'

'Oh, yes you do. You know exactly what I'm trying to say. But you're too embarrassed to admit it. Instead of weighing all the evidence before taking a decision, as someone in your position is expected to do, you allowed your judgement to be clouded by sympathy. And that didn't just spring out of nowhere. She seduced you, and you allowed it to happen, right from the start.'

Mihir is crestfallen.

Ravi asks, 'I do not want to embarrass you any further by going into all the little details. Did you disclose your identity to her?'

Mihir nods meekly, utterly ashamed.

Ravi gets up, 'It's all over, then. You're completely out in the open now. It'd be best if you took your things and went home.'

Mihir can't believe what he's hearing. He tries to defend himself, 'But sir, we can't assume that she deliberately misled us. Maybe somebody in the West Bengal police tipped them off, and so they aborted it at the last moment. She just told me what she'd heard. This happens all the time. Isn't it only fair that we give her another chance since she's also putting herself at grave risk for our sake?'

Ravi can't maintain his cool much longer, 'Are you even listening to yourself? Kid, she has completely played you, and it's time you admitted it. Since you're so convinced that she's innocent, let me give you the hard facts. After Jose voiced his suspicions, I arranged for a thorough background check. You see, she was born Rukmini Jaiswal, no doubt. But in college, she met a charming man named Tabrez known as Chocolate Boy, and they got married. She changed her name to Rukhsana, Tabrez founded an organization called Lashkar-e-Hind . . . Does that ring a bell? And even if you wanted to give her another chance, it's not going to happen. She has disappeared. The whole thing was a red herring deliberately constructed to waste two whole precious months. While you were busy being taken for a ride, I suspect they've been acting on their real plans.'

The guilt hits Mihir like a tsunami. He doesn't know what to say, and simply bows his head in shame.

Ravi with disappointment writ all over his face, tells him, 'Like I said, there's nothing to be done now. You should go home and reflect. I know the last six months have been very hard for you, and you have all my sympathies on a personal level. But you have to learn to shut out your personal difficulties, however tragic and insurmountable they might be. It might seem almost like an inhuman expectation, but that is what makes the work we do so very challenging. Most agents simply give up after a point. It's too painful and too traumatizing, to have to live in a constant state of denial about one's own demons. But the ones who persist, the ones who endure the pain, are those who never forget why they signed up for it in the first place. Go on leave for a few weeks and take a good hard look at yourself and see if you think you can continue serving this hallowed institution.'

Mihir has nothing to say. It is almost as if a shroud has been lifted off, revealing to him the bitter truth he has been trying so hard to deny. Finding it impossible to look Ravi in the eye, he simply turns around and walks out. In his trance-like state of shame and guilt, he doesn't even notice Cyrus who can tell from one look that Mihir is broken inside.

Ravi sighs deeply before walking out of the office himself. He too is completely preoccupied with his thoughts and doesn't notice Cyrus. Cyrus is puzzled and calls out, 'Sir . . .'

Ravi turns around, 'I completely forgot. Why don't you meet me in a little while?'

Cyrus nods and is about to walk away when Ravi changes his mind. 'Actually, why don't you come with me? Let's see if your insomniac friend is any good.'

The walk to Insomnia, the round-the-clock electronic surveillance unit of C3, is a quiet one. Cyrus has questions about Ravi's health, but Ravi doesn't acknowledge them. Cyrus knows not to persist when the boss is in a pensive mood and follows in silence as Ravi leads him to a dark projection room.

Jose is still poring over the images sent by Takshak, which are now blown up on the wall.

'Any luck?' Ravi asks.

'Not really, sir,' Jose replies, 'I mean, they're all reproductions of works by famous painters, and I'm comparing each of them, pixel by pixel, along with the originals. But the images aren't sharp enough for an algorithm to scan accurately and so I have to do at least some bit of it manually.'

'Very impressive,' Ravi replies, 'but it's like looking for a needle in a haystack. You might find it eventually, but at this rate, you're going to take weeks. With a heart like mine, I might be dead by then.'

Jose and Cyrus are visibly unsettled by Ravi's casual mention of death.

Ravi is quick to dispel their worries, 'Oh, you don't have to be all long-faced. I'm not dying. If anything, my heart is in better shape than yours. The doctor says I have decades left. But that's no reason to slack off. I'm telling you you're missing something crucial. Something that shouldn't need all this technology. Takshak is an old-fashioned, low-tech man. And he always had a fascination for all things European, including art. So, I'm sure the choices of images are very deliberate.'

Cyrus is intrigued, 'Who is Takshak?'

'A Michelin-starred chef in Monte Carlo. I will tell you all about it later. But first, let us figure out what Takshak is trying to tell us. Why don't you take a shot? These are some images he's sent us, and there's a message hidden in there.'

A look of recognition dawns on Cyrus's face. 'Like Jose was saying, these are all among the most iconic paintings of western civilization. That there is *The Birth of Venus* by Botticelli. Then there's the *School of Athens* by Raphael. That of course is *Mona Lisa* by Da Vinci. And finally, that is *The Persistence of Memory* by Salvador Dali. They're all Italian, except Dali, who was Spanish.'

Ravi is pleased, 'Very impressive. Looks like you really prepared hard for your civil services exam.'

'Actually, I've always been a bit of a connoisseur. My grandfather . . .'

'All very fascinating, I'm sure. Rich Parsi kid with a cultivated interest in fine art. But let's save that story for a drinking session. What else do you notice, apart from the fact that they're all Italian painters, and that Dali isn't?'

'They're separated by periods and style,' Cyrus replies. 'The first three are Renaissance paintings, all produced during or before the seventeenth century. The fourth one, the Dali painting, is a surrealist painting from the twentieth century. So, the message we're looking for ought to be hidden somewhere in there.'

'That's very plausible,' Ravi says, before turning to Jose. 'How about you pull down all the other images and just have this one on display?'

Jose projects *The Persistence of Memory* on the wall.

Ravi walks over to the whiteboard and announces, 'Let's start with the basics.'

'Looks like a bunch of melting clocks to me,' Jose remarks, 'possibly meaning to suggest that we're running out of time.'

'Fair point,' Ravi says, even as he writes 'running out of time' on the whiteboard, 'It might very well be one of the things Takshak is trying to tell us, we don't really need this painting to tell us that we're running out of time. Think at an even more basic level. Why is it called *The Persistence of Memory*?'

Jose hazards a guess, 'Perhaps Takshak is warning about a repeat of something that has happened in the past? Another series of blasts?'

'There's only one thing from the past that Takshak could possibly be hinting at. Before we helped him move to Monte Carlo and start a restaurant, Takshak was my most trusted asset inside the Khalistan movement. He was deeply embedded, and yet nobody ever found out that he was working for us. He still is an influential man with connections extending across the Sikh diaspora.'

Cyrus is surprised, 'But isn't the Khalistan movement dead?'

Ravi explains, 'For all practical purposes, yes. But it's quite evident that the Khalistani sentiment was never fully extinguished. But we've believed for a long time now that they no longer have the muscle to pose a direct threat to national security. Something has clearly changed on that front. Which means there's something we're missing here. Think more basic. Why are there three Renaissance paintings, and one surrealist painting, and not the other way round? And why this painting in particular? What's so special about it?'

'The thing about this painting, unlike the other three,' Cyrus explains, 'is that it is hard to pin down what exactly it is that Dali is trying to say. The surrealists, like Dali, differed significantly from the Renaissance painters at a very fundamental level. As opposed to simply painting one composite scene the way one might take a photograph, they tried deliberately to bring together different realities in unexpected ways.'

'Different realities coming together in unexpected ways . . . very interesting,' Ravi says, as he moves away from the whiteboard and stares intently at the image on the wall. A look of recognition flashes across his face, as his eyes land on a particular corner of the frame.

'Since you seem to know all these things nobody really cares about, tell me,' Ravi asks Cyrus. 'Did Dali ever add alphanumeric codes as his paintings?'

'I can't be sure, but I highly doubt it,' Cyrus replies.

'Then what's that?' Ravi asks, pointing at 'K2' embossed in the bottom right corner of the painting.

Ravi walks back to the whiteboard, and thinks aloud, 'We have "time running out", *The Persistence of Memory*, "different realities coming together in unexpected ways", Khalistan, and now we have K2. It's quite simple, really. Don't you see it?'

Cyrus and Jose shake their heads. They don't see it.

'Kashmir and Khalistan,' Ravi announces, as a shiver runs down his spine, 'Two different realities, being brought together. The persistence of memory.'

'What do we do now?' Jose is quick to ask, not quite allowing for the gravity of the discovery to sink in.

'We'll have to bring together two different realities of our own. I'd have tasked Mihir with looking into the Khalistani connection, but he's currently incapacitated. Besides, he was still in his diapers when the Khalistan insurgency was at its peak. He simply wouldn't know where to look. But I know just the man who can do it. He's retired, but it shouldn't take much persuasion to get him to return to the field. As for Kashmir, our in-house art connoisseur might want to establish contact with that bird friend of his . . .'

'Falcon?'

'Correct. But not right away. There's something else we're missing here. After this broad tip-off, Takshak would have followed up with more specific information that would tell us exactly where to start. It's got to be somewhere within these paintings, or in a separate email.'

'But there are no other emails. I've checked.'

'Check again. And then again. Until you find something. If it's specific information, like an address, or a photograph, basically anything concrete, then he wouldn't have made it easy to find. You're the expert. I'm sure you can figure it out.'

Ravi is about to walk out, when Cyrus stops him, 'But, sir . . . if K2 is what we think it is, then it is possibly the most terrifying scenario we can conceive of. Like Takshak has pointed out literally, it truly is surreal. And so, it can't just be Jose looking through emails, and me contacting Falcon. There needs to be a bigger game plan. I mean, it's probably none of my business but I think I'd like to understand exactly what it is that we're getting to, and where I fit in . . .'

Jose sighs, 'You can't have a game plan unless you know what, where, and against whom you are playing. And it doesn't help that we're dealing with an invisible enemy.'

Ravi announces, 'Operation Sudarshan Chakra. That's what this one's going to be called.'

'Sudarshan Chakra?'

'When Lord Vishnu was confronted with the problem of hidden enemies lurking in the nether world, terrorizing the innocent from afar, he hurled his chakra with such precise calculation that they were all slayed with not a single drop of innocent blood spilled. The task in front of us is something like this. But once the chakra is out of your hand, it truly is out of your hand. There's nothing you can do. And so, we must get our calculations right. One mistake, and you just can't tell where the chakra is headed.'

Chessboard

'Do you remember that time when we found a message in the park?' Ravi asks Jose, even as he paces up and down his office, squeezing a yellow stress ball. It's something his doctor has recommended as a surrogate for smoking in times of stress when the craving for a cigarette instinctively occurs.

'Yes, sir, I do,' Jose replies.

'In which case, you surely remember where exactly in the park we found it, don't you?'

Jose nods, 'Yes, in a dustbin.'

'What's the logic behind leaving a message in a dustbin, when a park is already the last place anybody would expect to find a secret message?'

'Well, I suppose it has to do with the fact that nobody would ever rummage through a dustbin. And so, even the chances of somebody accidentally discovering the message are next to none. If what you're suggesting is that there's a message in the trash folder, I checked. There isn't any.'

'When you come to think of it, it is a risky strategy, isn't it? What if, for instance, the designated receiver is unable to access the dustbin on that particular day? Dustbins are, after all, cleaned out on a daily basis.'

Jose is a confused. He wonders what Ravi is getting at. 'It is, I suppose, risky sir.'

'But if you remember, the letter wasn't exactly in the dustbin with the rest of the trash. It was taped to the dustbin. And so, even if it were to be emptied out, the letter would stay in place. Takshak knew I was in hospital. And so, he was aware that I wouldn't probably see his message until a month later. The question I'm asking you is, what is the digital equivalent of taping a message to a dustbin?'

Jose shrugs his shoulders, 'I don't know. Most email service providers automatically delete all messages in trash after thirty days. So, it's by design impossible to retrieve them after they've been sitting undiscovered in trash for over a month.'

'Most email service providers, you say. Isn't it curious that Takshak chose a little-known email provider? I don't know about you, but I've never heard of Photonmail. Perhaps it allows for things that the others don't? Perhaps Takshak isn't as low-tech and old-fashioned as I remember him to be?'

Jose's face lights up.

'No wonder I couldn't find anything,' he says, rushing to use Ravi's desktop, 'I ran my scans with the wrong initial premises, the sort that would be more appropriate for Yahoo or Gmail.'

Jose seems to know exactly what to do, and he deftly navigates a maze of dialog boxes and security checks to land finally at a terminal. He hammers away a series of commands and is finally presented with the option of recovering deleted emails.

'There is one message. Uploaded as a draft, and then deleted within a minute, thirty-five days ago.'

Jose retrieves the message:

Sending you a photograph, just so you can see what I look like now. It's been so long, what if you don't recognize me at the Himalayan airport on the third Saturday of next month? My old friend from the village, the guy who changed my life forever, is ready to pick me up in case you don't . . . If our friendship means anything to you, I hope I can expect to see you at the airport. Also, don't worry. Even my old friend from the village doesn't know what I look like these days. So, let's see if you can beat him to it :-)

PS: Old acquaintances are paying for my trip, but the new kid on the block is the one managing it all. You know, the one who ran away from his father's house recently.

Jose opens the picture attached to the email. An extremely fit and handsome man, not older than thirty-five, is seen posing with bikini-clad women on what looks like a beach somewhere in Europe. He is even more confused and asks Ravi, 'This is Takshak?'

'Of course not, don't be silly. This is either a top-level Khalistani leader or an ISI man. And he is coming to India, via the Tribhuvan International Airport in Kathmandu on the third Saturday of this month which is exactly nine days from now. I'm quite certain I know who the guy he is referring to is. He's an old operative of the dreaded terrorist organization—Khalsa Tigers. But as far as I remember, he never returned to

India after the organization collapsed. But anyway, I'll get that confirmed soon. As for the last part of the message, I'm sure you know who he's referring to.'

'The new kid on the block who ran away from his father's house recently? I can only think of one name—Tabrez.'

* * *

Gurmail Singh, Ravi's driver of nearly three decades, is taken aback when Ravi asks him to drive to Central Park in Connaught Place. It has been almost five years since Ravi has asked to be driven there, but Gurmail has no doubts about the agenda. Ravi wanting to go to Central Park can mean only one thing.

Ravi gets down from the car and walks towards a group of chess players—a motley mix of young and old, rich and poor—gathered under a canopy only a short distance from the entrance. Ravi watches from slightly afar, the back of a well-built man hunched over a chessboard, lost in thought, a beedi burning between the fingers of his right hand. Ravi can't think of a single time Madan Singh was in Delhi but wasn't to be found playing chess at this time of the day at Central Park.

Madan's instincts are as sharp as a hawk's, and he immediately realizes that somebody is staring at him from behind. His attention snaps and he turns around. He sees Ravi but does not acknowledge him immediately. Instead, he returns to his game, while Ravi walks back to his car. Madan's opponent, a college student, has been taking a long time to make his move. Finally running out of patience, especially now that he knows Ravi is waiting for him, Madan tells his opponent, 'Your cycle of perpetual checks has run its course. The only thing you can do is move your queen to d5. But then I will move my queen to e6, resulting in a check that will force you to trade queens. And then I'll just move my knight onto c6, and that'll be checkmate. Do you want to go through the moves, or do you want to quit?' The opponent looks at the board, realizes Madan is right, and extends his hand in resignation. Madan Singh quickly gets up and walks out of the park, into Ravi's car.

Gurmail salutes Madan, who in turn pats him affectionately on his shoulders, 'Looks like you'll be a great-grandfather by the time he lets you retire.'

Gurmail flashes a sheepish grin, even as he starts driving, 'On the contrary, sir, it is I who do not want to retire. With his health not in very good shape, I don't think I can trust anybody else to take care of him.'

'Nonsense,' Ravi snaps back in jest. 'I am healthier than I've ever been.'

Madan tells Ravi, 'You actually do look very healthy. I can't tell you how happy I am to see you.'

'Thank you, Madan Sahib. But the fact that I've come here to meet you must tell you the reason for my visit, doesn't it?'

'I do not know exactly what you have in mind, but I must tell you that I am an old man now. In the age of T20 cricket, what can a Test player like me have to offer? And if I remember, you have some of the finest young T20 players in your team already.'

Ravi chuckles. If there was one thing that had brought the two of them closer in the early years, it was their shared love for speaking in cryptic metaphors, even when there was no real need to.

'A Test player might somehow manage to play T20 but a T20 specialist wouldn't last a ball in Test cricket. And as it so happens, an all-star Test team of the past is planning on touring India, and I can't count on my swashbuckling stars, who were possibly still in their diapers when these veterans were in their prime.'

A quick look of alarm flashes on Madan's face. 'They've come out of retirement?'

From his briefcase Ravi pulls out an envelope containing Takshak's message and hands it to Madan.

It takes less than a minute for Madan to identify the 'old friend' from Takshak's village, 'It has to be Surjit Singh Sandhu. He's the only one alive. That's because we let him live. We let him get away.'

Ravi nods, 'That's what I thought as well, but I wanted you to confirm. Can I count on you to come up with a plan, and personally lead this on the ground?'

'If my captain thinks I can do it, then I most certainly can. But will the selectors agree to bring someone so old out of retirement?'

'That's for the captain to worry about. You start hitting the nets straight away.'

* * *

Back at headquarters, Ravi makes his way to Sarita's office. As if his troubles weren't bad enough, standing on the way to Sarita's office, quite literally at this moment, is Anil. Ravi keeps his head down and hopes to walk past unnoticed. But Anil isn't one to let go easily.

'Ravi!'

'Still alive, sir. Thanks for all the prayers.'

Before Anil can say anything, Ravi walks away.

The sight of Ravi in her office on his very first day back alarms Sarita and she immediately gets up from her seat, 'You didn't have to take the trouble to come here. We could have talked on the secraphone or I would have come over to your office myself.'

Ravi waves the suggestion away, 'The doctor said I must get as much light exercise as I can. I suppose the walk to your office helps.'

Sarita smiles. She's happy to have him back.

'So, what's the verdict? Have your blue-eyed boys been any good in your absence?'

'Much better than I'd expected, ma'am. Given how much they've had to endure in their very first year on the job, I must say I am proud of their fortitude. Of course, there have been mistakes, even crucial ones, but I take complete responsibility for them.'

'What do you mean? You weren't even around.'

'Precisely my point, ma'am. Perhaps I should have taken a more active and direct interest, even if only remotely.'

'You never cease to baffle me, Ravi. It's almost a hardwired instinct for officers to pass the buck at the first opportunity they get. You, on the other hand . . .'

As always, Ravi is embarrassed by the flattery, and he is eager to get to the point.

'I'm afraid I have ominous news for you, ma'am. Takshak has established contact after a decade and a half.'

A look of grave worry dawns on Sarita's face at the very mention of Takshak.

'And . . .?'

'It appears that long-dormant sleeper cells of Khalsa Tigers have been reactivated in Europe.'

The tense muscles on Sarita's face visibly ease up, 'That really shouldn't be all that worrying, Ravi. They keep trying every few years, but they always fail. They have no money, no arms, and most importantly, virtually no leadership. The old guard is all mostly gone. Besides, whatever presence they have is all outside the country. This used to be a real concern in the early years, no doubt. But we've come a long way since then. We're a stronger country. We can now count on nearly every important foreign intelligence agency to extend their cooperation.'

'Indeed, ma'am. This time too, a very important foreign intelligence agency is extending its cooperation. But, not to us.'

Sarita is stunned. 'ISI?'

'I'm afraid so, ma'am.'

'What exactly is their plan?'

'At this point, we can only speculate. For now, what we know is that an ISI asset is arriving at Tribhuvan International Airport in less than ten days from now. From there he will be picked up and driven into India by Surjeet Singh Sandhu, who was formerly number three in the Khalsa Tigers chain of command. If he's risked his safety at this old age, by coming back to India, my hunch is that something very big is in the offing. We must prepare to confront a huge storm. It's not just a professional collaboration between two enemy organizations that we're dealing with here, but a marriage in the true sense.'

Sarita is befuddled, 'I'm sorry . . . I'm not sure I follow.'

'What I'm trying to say is that this isn't one of those logistical and financial partnerships that the ISI usually establishes with most anti-India terror outfits. It's not purely transactional, and certainly not just about orchestrating attacks on civilians. It's much more sinister than that. What they're hoping to do is build strong networks of solidarity between the secessionist currents in Punjab and Kashmir. Since Tabrez is also an important cog in the wheel, they'll look to then manoeuvre those synergies to mobilize wider support by tapping into minority anxieties across the country. At this point, I can only speculate on how they plan on doing it. But I'm quite certain that if we let them succeed, they will have blurred the lines between political expression and outright secession. And if that happens, the integrity of our nation will be in peril. Again, this is all still partially just conjecture. If we are to discover anything concrete, we must act smartly. Instead of capturing the ISI agent straightaway, we must allow him to enter the country and commence operations. Within closely monitored conditions, of course. But in order to pull this off, I will need to ask for your permission.'

Sarita understands Ravi well enough to know that if he is asking for permission, he surely has a wild idea up his sleeve.

'What do you have in mind?'

'I'm proposing that we re-induct Madan Singh into the bureau. On a contractual basis, of course. He will impersonate Sandhu and bring the ISI man into India.'

'You don't mean the beedi-smoking Madan Singh?'

'The very same, ma'am.'

'Are you sure, Ravi? I mean, I understand your rationale. Nobody understands the Khalistani world better than him.

But he is sixty-five years old, if I'm not mistaken, and he hasn't been active since he retired. Instead, why don't you bring him in to train one of your boys, the way he always has?'

'I would have ma'am, but time is a luxury we simply cannot afford at this point. Madan Singh is our best hope. Most importantly, he's of the same age as Sandhu. It's a strange thing how fate pans out. It had been Madan Singh's idea to allow Sandhu to escape. It was a calculated gamble. You know what they say about trusting a known devil more than an unknown angel. And it might all now pay off, decades later, if we do this right. If age is what you're concerned about, you shouldn't be. He doesn't look a day older than fifty-five and can easily match up against a forty-year-old as far as fitness goes.'

'I have no doubt, Ravi. But is that all it takes? I mean, let's suppose things go horribly wrong and he is captured. Will a man his age be able to withstand the torture? Come to think of it, there's nearly half a century of secrets he's carrying with him. If they break him, we'll be done for. By we, I don't just mean you and I as individuals, but the IB itself. I hope I do not have to explain to you why a setback of that scale is also a luxury we simply cannot afford at this point . . . I'm sorry, I don't mean to question your judgement. It's just that I'm not sure I can permit such a risky move, not when there's so much at stake.'

'I completely agree, ma'am. Everything is at stake here. But that is precisely why I think Madan Singh should be the man leading this on the ground. If the ISI is as closely involved in this whole operation as I suspect it to be, the path ahead, wherever it might lead us, is going to be extremely treacherous. I don't think I can trust anybody else to navigate it for us. Besides, I have already spoken to Madan Singh, and he is eager to do this.'

Sarita sighs. 'One day, you're in here demanding that I induct rookies who still haven't even finished their training. And then another day, you come and tell me that you want to bring in a retired agent who should ideally be watching television and taking multiple naps in a day. What can I say? If this is what you think is best, then you should go ahead. But on one condition.'

'And that is?'

'That you step away from your administrative duties.'

Ravi is completely taken aback, but he keeps a straight face, 'If that is what you think C3 needs, then of course.'

Sarita does not respond, and there is an awkward silence for a few moments. Ravi grows restless, 'So, who is going to replace me? Please don't tell me . . . Anil?'

Sarita lets out a mild chuckle, 'That look on your face is just priceless. Who said anything about replacing you? I'm talking about appointing a deputy chief who can handle the dreary work of administration, while you train all your focus on the operational side of things. I'll leave you to decide who it will be. Take a day or two and let me know. Of course, the final decision lies with the home secretary, but it's just a procedural necessity. He'll approve of whoever you recommend, provided the individual conforms to the eligibility criteria as far as experience, cadre, and rank are concerned. I'm sure you know this, but I'm just saying it anyway, just so you don't come in tomorrow and tell me that you want to make Jose your deputy.'

* * *

As Madan drives through the main streets of the city in a swanky SUV, still several kilometres from Sandhu's farm, the thought that he might be recognized by an old-timer crosses his mind a few times. But he reminds himself that he has nothing to worry about. He is presumed to be dead in these parts, having been declared so by the police. It was a strategy the Intelligence Bureau had employed to extricate its assets embedded within the Khalistani fold.

Memories come flooding through Madan's mind as he passes by several familiar sights, strangely comforting despite their inextricable association with the toughest years of his life. It was about thirty years ago that Madan Singh, posing as a Bihari labourer, had landed up in the sacred city of Anandpur Sahib in north-eastern Punjab. He had arrived in tattered clothes, carrying no money, no possessions. Sympathetic locals had taken him in and offered food and shelter. He had narrated to them a deftly scripted story—rehearsed down to every single emotional detail—about how his entire family had been wiped out in a genocidal spree by the upper castes in his village. He had then made his way on foot all the way to Anandpur Sahib, under the firm hope that he would be accepted and cared for. They had bought into his story entirely and allowed him to settle down and carve out a new life for himself. He had found work on a farm on the outskirts of the city. His foremost task was to keep an eye on Surjit Singh Sandhu, a rising star within the Khalsa Tigers, who fancied himself as potentially being a major political figure within the Khalistani nation they were trying to establish by seceding from India.

Over the next couple of years, even as he worked on the fields during the day, Madan weaselled his way into Sandhu's inner circle. Madan—or Nagendra or Nago as he had called himself then—penetrated a vast web of recruitment, training and arms procurement networks to help the Indian government bring it all crashing down, along with the rest of the Khalsa Tigers. It was a massive operation that had involved multiple agencies and organizations. Sandhu escaped and went into hiding somewhere in Europe and had never since returned.

Madan exits the main city area, onto the highway and stops at a dhaba that stands right by the side of a small road that leads straight into Sandhu's massive farmhouse. It is a ramshackle establishment that seems to cater primarily to truck drivers. And so, the sharply dressed Madan in his fancy SUV, asking for a glass of buttermilk and something to munch on, immediately attracts attention. Eager to earn a handsome tip, Monty, the owner of the place, who also doubles up as its sole waiter, is exceedingly polite towards Madan.

But after a few moments, Monty grows slightly suspicious as he looks carefully at Madan. Suspicion finally gives way to recognition, but before he can articulate the words, Madan puts his arm around Monty's shoulder. 'Yes, it is me.'

'But you were dead.'

'Young Nagendra is dead. I am very much alive, as you can see.'

'I should have expected you. He came back a week ago—Sandhu. From what I've been hearing, he's looking to dispose of his property and permanently end all connections to his homeland. He has already found a buyer, I heard, a very wealthy foreigner, and Sandhu is planning to personally pick him up from the airport.'

Madan hands over a wad of notes to Monty. 'When he leaves, you let me know. Somebody's going to be keeping a watch on you as well, and so if you try to strike a deal with Sandhu behind my back, I'll know.'

Madan drives back towards the main streets, and finds his way to a gurudwara, one of several scattered through the holy city. It is time for langar, and Karnail Singh, the *langri*, is particularly generous to Madan, who eats his meal with genuine relish. After he's done with eating, Madan finds a moment with Karnail and explains the reason for his return.

'Just in case Monty fails to do his job, for whatever reasons, can I count on you to keep an eye on Sandhu and inform me when he leaves? If we let him get away, the horrors of those godforsaken decades might return. I hope you understand what is at stake here.'

Karnail Singh nods sombrely. He understands better than anybody else having lost his entire family at the peak of the insurgency. He too had been a rich landlord like Sandhu, but he had given everything up and turned to a life of service at the gurudwara.

Madan bows in respect, and quietly sneaks in a generous amount into the donation box, before driving back to Delhi.

The Switcheroo

On the outskirts of Gorakhpur, only a hundred and fifty kilometres away from Nepal, Sandhu's SUV is waylaid by a convoy of unmarked black vehicles that quietly surround him from all sides, leaving no room for manoeuvre. It is a completely quiet operation, and before Sandhu can even register what is happening, he is herded into one of the cars, blindfolded, and driven away. Only one car stays behind, and Madan emerges from its passenger's seat, and gets into Sandhu's car. Even as the other car follows at a distance, Madan drives towards Kathmandu. Only moments later, he is informed by the unit ferrying Sandhu that he is to receive someone named Suleimani at the airport.

At the Tribhuvan International Airport, Madan parks the car and retrieves from the back seat a printed placard that reads, 'K2 Tours and Travels Welcomes You to Kathmandu'. The flight lands only in an hour's time, but Madan Singh diligently waits at the arrivals gate with the placard in hand. All the while, he keeps his eye out for any suspicious characters loitering around. For if there is a third person designated to watch over Suleimani's reception, Madan could be in trouble. But as far as he can see, there is nobody else.

It takes little time for Suleimani to find Madan and his placard—held upside down as part of the pre-decided protocol—in the crowd. They walk to Sandhu's car in silence. Suleimani is an imposing figure, a six-foot something who looks like he could take down ten men in one go, but Madan Singh isn't intimidated. He coolly gets into the car, even as Suleimani pulls out a bug detector and subjects the car to a quick scan. There are no bugs, and Suleimani is assured. It becomes clear to Madan that Suleimani is a trained professional, possibly a senior ISI man, just as Ravi had predicted. Madan Singh reaches into the glove compartment and retrieves a fake Indian passport for Suleimani, which identifies him as Rizwan Qureshi, a resident of Hazratganj in Lucknow. Suleimani closely inspects the passport, before asking Madan Singh, 'Can I see your ID? Just to be absolutely sure, before we cross over into India.' Madan is well prepared, and pulls out an Overseas Citizen of India card of Surjit Singh Sandhu that has Madan's photo. Suleimani is convinced as the details matched those provided to him. They begin driving.

Suleimani is a man of few words, and Madan is equally happy to drive in silence. But as they get closer to the Indian border, passing through the town of Birganj, Madan notices an unmistakable restlessness growing within Suleimani. At the Indian border, they are stopped and asked to step out of the car. Suleimani grows even more anxious, and the possibility that he might have walked into a trap begins to play on his mind. The officer on duty casts a suspicious glance at Suleimani's passport and has all kinds of questions to ask. But Madan, posing as Sandhu, swiftly defuses the tension and convinces the officer to let them go. Suleimani is relieved, but little does he know that all of this is simply part of an elaborate scheme designed to induce him into trusting Madan Singh.

As they commence their long drive to Lucknow, Madan tries to strike a conversation, and see if it rings any bells, 'Twenty years ago, when I received Major Ifthikar from the same airport, we managed to go through a route that had no checkposts. Now, they've completely tightened the borders.'

The mention of Ifthikar puts Suleimani completely at ease, and he is now happy to talk, 'Twenty years ago, I was still a school student. I suppose it was a different time. Now Major Sa'ab is a Brigadier'

Madan is happy to have broken the ice, and continues, 'Brigadier Ifthikar saved my life, you know . . . Our movement was almost entirely dead, and the Indian government was closing in on me. It was Brigadier Ifthikar who personally arranged for me to flee to Canada, and from there to Europe. He stayed in touch with me all throughout, always concerned about how I was doing. When he proposed the possibility of reviving our movement, I immediately said yes. He's always had more concern for the realization of the Khalistani dream than my own people.'

Suleimani nods along, 'He is a real gem. Despite being so senior, he takes a keen interest in mentoring young officers like me. All that I've learnt is thanks to him.'

'In which case, he's also taught you the importance of never missing out on prayer time, no matter what. Isn't that correct? Let's stop at the next village. There's a small mosque where you can offer namaz. We can then stop for lunch a little further ahead. There's a nice spot I know.'

Suleimani nods, evidently impressed by how well Madan seems to know his boss. Madan, of course, has never met Ifthikar, but knows enough—from hearsay, anecdotes, and the ever-fattening file in the IB's archives that had first been created by a young Ravi—to easily pass off as a close friend. Ifthikar, or Brigadier Ahmadi as he is formally identified, heads the ISI's India operations.

When the Khalistan movement had collapsed two decades ago, Ifthikar had gone out of his way to persuade his bosses to help the fleeing leadership of the Khalsa Tigers safely relocate to other countries. He had held the firm belief that someday, the insurgency could be revived, and they could exert complete control over it. Several attempts had taken off in the years since, only to quickly be nipped by alert Indian agencies. Project K2 is the most ambitious attempt by far, and with Abu Jihad Al-Brittani personally overseeing all the moving parts, Ifthikar is confident of finally making inroads.

The mosque Madan stops at is no random one, but one that has been identified, vetted and secured by a C3 unit. Even as Suleimani enters the mosque, Madan walks over to a nondescript toddy-shack-turned-restaurant where a mobile phone is handed to him. Ravi is on the line.

'Looks like Ifthikar is copying your style, Ravi. Sending out young officers on critical missions. He can't be older than forty, at least partially European. But unlike your boys, this chap is a gullible fool. It's looking good for us.'

Even as Madan talks to Ravi, the number plates on Sandhu's car have swiftly been replaced with exact replicas by another C3 unit. Only, these new plates have GPS trackers embedded in them. The conversation with Ravi is a quick one, and Madan picks up a parcel that's been left there for him, before exiting the shack. It's all timed perfectly and just as he expects, Suleimani is already waiting for him by the car. Madan holds up the parcel and tells Suleimani, 'I managed to get some lunch packed. Nihari and khamiri roti, the Brigadier's favourite.'

If there was any doubt at all lingering in Suleimani's mind, it is now laid to rest. A little further ahead, they stop at a scenic location on the banks of the Gandak river, close to the border between Uttar Pradesh and Bihar. Madan unfurls a silken rug over the grass and serves lunch in two plates. Suleimani eats the nihari with relish, and Madan partakes without flinching an eyebrow. Left to his own devices, Madan is the sort who wouldn't touch non-vegetarian food with a barge pole. But whilst on the job, his personal preference and beliefs—regardless of how profoundly dear they might be to him—are cast away with the remarkable swiftness and regularity of a snake shedding its skin in the course of natural order.

After lunch they set off on the drive towards Lucknow. They are taking a longer route, as Suleimani wants to stop at Varanasi on the way, to quickly scout a few locations of interest. Madan is only too happy to oblige. After they've finally run out of anecdotes about Brigadier Ifthikar to share, there is awkward silence for a while. Madan is determined to cement the relationship by finding more things to bond over. Given the vast gulf in age that separates them, Madan knows that there are possibly only a few things that they hold in common. He decides to play it safe and asks Suleimani if he can put on some music. Suleimani isn't exactly enthused, for he has no idea what music Madan might play and ruin what has so far been a perfect afternoon. But he agrees anyway.

As 'Ranjish Hi Sahi' by Mehdi Hassan pours out through Sandhu's expensive stereo system, Madan takes in with quiet delight the sight of Suleimani's ears perking up. It is just as he had expected. He had picked up the music from Examiner, who had over the course of his career, developed a nuanced understanding of the ordinary Pakistani psyche. Just as one couldn't go wrong with Kishore Kumar or Lata Mangeshkar when choosing music for an Indian, so too was the case with Mehdi Hasan and Pakistanis.

And so, by the time they reach Varanasi, just in time for Suleimani's evening namaz, Madan has completely won over the young Pakistani officer. Even as Suleimani enters the Alamgir Masjid, Madan sneaks into a bhang shop, where yet another mobile phone with Ravi at the other end, awaits him.

'So, what's the verdict, Sandhu Sahib? We have an ATS squad standing by, waiting for your confirmation. They can get there in two minutes and whisk your man away.'

'I think we can afford to hold off an immediate capture. He's ours to be had. Let him go about his business for a while.'

Ravi is thrilled. If there is one man who shares his enthusiasm for taking the highest risk, highest-payout approach to intelligence operations, it is Madan Singh.

'That is excellent news. What's the plan of action?'

'We're going to scout around Varanasi for a short while, and then we're going to Lucknow. I'm going to stay with him for a few days, while he carries out some pre-arranged meetings. Please instruct all units to refrain, at all costs, from acting in haste. Surveillance is fine, but we must allow him to carry on with his plans. After he's done with his engagements in Lucknow, we'll return to Delhi, and then the ball is in your court, chief.'

Ravi hangs up, and summons Subramaniam.

'I am heading home for the day, Subramaniam. Is there anything on the agenda I must look into before that?'

Subramaniam straightens his glasses and looks at his planner, although he doesn't really have to. Ravi's itinerary is something he etches into his memory at the start of every day. And as the day progresses, and additions and subtractions are constantly being made to the schedule, he effortlessly keeps track of it.

'Nothing for today, sir. But I must remind you that by tomorrow you are supposed to forward your recommendation to Sarita ma'am.'

Ravi raises his eyebrows, 'Recommendation?'

'You've forgotten sir, as usual. A deputy chief is being appointed to serve under you, and you are expected to recommend a name.'

Ravi shakes his head in disbelief at his abject memory when it comes to administrative matters.

'Thanks for reminding me, Subramaniam. I have actually taken a decision already. Just want to give it some more time in my head before passing it on to the chief.'

'Anything else, sir?'

'Yes, there is one thing. I'd like you to call up Mihir and tell him that he'll be having dinner at my residence tonight.'

It is now Subramaniam's turn to raise his eyebrows, 'Are you making Mihir your deputy, sir?'

Ravi doesn't acknowledge the question, and moves on, 'Is there anything else?'

'Jose has requested an appointment, sir. Should I also invite him to dinner at your residence?'

'No, tonight's just Mihir. Ask Jose to meet me in the morning. He'll know when and where.'

* * *

Ravi steps out into his garden in anticipation of Mihir's arrival. It has been a fortnight since their last interaction, and Ravi is eager to see how Mihir has been coping with his punitive exile. At 8.30 p.m. sharp, Mihir arrives in a cab. Ravi waves warmly at a sharply dressed Mihir, who smiles awkwardly as he walks towards his boss. The beard that he had grown after his mother's death has been shaved off, and Mihir is looking as sharp as ever.

'I'm impressed,' Ravi tells Mihir. 'I was half-expecting you to turn up looking even more dishevelled than before, perhaps reeking of rum.'

Mihir tries to muster a chuckle but can only manage a weak smile. Ravi can tell immediately that for all the appearance of normalcy and order, Mihir is a broken man still fighting hard to bury his demons. As he follows Ravi into the living room, Mihir notices the conspicuous absence of the fixtures in Ravi's domestic life—Rita and Ranger, the black Labrador pup.

'I-is ma'am asleep, sir?'

Ravi taps on a wooden table. 'Touch wood, no. She's back on her feet now. She's just stepped out with some friends. And Ranger has gone along. Suits me well. I get to spend some quiet time with my thoughts. Why don't you sit down and make yourself comfortable, while I fix some drinks? Whiskey?'

Mihir shakes his head. 'Sorry sir, I don't drink any more.'

Ravi chuckles. 'Good. That was just a test. I wasn't going to offer you one even if you said yes. But of course, you can sit down and make yourself comfortable. That bit, I was serious about.'

Mihir smiles. 'You should go ahead and pour yourself one, sir.'

'I've stopped drinking too. Not even a glass of wine at dinner, at least for a few months.'

'Bearing in mind your health, I suppose, sir?'

'Not really, at least not directly. My liver is in better shape than Cyrus Bandookwallah's, I'm told by Dr Himwal. Besides, there are studies that show that moderate drinking is beneficial for cardiac well-being. Did you know that?'

'I did, sir. Cyrus himself told me, actually. And he found out from Jose, who knows all these random facts about everything in the world for no good reason at all. Anyway, ever since he found out, Cyrus has been using it to justify his love for alcohol. Of course, it's a different matter altogether that the amount he consumes is far from being moderate.'

'I'm sure you're getting all sentimental thinking about your friends. But I hope you'll forgive me for not being particularly interested in the details. Getting back to the question of why I've given up drinking, any hypotheses?'

Mihir shakes his head.

Ravi is unimpressed. 'What sort of an intelligence officer are you who can't come up with a hypothesis? Just say something. Has three weeks of staying at home completely quelled your instincts for speculation?'

Mihir sits upright, trying to sharpen his focus and gather his thoughts. He knows Ravi well enough to realize that the question has little to do with why Ravi has given up drinking.

'Since you left open the possibility that it might at least indirectly have something to do with your health, I'm assuming . . .'

'Smoking. Every time I'd drink, since the time I was a freshly minted police officer, I'd smoke an entire pack of cigarettes. I'd allowed them to form such a deep-rooted connection without even realizing it. I found out last Sunday, when I decided I'd have a small glass of wine with dinner. As soon as the alcohol hit my blood, I was craving desperately for a cigarette. I rummaged through my drawers, and finally found an unopened pack. I opened it and lit one with much relish. But as soon as I'd taken that first drag, I realized what a terrible mistake I'd made and immediately stubbed it out. But only five minutes later, the craving returned, and it was even stronger. I don't want to bore you with all the painful details, but the point I'm trying to make is, we all make mistakes. And sometimes, as I was hoping to demonstrate through this example, these mistakes arise out of associations and conflicts within ourselves that we are barely aware of. But once you recognize that you've made a mistake, what do you do next? Do I resolve to never smoke again—and in order to achieve that, not drink again until I'm reasonably settled in my convictions—or do I convince myself that a few puffs once in a while will do no harm?'

Mihir is visibly uncomfortable, and this doesn't escape Ravi's attention. He asks Mihir what the matter is.

'I get where you're going with this, sir. Behind all these trivial matters you keep bringing up, I'm sure there are profound insights. But I don't understand why you're wasting all this time on me?'

Mihir begins to quiver in his seat, and his face turns pale as he continues, 'I-I've completely let you down. To be honest, I'm embarrassed to even be in your company right now. I should at the very least be permanently discharged from duty, if not thrown into prison for treason.'

A poker-faced Ravi glares at Mihir. 'If I thought you belonged in prison, trust me, you would have been there by now. Listen here, boy. You made a mistake, you're evidently repentant, and that's a good enough sign for me. When I decided to fast track your induction into the organization, I was well-aware that you were a hot keg waiting to explode. It's a time-honoured truth known to all spymasters—individuals with turbulent pasts make for erratic and unreliable agents. It's common sense if you come to think of it. The more baggage you're carrying, the harder it becomes to set it all aside in an instant. But I still took the chance, because I saw in you a burning passion that eclipsed all the wounds you were carrying. To persist with the alcohol analogy, I saw in you the will and courage to have a drink without succumbing to the urge to smoke. It's not a straightforward analogy, but I'll trust you to make what you will out of it. What I'm essentially trying to tell you is taking one drag of a cigarette when you're recovering from a decades-long addiction is by itself not a grave mistake. But to then assume all hope is lost and give in to that addiction all over again would be a grave mistake. I stand by what I felt the first time I met you. I think I can trust you to be more conscious of all the battles being fought inside of you and put this debacle behind you, unless you're absolutely sure that you're a spent force. Do you want to report back to duty?'

Mihir is left dumfounded. He struggles to find the words, as tears trickle down his cheeks. 'I-I don't know how I can ever . . .'

'Save it. You'll only embarrass yourself further. Report to my office at 9.30 in the morning. You've been exposed, and so we'll have to put you to work far away from here.'

Weathermen

A minute before his 5.30 a.m. alarm can go off Jose wakes up on his own. It's a far cry from the time a year or so ago when having to wake up so early to join Ravi on his morning walk was something he dreaded, despite the obvious rewards that lay in store. But now he doesn't even need an alarm. His body seems to effortlessly rouse itself out of slumber at the designated hour each day, regardless of how late he's slept the previous night. It's almost as if his body is seeking to emulate the battle-hardened adherence to routine that his boss has cultivated for himself over the years.

Ravi has only recently resumed strenuous exercise and so the walk around Nehru Park is likely to be much shorter than usual. Jose knows that this can mean only one thing, that although Ravi intends to carry out a holistic assessment of Jose—which is why he isn't being summoned to Ravi's office—Ravi doesn't intend to allow Jose too much time to make his point.

As they break into a brisk walk, Jose tells Ravi, 'Thanks for inviting me on the walk, sir. I've been trying to set up an appointment to meet you for several days. I was hoping to actually see you in your office. There's something very important that I need to talk to you about, and I'm not sure if this is the right place.'

Ravi pretends not to hear Jose and begins talking about the weather.

'I've been feeling very nostalgic about the Delhi weather of the 1980s and the 1990s, and it looks like my wish for a return to that time has been granted. Don't you think the weather's been a lot like the way it was back then?'

Jose is befuddled. 'I wouldn't know, sir. One, I was very young. Two, I wasn't even in Delhi.'

'Oh yes, of course. But you do have access to historical weather data, don't you?'

Jose shrugs. He knows that Ravi is talking in code, but the cipher eludes him for now. 'If I wanted to, I guess I could get access. But it's not something that really interests me.'

'Really? It's no wonder so many people are always grumbling about the younger generation lacking integrity or commitment. Do you even hear yourself? You work for the meteorological department, you're paid from taxpayer money to keep track of weather patterns, and you're telling me it doesn't interest you? If I'm not mistaken, I'd asked you to keep track of weather patterns in the northern and western frontiers of the country. What's the forecast?'

'Oh . . .'

Ravi is talking about Kashmir and Punjab—two regions Jose has been asked to intensify interception efforts in. But Jose hasn't been able to make much progress, and he takes a few moments to figure out a way to convey this in weatherman terms.

'We still don't have a very clear understanding of the patterns sir, because our satellites simply haven't been able to pick up the right kind of data that would allow us make reliable predictions.'

'Then deploy more satellites. Do whatever it takes. If flood and drought strike again in the north and the west, and it turns out that we had done nothing to prevent it, it'll all be because of an incompetent weatherman who was slacking off on his job. You do not want to be that weatherman, do you?'

'We can deploy every satellite in the world, but that might not really solve our problem. What we need is something much more primitive, something that will allow us to figure out which way the wind is blowing on the ground. Something like a weathervane . . .'

Ravi doesn't immediately respond, and Jose feels the need to explain further. 'A weathervane is one of those things with a cockerel head, and lettered arrows marking each direction, which turns according to which way the wind is blowing.'

'I know what a weathervane is. I'm the head of the bloody meteorological department.'

Jose can't help but chuckle, and Ravi glares at him, forcing Jose to suppress his amusement.

Ravi continues, 'We already have weathervanes on the ground, but the information is very sketchy at the moment because it's possible that these weathervanes aren't properly located. What I need from you is a bird's eye view, or a satellite-eye view, of what it is looking like from above, so I can plan out my on-ground strategy accordingly.'

'I'm afraid that might not work, sir. And that's what I've been trying to bring to your attention. You see, all the turbulence that's expected exists right now only within a simulation. And so, what we need is a virtual weathervane of sorts. Something that seems like it's out there on-ground physically but is actually just a computer model being operated by a human being.'

The walk is over, and Ravi abruptly bids goodbye to Jose before heading to his car. A perplexed Jose decides to follow. Ravi can see that Jose isn't satisfied, and so he asks him to get into his car.

Ravi tells Jose, not looking directly at him, 'You wanted to give me an update, and you've given me one. What is it now?'

'I'm sorry sir, but I'm not entirely sure if you understood. It's technically complex information, and I don't understand why we even need to be talking in code when we could actually just discuss all of this in plain terms within the secure premises of your office or mine.'

'You know, I discovered during my recent illness that the average doctor is expected to closely study at least ten thousand electrocardiograms, before they can begin to consistently detect anomalies. Because apparently, heart attacks and other cardiac problems manifest in many different ways. But that doesn't mean that simply by looking at ten thousand electrocardiograms one after the other, you've learnt to diagnose heart attacks. The best cardiac diagnosticians are those who don't just remember what an abnormal wave roughly looks like, but somebody who can look at an abnormal wave and be able to visualize in their mind's eye exactly what's going on in that patient's heart.'

Jose feels hopelessly lost. In response to a question about the need to talk in code even when they don't really have to, all he's received is even more codes!

Ravi decides to spare Jose the suspense. 'Deliberate practice, that's what it's all about. Imagine how much more difficult it is when what we're dealing with is not something specialized like an electrocardiogram, but plain old ordinary language. It's astounding if you come to think of it, just how potent language is. The same piece of information can be communicated in an infinite number of different ways. You're the expert, and so I don't really need to be telling you all this. But the more practice you have transposing and translating complex pieces of information into completely unrelated contexts, the better your chances are of recognizing such transpositions when you encounter them in the material you're expected to scrutinize. And so, although you're not a field officer who doesn't for the most part actually need to communicate in code, you do happen to be someone who examines and analyses clusters of hundreds of thousands of messages. Unless you're always working on training your mind to come up with newer and more inventive ways of encoding complex information, you're bound to eventually be outsmarted by the enemy. Anybody can invent a metaphor—even five-year-olds come up with private languages in play, to retain that sense of play and wonder, that's what it takes.'

'I get all of that, sir. And I know that's why you're always joking around. It's like gymnastics for the brain. But surely, you'd agree that there are times where it simply makes more sense to talk in plain terms, especially when we have the privilege of having access to completely secure spaces where a spade can be called a spade. Like the problem I'm currently up against, the one I'm hoping to talk to you about is already difficult to explain, forget having to translate it into weatherman language on the fly. So, I'd really appreciate the opportunity to take you through it in detail.'

Ravi glares at Jose. 'All right, Professor Cherian. I suppose you won't be satisfied until I demonstrate to you that I have understood. I'd hate to be seen as somebody who's always joking around . . .'

'That's not what I meant, sir.'

'Going back to how all this started, the problem of satellites and weathervanes. Unless I'm mistaken, what you're saying is that the usual channels of information have gone quiet. But because sources on the ground, and elsewhere, are telling us that something massive is brewing, we're clearly missing something. Which, from what you're saying, is to be taken to imply that they've started using completely new channels of communication, and these are outside the purview of our surveillance modules. And this is not because we're lacking in technical skill or infrastructure, but because the internet by design allows for such channels. If I am for instance, sending you a message, I need to physically be me, and you need to physically be you in order to access the message. End-to-encryption is the technical phrase, I believe. And so finally, unless I've got every bit of this completely wrong, the only way to figure out what's going on in there is to infiltrate these channels in much the same way that Madan Singh infiltrated the Khalsa Tigers. The metadata you are collecting is giving you only rough patterns. Only infiltration of these channels by a digital entity would give a complete picture.'

Jose is stunned. This is exactly what he'd have said, if he'd been asked to speak in plain terms.

Ravi takes in the shock on Jose's face. 'I wonder why you seem to automatically assume, every single time, that if something's even remotely technical then it needs to be spoon-fed to me. There's something I've hidden from you all this while, just to test your competence. You see, I happen to have a PhD in computer science.'

Ravi relishes the shock on Jose's face. He lets it linger until they're only a minute away from Ravi's residence. And that's when Ravi can't hold it in any longer.

'I'm just messing with you, young man. I already received a thorough briefing from the head of Insomnia, Jyotirmoy Saha, which is why I didn't see the need to entertain your requests for an appointment. I knew that if you'd actually made a breakthrough, then you wouldn't have bothered seeking an appointment, and would have simply walked into my office. But I thought I'd see you anyway. Not just to have a good laugh, which I'm very glad to have done at your expense, but to also tell you about some impending changes at the headquarters. I've realized I can't delude myself into believing I'm just as fit and healthy as ever. I obviously cannot afford to take a back seat and let someone else take over at this critical juncture, but C3 will henceforth have a deputy chief, who will actively co-ordinate operations while I focus on strategy—Anjali Malik from the Gujarat cadre of the Indian Police Service, who in my view is the brightest officer in the country. I think you in particular might enjoy working under her. You see, before she became an IPS officer, she was a gold medallist in computer science from IIT Bombay. She's exactly the kind of person we need at this make-or-break moment in the history of our organization. Somebody with a strong foundation in the gritty nuances of the flesh-and-blood worlds of conventional intelligence and law enforcement, but also somebody who truly understands what it would take to lead the bureau into a digital future.'

* * *

The knock on the door alarms Cyrus. Only Falcon's brother-in-law knows where the safe house in Baramulla is. It has been a while since he got here, and Cyrus is close to giving up hope. The prolonged isolation has been playing tricks with his mind, and he half expects to find armed militants led by Falcon himself waiting at the door, guns and grenades in their hands. Banishing these thoughts from his mind, Cyrus stubs his cigarette and quietly makes his way to the door. He looks through the peephole, and there is nobody outside. He slowly opens the door and finds a brick on the doormat. He scans the horizon and finds the unmistakable silhouette of Falcon's brother-in-law, a tall man with a pronounced limp on the right side, trying to quickly get away.

Cyrus heaves a sigh of relief as he takes apart the envelope taped to the brick. Inside it is a handwritten note from Falcon's brother-in-law:

Impossible for my brother-in-law to communicate at length without getting exposed. But a man going by the name of Karim has been arrested in Kolkata for possession of fake Indian documents. But he is not a poor Bangladeshi immigrant as he claims to be. He knows everything you're seeking.

This might be the most valuable piece of information he can provide. He fears that he will soon get caught. Appeal to you to kindly arrange for his return, as his health is worsening.

Cyrus burns the letter, before pulling out a fresh sheet of paper. He writes on it, 'If this information helps us, then will consider matter of return. Do not lose hope.' He puts the paper into the same envelope, before taping it to the brick and placing it back on the doormat. Although Falcon has been thrust into this miserable situation on account of his own deeds, Cyrus knows that he must do his best to help secure Falcon's return. The founding principles of his organization compel him to do so. He shuts the door and picks up the half-smoked cigarette before dialling Ravi's number on the secure landline receiver.

As soon as he picks up, Ravi hears the click of a lighter.

'Still haven't quit, Bandookwallah?'

Cyrus chuckles. It's comforting to hear Ravi's voice.

'Not a chance, sir. When you're all by yourself in one of the coldest regions in the world for weeks on end, nothing keeps you better company than a cigarette.'

At the other end, Ravi shakes his head.

'Looks like only a heart attack can drive that foolish romanticism out of your mind. Like it had to in my case. Anyway, what's the bird's eye view of this K2 rubbish looking like?'

'A man going by the name Karim has been arrested in Kolkata. But from what I could deduce from the input, the police don't seem to know who he really is.'

'And who is he?'

'Somebody who can give us a worm's eye view of this K2 rubbish.'

'Excellent. Head to Kolkata and await further instructions from your new boss.'

Cyrus is intrigued.

'New boss? Who's the new boss?'

'You'll find out soon enough. Like I said, await further instructions. Before you go, check on Falcon's family. See if they're doing okay, and if there's anything they need that we can help with.'

But before Cyrus can tell Ravi that he has already done that, Ravi has hung up. Ravi turns to Subramaniam, who is frantically trying to organize a sheaf of papers for Ravi to review and sign on, 'Looks like you need a deputy as well, Subramaniam. Should I speak to the chief about getting you one?'

Subramaniam smiles sheepishly. 'That's very kind of you, sir. But I'll probably be retired, and you'll probably be retired, by the time I finish teaching that deputy to make sense of your instructions and keep track of your schedule.'

Ravi laughs. 'That's a fair point. Anyway, are we good to go?'

Subramaniam looks at his watch. 'If you leave in exactly two minutes, you'll get there right on time, sir.'

Ravi gets up from his chair. 'In that case, I guess I'll just walk a little slower.'

Ravi walks out of his office and finds Mihir sitting outside. Ravi gestures to him to follow and gets into the elevator which takes him all the way down to the ground floor. Just as he walks out of the entrance, Gurmail Singh drives in with the new deputy of C3—Anjali Mallik. Anjali is embarrassed to find Ravi waiting to receive her.

In her mid-to-late thirties, Anjali is dressed in a plain yet elegant cotton saree and wears minimal jewellery—tiny studs in her nose and ears, and a single bangle on each hand. Like Ravi, she is a woman of fine tastes and a highly cultivated intellect. But much like in the case of Ravi, one would never suspect just by looking at her that she is now among the most important officers in the country's vast counterterrorism infrastructure.

Anjali had first caught Ravi's attention over a decade ago, right after her induction into the Indian Police Service. He had noticed her making the most notorious horse in the academy's stable canter and gallop at her command while some of her male counterparts fed jaggery and black gram to entice their horses to behave. Her unarmed combat skills were admired by trainers. During a series of lectures on counterterrorism delivered by Ravi at the academy, she had posed the sharpest questions. Her gift for deduction and nuanced understanding of geopolitics and technology had impressed Ravi. She came back to his attention a year ago, during the interdiction of arms in Gujarat, an operation that had succeeded largely because of Anjali's tactful leadership on the ground. Ravi had been convinced that she belonged at the Intelligence Bureau. He was waiting for an opportune moment to recommend her. Ravi is the sort to snap up talent the moment he sees it. When Sarita explicitly asked Ravi for his recommendation, his choice was Anjali.

Ravi invites Anjali into his office. Subramaniam gets up to hand her a bouquet. 'Welcome to C3, ma'am. If there's anything at all I can do to help you settle in, please let me know.' Anjali thanks Subramaniam and takes a seat opposite Ravi. Ravi turns to Mihir. 'Get yourself up to speed on things. I'll meet you soon,' Ravi says, and then turns to Anjali. 'That was Mihir Kaul. Because he's been exposed, he is currently useless to us within the country. But he's still one of our brightest talents and I want to draft him back into service. But I can't seem to make up my mind on what to do with him. I'd like you to take him under your wing, let him shadow you. But that can wait because something more urgent has come up. I've received information about an arrest in Kolkata, a man called Karim. We have learnt from a deep asset that he is an important player in operation K2. The police have picked him up because they found fake documents in his possession, and apparently have no idea who Karim actually is. What do you think we should do?'

'The first step would be to seek custody and bring him to Delhi. But if that's what you wanted to do, then we wouldn't even be having this conversation. I'm assuming you have something completely off the books in mind.'

Ravi chuckles. 'Liberation from the tyranny of law and order, that's how my first bosses at the bureau had described the transition, just after I'd been inducted.'

Unlike Ravi, Anjali is not the sort to indulge in banter or small talk when business awaits. 'One possibility that immediately strikes me as being worthy of considering is that we simply let him go. We let him linger in the illusion that we have no clue who he is. However, keep a close watch as he goes about persuading the police to let him go, and then we put him under close surveillance and figure out what his plans are.'

Ravi can already see why Anjali Mallik is the best choice he could have possibly made. It's almost like she is a more polished version of himself—a flair for radical ideas, but without the eccentric humour that makes Ravi a much-despised figure within certain circles.

'That was my first impulse, too. But then I decided against it, because it might be too much of a risk. We already have Suleimani operating out there under a similar arrangement. If there's too many moving parts on the ground, things might easily slip out of control, and we'll be back to square one. But at the same time, if we seek custody, the ISI will realize that we know exactly what they're up to, and trigger whatever contingency plan they have in place. The problem is that we have absolutely no clue what Plan B is. And so, we must allow them to carry on with Plan A for as long as we can without risking civilian lives. It's our only chance to get to the masterminds behind the whole thing. They'll otherwise just go cold for a while, only to strike back with an even harder vengeance. And if we do manage to pre-empt even that, we still wouldn't be any closer to nabbing Tabrez. Which is another thing that will have to be figured out at some point down the line. How do we bring him back to India? Pakistan will not hand him over to us in a million years. But we can get back to that later.'

Anjali is quick to process all of this, and a light bulb seems to go off in her head.

'What we need sir, is a proxy. Somebody who Karim believes can be trusted to carry out his bidding but is in fact one of our men. The specifics would have to be fleshed out, but the way I'm envisioning it, our man's objective will be to completely win Karim's confidence and learn as much as he can about operation K2. But the tricky part is that we will have to set up the whole thing in such a way that it is Karim who feels the need to open up to our operative. Not to mention the fact that all of this will have to happen inside of prison, without the police finding out. I'm sorry if I'm being vague, sir. I'm not sure if something like it is even feasible. I'm just thinking aloud, really . . .'

Now, a light bulb goes off in Ravi's head.

'Tell me, do you have any contacts in the Kolkata Police? Somebody from your batch perhaps, who you can count on for a personal favour? Something completely off the books?'

'As a matter of fact, I do, sir. Additional Commissioner Vikas Bose is a good friend of mine. We go a long way back.'

As he considers the possibilities, a mischievous smile dawns on Ravi's face. He picks up the phone and dials Cyrus.

'How long do you think it will take you to get to Kolkata?'

'There are no direct flights from Srinagar to Kolkata, sir. And so, I'm guessing I'll get there only later in the evening.'

'Perfect timing. What I want you to do as soon as you land, is this—walk into a bar.'

'Which bar?'

'Any bar, it doesn't matter. Once you get there, create such a horrible ruckus that the police is summoned. I'm not saying beat people up, but maybe smash the bar cabinet into smithereens, or whatever. Use your imagination. But it's essential that you do not stop until the police arrive and arrest you. And when they do, you will use your Baramulla cover of Saqib Khan. Just the name. You're no longer a researcher, but the wastrel son of a multimillionaire based in the UK. At no cost must you reveal that you are an undercover officer.'

Cyrus is stunned.

'A-and then what, sir?'

'Get to Kolkata first. We'll talk then.'

Bacchus

Cyrus swaggers into the Polo Bar on Park Street, Kolkata. It's an old colonial-era establishment that mostly attracts the same set of loyal drinkers every evening. And so, the arrival of a new face never goes unnoticed. As Cyrus looks around, he realizes that all the tables are already taken. A waiter comes up to him and asks him to take a seat at the bar.

But Cyrus takes offence at this perfectly reasonable demand, 'How dare you ask me to sit at the bar like I'm some street drunkard? I want a table.'

The waiter is taken aback by this unexpectedly curt rejoinder. But because of the evidently expensive clothes Cyrus wears, and the clipped British accent with which he speaks, the waiter is careful not to mess around, lest Cyrus does turn out to be some big shot as he claims. He tries to calm Cyrus down. 'I'm sorry, sir. But as you can see yourself, all the tables are occupied. You can take a seat at the bar for now. As soon as a table is vacated, I will let you know.'

But Cyrus won't budge. 'You expect me to wait? Do you know who I am? Kick some people out if that's what it takes. All I see are old farts who ought to be at home anyway.'

Cyrus deliberately raises his voice as he utters that last line, and it is enough to incite the crowd of loyal patrons into rising in unison against the unruly interloper. They are all mostly retired people, and so they do not want to risk getting into a physical fight with the well-built Cyrus. Nevertheless, a heated argument ensues, and the manager steps in to ease the tension. But Cyrus is in no mood to let tensions ease and he walks towards the bar counter, where he grabs an expensive liquor bottle and smashes it onto the ground. He picks up a large shard and holds it up threateningly as he walks towards a table and forcefully takes a seat. 'If anybody dares evict me, I will slit their throat with this piece of glass.' He then turns to the waiter, who is left speechless like most of the crowd, and shouts, 'What are you looking at? Get me a drink!'

By the time Cyrus's second drink comes, the police have also arrived. Just before they can pick him up, Cyrus swiftly types into his phone, 'arrested' and hits the send button.

At the police station, Cyrus is led into the SHO's cabin. The SHO, a stout, balding man, sizes Cyrus up from top to bottom and shakes his head in disgust. 'What, hero? Just because you're a rich kid, do you think you can barge into a respected establishment, pick up a fight with decent retired people, and expect to get away with it?'

Cyrus hasn't yet been briefed on what exactly is expected of him after the arrest, and he does not know what to say in response. And so, he simply stands with his head bowed in shame, scratching his head for a suitable response. But just then a constable walks into the cabin and informs the SHO that a woman claiming to be a representative of Cyrus's family has arrived at the station.

Cyrus is perplexed. He knows that it is undoubtedly somebody Ravi has sent, but wonders who it might possibly be, even as the SHO asks the constable to let the woman in. Cyrus raises his eyebrows as a hint of recognition flashes in his head.

Anjali Malik, or Rani Kothari as she goes by now, looks vaguely familiar, but he can't put his finger on it. She doesn't meet his gaze and hands the SHO a business card that identifies her as a senior legal executive of 'Khan Global Industries Inc', which as she explains is a multimillion-dollar corporation headquartered in London, but with business interests across the world. And Cyrus, or Saqib Khan as he is now being identified, is the only son of its chairman and managing director.

The SHO tells her plainly that influence and money won't work with him. Anjali is quick to clarify that she is not going to attempt to use either. All she wants is for a chance to speak to her client in private. The SHO relents, for it is a petty matter after all, and a constable leads Cyrus and Anjali into a separate room.

As soon as the constable leaves, Cyrus asks, 'I'm sorry, but you are . . .'

'It doesn't matter. Now's not the time for introductions. Listen to me carefully.'

'I'm sorry, but I can't. Without speaking to my father, how can I believe that you are who you claim to be?'

Anjali pulls out her phone and dials Ravi's number.

'Your son wants to speak to you before deciding if he can trust me.'

Anjali hands the phone to Cyrus, who gets a mouthful as soon as he puts his ear to the receiver, 'You ungrateful excuse for a son. First you go and terrorize unsuspecting old people, and then when I decide to help you out, you're suspicious of the person I send?'

Even if it were possible to somehow pull off a flawless mimicry of Ravi's voice, it is unlikely anybody could possibly hope to imitate Ravi's unique brand of humour.

'Like father, like son. You taught me to be suspicious.'

'That's good. Now stop fooling around and get to work.'

The line goes dead, and Cyrus hands the phone back to Anjali, who wastes no time in getting to the brief. 'A top LeH operative named Karim was arrested in Agartala a week ago. The police do not know who he is, and it is essential that it remains that way. I'm going to arrange for you to be lodged in the same cell as him. Once there, you will strike up a rapport with him. Karim should believe that you actually are the wayward son of a Muslim millionaire, desperately seeking a purpose in life. Once he's sufficiently convinced, he will try to radicalize you, and you must give in completely. I will meet you in jail after a few days, and we can take stock of the situation before figuring out our next plan of action. I hope I do not have to remind you, but nobody including the police can know that you are undercover.'

The authority that Anjali effortlessly commands, as she gives him these instructions, leads Cyrus to conclude that he is dealing with a senior officer.

'Understood, ma'am.'

* * *

Madan Singh and Suleimani finish their extensive scouting trip through the hinterlands before arriving in Delhi. Madan drives them to a large bungalow in the posh Defence Colony of South Delhi. Suleimani thoroughly inspects the house and is satisfied when he discovers that there are no bugs. Little does he know that he is under the surveillance of an older and more insidious sort. The caretakers of the house, an old Muslim couple, are C3 assets installed by Ravi in advance of Suleimani's arrival. There had been much debate at the headquarters on how best they could keep track of Suleimani. Jose had insisted that this was their best chance to try out a new gadget that supposedly could evade existing surveillance-detection scanners. But Ravi had rubbished the suggestion and pointed out to Jose that they didn't need bugs when they had access to and control over something even the most sophisticated scanners could never hope to detect—human assets on the ground.

After helping Suleimani settle into his new base, Madan decides to go on his way. He hands Suleimani a new phone and SIM card and instructs him to discard his existing phone. Suleimani chuckles and flings the new phone into the dustbin.

Suleimani explains, 'Phone calls can't be trusted any longer. The bastards are listening to everything. In fact, you too shouldn't be using a phone to communicate with me.'

Madan is taken aback and wonders what the alternative is. Suleimani reaches into his bag and pulls out another phone and hands it to Madan, who is curious to know how this phone is any different. Madan also realizes that in one of Suleimani's bags, there are nearly a hundred identical phones.

Suleimani clarifies, 'This one can't be used to make regular phone calls. It's a lot like a satellite phone, except that it's connected to the internet. This is as secure as it gets. Even the CIA can't track us.' Madan hasn't used a smartphone before, and confesses as much to Suleimani, 'I'm an old man. You'll have to teach me how all of this works.'

Suleimani chuckles as he pulls out his laptop and attaches a fingerprint scanner to it. He logs on to an encrypted portal using his fingerprint, and after a few quick keystrokes, tells Madan that the new phone has been activated. He then turns on the phone and tells Madan Singh that there is only one app on the phone—a comprehensive communications portal that encompasses voice, text and email—and it can only be accessed using a secure password that has to be keyed in each time. Suleimani then explains to Madan that if he is ever captured, he must press the power button five times in a row. That would permanently erase all data. Technology has never really been Madan's strong point. But memory is, and so Madan decides to remember every little detail for the sleuths at Insomnia to work their way around.

As he walks out of the house, Madan instructs the caretakers to ensure that their guest is comfortable and gets whatever he needs. Despite the obvious consternation he feels towards Suleimani and his agenda, Madan has managed to strike an excellent rapport with him, and it now almost borders on friendship. And so, as they bid goodbye, Suleimani and Madan embrace each other warmly.

As Sandhu's car is being left behind for Suleimani to use, Madan Singh has to take a rickshaw. He pulls out his old phone and sends Ravi a text message, 'Up for a game of chess?'

* * *

Tabrez is even more anxious than he usually is in anticipation of Rauf's visit. And so, as Rauf's convoy pulls up in the garden, followed by the routine security sweeping protocol, Tabrez has to put in a conscious effort to maintain a veneer of calm. But Rauf is sharper than anybody Tabrez has ever met, and so it is no surprise that he can tell immediately that not all's well with Tabrez.

Putting his arm around Tabrez as they walk into the house, Rauf asks, 'What's the matter? I assumed you'd be very happy about operation K2 taking off.'

'I am, Rauf Miyan, trust me. But I'm also a little concerned. If Karim spills the beans, then it's all over.'

'Would it comfort you if I were to tell you that I am the reason he got arrested?'

Tabrez is stunned. 'What do you mean?'

'Do you really reckon a soldier of Karim's training and capabilities would get arrested on his first day in India? And that too by the state police?'

Although Tabrez can't bring himself to say anything in response to this startling revelation, it is almost as if Al-Brittani can read Tabrez's mind. 'Relax, old mate. I'm not sabotaging the mission. If anything, you will thank me later for saving it from getting foiled. You see, the Indian agencies aren't to be underestimated. Our IT cell has picked up on attempts by C3 to break into our communications networks. While it is theoretically impossible for them to actually break in, just the fact that they know of its existence means that we've got to tread carefully. They've got their eyes wide open.'

'B-but Rauf Miyan, what does that have to do with Karim getting arrested?'

'The task he's set out to accomplish is not something that can be done in hiding. Karim was sent through the

Bangladesh border, along a route that's typically used by illegal Bangladeshi immigrants. These routes are well-known to the Indian security forces, and most people end up getting arrested. But depending on why a person was crossing over, the Indian authorities decide on what is to be done with them. If, for instance, they realize that you are a militant, then, of course, you're put in jail for life. If you're just a poor labourer seeking a better life in India, they'll deport you.'

'And how would him staying in jail or getting deported help us?'

'There's a third category as well. If you are seeking asylum on humanitarian grounds, then you are taken in as a refugee and granted permission to reside in India. And so, Karim is for all practical purposes an Ahmaddiya fleeing religious persecution in Bangladesh. The Indians love sheltering those infidels, and so he'll have no trouble getting asylum. He'll have to stay in jail for some time while the Indian authorities inquire into his antecedents. But I've ensured that Karim is listed as an Ahmaddiya in the Bangladeshi records as well, and so he will easily make it past their vetting. After that, he'll be a free man with official Indian papers. I know it sounds like it'll take time, but we have to be patient. Don't forget that impatience is what got you into trouble the last time around.'

'Rauf Miyan, please don't take this the wrong way, but I expect you to keep me informed about these decisions before they are put into action. It is not just about how much time this is taking, which too is a real concern, but more importantly, about there being complete transparency between us. I and my organization are an integral part of K2 as well, right? We can't go in blind.'

Rauf lets out a loud chuckle, in the way a mother would laugh at the naive complaints of her child. He pats Tabrez gently on the shoulder, 'I did not tell you, because these are all small little operational details that I don't want you to waste your time worrying about. You should focus on the big picture. Tell me, what's your next course of action?'

Tabrez isn't entirely reassured, but he can't bring himself to say it.

'Hussaini has performed an extensive recce at key locations across Uttar Pradesh and has sent me blueprints and photographs. I am studying them currently. There are some historic temples in Varanasi that I'm particularly keen on attacking. And then there's also the assassination plan. Iqbal is already on the ground, equipping the list of madrasas and mosques approved by you with projectors and internet access. Hussaini will then put in place the indoctrination module, which will allow us to recruit lone-wolf assassins who can target the politicians involved in the demolition of Babri Masjid. But until Karim is released from jail, we cannot move on to the most critical phase.'

'And what is that?'

'Establish and secure a new arms route. With the explosives that my men have access to, we can only pull off a few attacks and that'll be it. All our access points have been cut off.'

Rauf shakes his head as he processes the entire sequence of events described by Tabrez. 'Tell me this, do you want to destroy India or do you want to just inflict minor injuries that the country will heal from, and only get stronger?'

'Destroy India, of course.'

'Then why are you still stuck in the ancient ways of warfare?'

Tabrez is confused. 'But Rauf Miyan, a large part of our effort is entirely digital, just as you'd suggested. What I described is just the final outcome of it all.'

'Let me ask you a simple question. If I served you some biryani, would you call it a modern dish simply because I cooked it in a microwave oven?'

'No, not really. It'd still be biryani.'

'But if I were to change the composition of the dish, using the same recipe broadly but with an entirely unique combination of ingredients, would you call it a modern dish?'

'Perhaps, yes.'

'That's exactly how I want you to look at operation K2. You've got the recipe right, no doubt, but it's the ingredients and their combination that needs a little tweaking.'

'What do you have in mind, Rauf Miyan?'

'Instead of temples, target mosques and gurdwaras. If we do it with due care, as I fully expect you to, nobody will suspect us of having a hand. After that, we carefully manipulate the narrative to ensure that communal tensions automatically flare up to a point where the next step of your plan, of assassinating those who destroyed the Babri Masjid, will seem like an organic retaliation. And you won't need Karim for all of that. If mosques are bombed, then the atmosphere will be ripe for Muslim youngsters across the country to be radicalized and carry out these attacks simultaneously. And this will only stoke even more tensions, and if all goes well, we can expect a full-blown civil war that will bring the country down on its knees.'

Tabrez is stunned. 'But Rauf Miyan, bombing mosques? Isn't that blasphemous? What about our brothers and sisters who will be killed?'

'The ends justify the means, Tabrez. This is a holy war we're fighting. In that country, our brothers and sisters are going to die anyway, and our mosques are going to be destroyed anyway. But it doesn't have to all be in vain, and we can ensure that. Our brethren will be rewarded in heaven for their sacrifice. And if these alone don't stoke sentiments organically, then hire contract killers to push things to the brink. It's the optics that matter, nothing else.'

Brainwash

Examiner stares one last time at the name and address written on a small piece of paper, and puts it back into his pocket. He asks a coolie to pick up his bags and walks towards a waiting vehicle. Close to a fortnight's worth of careful scouting and strategizing has gone into planning this operation to infiltrate Suleimani's radicalization module. First, a team of field operatives had kept a careful watch on one of the mosques Suleimani had visited during his scouting trip with Madan Singh and identified some of the most regular young visitors. Then, posing as real estate agents making enquiries about the possibility of a property sale, they had visited each of their homes and tried to uncover as much detail as possible about the internal dynamics of each household.

After assessing further background checks, they had finally zeroed in on Altaf Ansari, a twenty-year-old who lived with his widowed mother at their ancestral manor and survived on the rent earned from smaller tenements attached to the property. He seemed to spend an inordinate amount of time with the people Suleimani had been regularly meeting, and was therefore the perfect target, apart from the specific circumstances of his family arrangements that made him particularly vulnerable to being cultivated by Examiner.

As the car pulls up outside the dilapidated manor, Examiner gets into the character he is playing and steps out with a calculated sombreness. Zabeena, Altaf's mother, is winnowing grains in the courtyard when she notices the slightly aged man lugging his bags towards the gate. Wrapping a veil around her face, she walks out to find him staring with nostalgic longing at the peeling yellow façade.

'Are you looking for something?'

Examiner stirs out of his absorption.

'Zabeena?'

'Yes. And you are?'

'I'm Rasheed, your husband's uncle. Your father-in-law, Salman, was my elder cousin.'

Zabeena doesn't seem to recognize the man, although the name does ring a bell.

Examiner puts her at ease. 'I don't expect you to remember. I was at your wedding if that might help you recall . . .'

'Sorry, I don't remember your face. But it was such a long time ago. I definitely recall having met you. You were in the Gulf, right? All these years?'

The real Rasheed had died a few years ago in Oman, but because he was single, he had fallen out of touch with his relatives a long time ago. Nobody had heard from him. And because nobody has seen Rasheed since the time he was in his twenties, Examiner is able to easily persuade Zabeena of his identity.

She asks him to come in and allows him to freshen up and make himself comfortable. She brings him a hot cup of tea and tries making conversation, although she still feels a little awkward in the company of this unexpected relative.

'So, what brings you back to Lucknow? How long are you planning on staying here?'

'I'm back for a few months, at least. I am going to retire next year and so I am hoping to come back for good, but I would like to first see if I can get used to living here once again.'

Examiner notices the slight discomfiture in Zabeena's posture and is quick to allay her concerns, 'I don't intend to be a burden on you, nor do I have any interest in taking this property out of your hands. As the daughter-in-law of the eldest son of my uncle, this house is rightfully yours. All that I'm asking is that you evict your tenants and let me take up that entire floor. Whatever rent they are paying you, I will pay you double.'

'There is no need for all that. You can definitely stay here with us for a few months. I will just have to speak to my son once. He'll be back from the mosque soon.'

'Please, I insist. I have worked very hard in life and have been blessed with abundant wealth. It is my duty to share my wealth with my family. I have nobody else, and if everything goes well, I would like to do whatever I can to help restore this manor to its earlier glory.'

Zabeena is touched by Examiner's words, and a bond is immediately established. Altaf returns home only late in the evening and is pleased to discover that their guest has brought expensive gifts for him. But Altaf doesn't have the time for a more extended introduction as he has to eat dinner and hurry back to the mosque where he is helping with arrangements for a special sermon being organized the next day. Examiner knows all about the sermon Altaf is referring to. Indeed, his arrival in Lucknow had been timed to coincide with the sermon, which Madan Singh had gathered from Suleimani's schedule.

Nevertheless, he chooses to ask innocently, 'What sermon is this? Can I also attend?'

Altaf isn't so sure. 'It's by a foreign Imam, Dadajaan. It's mainly intended for young people. You might feel out of place.'

'Where is it happening, though? Is it that same mosque where your father and grandfather used to go?'

Altaf nods.

'Then I have to come. You know, it's been ages since I've prayed in that mosque. Brings back so many memories, just thinking of it. Because I was closest in age to your father, out of all his uncles, I would be the one taking him there. His pyjama would keep falling off.'

The mention of his father puts a smile on Altaf's face. 'Okay, you can come. Around ten in the morning.'

Examiner thanks Altaf and decides to retire to his room. Just before tucking in for the night he types out a message to Ravi, 'Settled down well in family. My grand-nephew is a sweet boy who's unfortunately been misled. Apart from the main reason I'm here, I'm also going to try and set him on the right path in life.' As soon as the message is sent, he deletes it and turns off his phone.

The next morning, Examiner slides in with the regulars as they make their way into a small mosque tucked away inside a narrow lane in one of Lucknow's many business districts. A special sermon is to be delivered by a visiting dignitary, and the organizers seem to be taking extra precautions today. Every visitor is scanned and frisked, apart from being asked to deposit their mobile phones at the entrance. Most of the attendees are familiar faces and are therefore allowed to pass without much ado. But one of the organizers guarding the entry—a boy around the same age as Altaf—isn't sure if Examiner should be let in.

'I have never seen you here before.'

'Yes, you haven't, because I'm coming after a long time . . .'

The young organizer's suspicions aren't allayed, and he stares at Examiner, whose clean-shaven appearance stands in contrast against the mostly bearded crowd.

'And you are a Muslim?'

Examiner pretends to be annoyed. 'Listen, kid. I went away before you were even born perhaps, and now I've returned.'

The young organizer is unmoved, 'Recite the Shahadah.'

Without batting an eyelid, Examiner recites in impeccable Arabic, 'I bear witness that there is no God but Allah, and Muhammad is his messenger.'

The young organizer is somewhat reassured, but is still reluctant to let him in.

'How did you find out about today's sermon? We only announced it to young worshippers.'

'My grand-nephew Altaf. He told me.'

Examiner scans the room and spots Altaf. 'There, that's him.'

The young organizer is finally convinced. Altaf notices Examiner pointing at him and hurriedly walks towards him,

'Dadajaan, please quickly come in and take a seat. We're starting in a minute.'

Apart from Examiner and a few other senior worshippers, the nearly hundred people that pack the room seem to be all in their twenties. Examiner even spots a few teenagers at the back. There is palpable excitement in the room, but as soon as the maulvi enters, it gives way to complete silence.

The maulvi welcomes the gathering, 'Thank you all for attending this very special event. We are privileged to have with us today a very special guest who has travelled across the length and breadth of the Islamic world. From Bosnia to Sudan, Afghanistan to Palestine, he has put his blood and sweat into upholding the commandments of our Prophet. He has lived and fought alongside our brothers and sisters, wherever they have faced oppression. But such is the humility of this great man that he does not deem himself worthy of addressing us all today. Instead, he carries with him a message from another great man.' The audience waits with much anticipation for their unnamed guest to come forward. But instead, a portable white screen with an inbuilt projection unit is rolled into the room by one of the volunteers.

The lights are turned off, and the screen comes to life. After a short sequence of selected Quranic verses, a tall and fair man begins addressing the camera in Arabic, while Urdu subtitles appear on the screen. His speech is to the 'young Muslims of Lucknow', making it evident that the video has been customized for this occasion. The footage is extremely grainy, and Examiner trains all his attention on the screen to try and identify the speaker. As he begins to listen more carefully, the thickly British-accented Arabic gives it away. It can only be Abdul Salim Rauf, the brilliant British–Pakistani computer scientist better known by his dreaded nom de guerre, Abu Jihad Al–Brittani.

Examiner is intrigued. Although Al–Brittani's fiery speeches have a global appeal and are employed by numerous organizations as part of their radicalization programmes, it is unusual for his talks to begin with a customized address. Putting his famed oratory skills on full display, Al–Brittani then launches into a fiery tirade against the greed of the western world, urging upon young Muslims around the world to fight the imposition of western values by embracing their Islamic identity.

He then continues: '. . . but this embrace cannot be half-hearted. Only if you are prepared to sacrifice your trivial ambitions for the higher good are you worthy of joining this fight. But embracing your Islamic identity does not mean turning your back on modernity. Not at all. That is a fatal mistake, I warn you, which will set us off on a path of decline, inevitably culminating in our extinction . . .'

As Al–Brittani's spiel goes on, the captivated audience listens to each word. Apart from the customized introduction, Examiner has heard it all before, and he knows better than to expect anything beyond empty rhetoric in an open meeting such as this one. But he also knows that Suleimani hasn't come all the way here just to screen a generic propaganda video. This is a screening session of another sort, meant to identify potential recruits. And so even as the others have their eyes and ears glued to the screen, Examiner decides to discreetly scan the dark room. He knows that somebody, somewhere, is watching carefully. And sure enough, at a far corner of the hall, he notices Suleimani standing behind a pillar and intently watching the crowd. Next to Suleimani is the maulvi who makes notes as Suleimani points at particular faces. Eager not to push his luck, Examiner decides not to stare any further and returns his attention to the screen.

The video finally comes to an end and the lights are turned on. Even as the awestruck youngsters exchange hushed whispers, Examiner steals a quick glance at the pillar. Suleimani has disappeared, leaving only the maulvi who is handing out the list of names to Altaf, who quickly spreads the word among the other organizing volunteers. The maulvi steps up to the front of the room and announces that the session is over. As the attendees get up to leave, the volunteers individually go up to the people specifically identified by Suleimani and ask them to wait.

Examiner knows what is likely to happen next. The selected individuals will be taken into a more private space where Suleimani will speak to them in more explicit terms as a preliminary step towards recruitment. Examiner does not want to arouse any suspicions by asking to stay back and decides to make a quiet exit. But Altaf himself comes running towards him.

'Dadajaan, I have some more work left here. You go home, I'll come later. But please don't tell my mother what the speech was about. She doesn't understand all these matters, and so she'll get angry at me. I've just told her this was a motivational talk for youngsters, which is all it was, but she'll get the wrong idea. So, if you can also say the same thing . . .'

Examiner chuckles, 'Okay, I won't tell her. But come back soon. I want to spend some time with you.'

He walks out of the mosque and makes his way through the narrow alleys of the old neighbourhood, until he reaches a single-screen cinema hall just in time for the 11 a.m. show of a Bhojpuri film. It is a weekday morning and except for a few people sprawled on the floor right in front of the screen there is nobody in the hall. This suits Examiner perfectly, and he staggers up the unlit stairs to the topmost corner seat. The film has already begun, and there's a sleazy dance sequence on the screen at the moment. But Examiner is not here to be entertained. He pulls out his mobile phone, turns it on, and dials a number from memory.

The music's blaring at full volume, and so Examiner presses the phone into his ears and cups his palm around his mouth.

'A British mountaineer is leading the expedition to Mount K2.'

At the other end, Ravi thinks for a few moments.

'Every mountaineering company claims that its expedition is led by that British mountaineer you're referring to. It's a marketing trick. He's a superstar, and so they get instant brand appeal. But in reality, he's probably working on an Everest expedition. He's a big game player.'

'This is different. His motivational talk to the trainee mountaineers began with a customized introduction addressed to the trainees at that particular camp. Imagine, if he's put in the effort to record customized introductions like that for every single camp in the country, he's got to have some stake in it.'

'Got it.'

With that, Ravi—who's in the midst of a dreary marathon of paperwork with Subramaniam—abruptly disconnects the call, leaps out of his seat, and bolts out of the door. Subramaniam is caught off guard and he runs after his boss, 'Sir, you have to take it easy. It's not good for your health.'

'Not now, Subramaniam. Don't be my doctor.'

'But, sir . . .'

'Get back to your work and let me do what I have to. These are my orders.'

Ravi continues walking at a brisk pace, and Subramaniam—who is over a decade older—struggles to keep up.

'But, sir . . . I also have orders from Sarita ma'am.'

'She's my boss, but I'd say the exact same thing to her. Now please, go back. You're slowing me down.'

Subramaniam gives it one last shot, 'Whose office is it that you want to barge into, sir? Why don't you just tell me, so I can ask them to come here and see you? You head this organization; I hope I don't have to remind you.'

Ravi stops in his tracks and pulls Subramaniam to the side.

'You've ever heard that saying, Subramaniam, about how every cat is a lion in its own cave, and how every pigeon is a hawk in its own nest? It's the other way around in this place. I've got a fancy, well-trained hawk here, or least that's what he pretends to be, and so I asked him to keep a careful watch from his nest. But I'm worried when he's actually back in his nest at the owl colony, he's just being a rustic pigeon, catching afternoon siestas and long dinners. And because of that, I'm afraid he hasn't noticed the huge robotic monster marching towards us from the mountains. It took an old jackal, who wasn't in the air or even up high on some tree, to alert me to this impending invasion.'

Subramaniam is stumped.

'I have no clue about what you just said, sir. If you don't mind me asking, and I mean no disrespect, is everything okay? Have you been taking too many painkillers? I've noticed that ever since you've come back from the surgery, you've been speaking cryptically far more than usual. I rarely hear you speak normally these days. I'm just asking because these pills sometimes have very strong effect.'

Ravi is amused.

'I'm not high Subramaniam, if that's what you're hinting at. I wasn't around for almost two months, and that's a long time to be away from a jungle like this. In that time, allegiances can change, new hunting packs may form, anything's possible . . . But mostly, it's these rats you can't trust.'

Subramaniam follows Ravi's piercing gaze to arrive at what he's hinting at. Only forty metres away, Anil is standing at the door to his office, evidently trying his best to eavesdrop on the conversation. Ravi waves at him with a broad plastic smile, taking Anil by surprise. He musters a weak hello in response, before going back into his office.

* * *

As he narrates yet another elaborately concocted tale about one of Saqib Khan's innumerable misadventures all around the globe, Cyrus can tell that Karim is losing interest. But he continues narrating anyway, there being little else to do within their cramped jail cell in Kolkata. In any case, it's part of the plan. Cyrus knows that ideas are already brewing in Karim's head, and it won't be long before he'll want to confide in Cyrus. He knows that the time is ripe to catch Karim off guard.

'. . . and so, that was when I decided to go to Africa. I started off in Sudan. The capital city is called Tripoli . . .' Cyrus continues with his story.

Karim looks at him with scepticism.

'Khartoum is the capital of Sudan . . .'

The shark has caught the bait, and Cyrus is keen on reeling it in.

'Yes, yes, of course. I'm sorry, what I meant to say is, I started off in Libya. That's where Tripoli is. The phase in my life where I went astray, the one I was telling you about where I moved away from God and took to intoxication? That started when I was in Morocco, on this very tour, after I did Libya and Sudan. And so, because of all the sinful substances I was putting into my body, my memories of that entire tour of Africa are quite vague. That's how I got confused.'

Karim nods, convinced by yet another meticulously fabricated account. But he has unwittingly given away the fact that he's no illiterate peasant from Bangladesh.

Cyrus subtly broaches the matter, 'But I'm surprised, Karim Miyan. For somebody who's never gone out of his village, and never read a single word in his entire life, you seem to have a fairly decent grasp of world geography. I saw your face light up a few times when I was mentioning places in the Middle East as well. What is it I'm missing here?'

Karim smiles. He's glad Cyrus has caught his bluff.

'You're not the only man who's gone around the world trying to find himself, *janaab*. I have done my fair share of soul-searching. That deeply felt sense of injustice and that

irrepressible impulse to fight that you've been talking about.
I felt all of that too, and just as strongly as you. But unlike
you, I haven't wandered aimlessly. I found a long time ago
the path you are still so desperately searching for in your life.
And I had none of your privileges. Imagine what a man of
your education and resources can accomplish. You would not
only find your own purpose, but also be a beacon of hope to
millions of others all around the world who are similarly lost
and disillusioned.'

'What exactly is this path?'

'You are an intelligent man. I believe I do not have to spell
everything out. Not immediately, at least. Your bail hearing
comes up only in a week, and I'm possibly going to be in here
for longer than that. We have all the time in the world to
discuss what exactly this path is, and how you, Saqib Al-Hindi,
can help move it ahead into uncharted territory.'

The solemn look on Cyrus's face tells Karim that he's
understood exactly what he's hinting at.

* * *

Jose is staring blankly at the faintly illuminated wall in front
of his desk. But in his mind's eye an enormously complex
maze of thoughts and images keep circling one another much
like the problem he's been trying to tackle. He's stirred out
of this frustratingly deadlocked puzzle when Ravi barges into
his office unannounced, accompanied by a highly circumspect
Subramaniam who closes the door behind him.

'How is it that one of the world's most wanted men,
somebody's who particularly renowned for his expertise in

cryptology and computer science, has been conspiring to wage war against India, and you haven't caught a single whiff of it so far? It took a long-retired agent, who can barely use a smartphone, to discover this.'

Ravi's thundering tone sends a mild shiver down Jose's spine. Unlike Mihir and Cyrus, Jose never really has had to bear the full brunt of the boss's wrath. But if what Ravi is saying is indeed true, then Jose knows that he is well deserving of far worse than what he's receiving. He thinks for a full two minutes, while Ravi looks through Jose's whiteboards, before responding.

'It's no excuse, sir, nor am I making this up to exonerate myself. But I'd come to a similar conclusion myself quite some time back. It's just that I had no proof, and so I didn't come to you. Only Al-Brittani could have conceived of such a foolproof system, and actually implemented it. But knowing this still doesn't change the fact that there's no way of breaking in. All entry points are sealed off, end-to-end. We'll just keep going around in circles looking for backdoors when none exist, and so . . .'

Ravi raises his hand, asking Jose to stop.

'Please spare me the poetry. Every time we've discussed this, you've said the exact same thing. There's no way of breaking into this. Any fool with a computer science degree, if given access to all this data and infrastructure, will probably be able to tell me what you're saying. Brute force won't work, and we need to come up with a different strategy, I've been telling you every single time you've brought this up. I was questioning myself on the way, why I even hired you, and then I was reminded of a conversation I had with Subramaniam when I was considering fast-tracking you from the academy. Do you remember, Subramaniam?'

Subramaniam is caught off-guard, 'Yes, sir. About my granddaughter.'

'Would you mind repeating it, Subramaniam? I think it's quite appropriate that Mr James Bond here listens to it.'

'If you say so, sir. So, I gifted my granddaughter a computer for her birthday a few years ago assuming it would help her with her studies. But she spent more time on the internet talking to strangers from all over the world and playing games with them. Nothing we said or did would deter her, and she would never say anything regarding what she was talking to these strangers about. Finally, my poor daughter-in-law had to create a fake account online to get into my granddaughter's circles and see what was happening. She used the fake account not only to see what my granddaughter was up to, but also to subtly manipulate her in the direction that she wanted her to take. Instead of stupid car racing games, she started playing chess and Scrabble because her close online friend kept pulling her in that direction. She was hooked. Little did she know that this "friend" was actually her mother!'

Ravi takes over. 'Subramaniam had brought this up when I was unsure of whether or not it made sense to take you directly under my wing. Because field operations are where my expertise lies, and I didn't think that a technical officer like you would fit actively into my scheme of action. But Subramaniam pointed me in the right direction. There was a time when monitoring and fieldwork was separate, but the internet changed it. Your addiction to metadata is of no use. Like Subramaniam's daughter-in-law, create a fake digital persona and try to penetrate the seemingly impregnable network. Is that clear?'

Subramaniam clears his throat. 'And there's something else that I added, sir. That this is like astrology. It doesn't matter if you believe in it or not, it is what it is. But the point of astrology is not to prove that what is bound to happen will happen. Rather it is to prove that you can change what is bound to happen if you take the right steps, modify your behaviour and perform the correct rituals.'

Bird Cage

The phone rings in Tabrez's study, startling him. It's the secure line to Islamabad. He picks up with some trepidation, although he knows it can only be his ISI handler, a very senior officer who Tabrez knows only by the nom de guerre Karbala.

Karbala is a busy man with little time, and cuts straight to business, 'Tabrez, I have been briefed that K2 is ripe for execution. God willing, we will succeed. But once we put this into action, there's no going back. The backlash is going to be severe, and soon enough India will catch on to the plot. There are suspicions already; we've picked up some chatter. But I don't think they really know yet. But when that happens, and it will happen, we cannot be seen as having anything to do with this operation. For it to work at the scale we've envisioned it, it is essential that the chain of events that will follow is perceived as both indigenous and organic. Which is why after things have heated up to a certain point you will have to leave Pakistan. We will continue to support you, but we will not be able to shelter you any longer.'

Tabrez is stunned. 'I-I have to leave . . . Right now?'

'No, not right now. We will tell you. I'm just warning you to be prepared. Right now, you must stay focused on guiding your soldiers in India. We cannot afford mistakes. In how many days are we ready to strike?'

'Immediately. Inshaallah, tomorrow will mark the beginning of the final chapter in this holy war.'

'Good. I'll keep an eye out for the news.'

With that, Karbala hangs up, leaving Tabrez with mixed feelings.

Little do Karbala or Tabrez know that India has more than picked up on their plot. Through Suleimani and Karim, C3 has already infiltrated their ranks and its topmost officers are well aware of the larger scheme of fomenting internal strife across the country. But because of how their operation has been designed, where Suleimani is unaware of Karim's briefing and Karim is unaware of Iqbal's networks, even the sharp cookies at C3 are clueless about exactly how it is all going to begin.

* * *

Ravi's heart stops for a moment when he hears Sarita utter the most dreadful words in the vocabulary of a spymaster, 'Turn on the news.' If he's being asked to learn something from the news, it can only mean one thing—he's failed to anticipate something. And when it's the chief of the Intelligence Bureau calling personally, it's almost certainly very bad news.

'And after you have, come over to my office.'

Ravi turns on the TV. This is what is being telecast:

'. . . It is of course too early to speculate, but authorities certainly have their task cut out as far as uncovering the perpetrators of this highly unusual series of coordinated attacks is concerned. For those just tuning in, this is our breaking news for the moment. We've had reports coming in of a series of low-intensity blasts across Uttar Pradesh. In what is possibly a first in the history of terror in the subcontinent, mosques and gurudwaras have been simultaneously targeted.'

Ravi reaches for the stress ball on his desk, desperate to vent the rage that in his pre-morbid state would have been directed at the TV, or any physical object in sight. He sinks into his chair, and takes in a few deep breaths before leaping up onto his feet and rushing out of his office. After a few seconds, he stops in his tracks and runs back. He pulls out a sealed envelope from his safe and tucks it into his pocket.

Anil is already in Sarita's office, and along expected lines, is trying to play knight in shining armour. 'This is something unprecedented, and a clear sign that our best resources are being diverted towards questionable operations. When will Ravi move past Tabrez and LeH? He is not in the right space, physically or mentally, to be investigating such a complex attack. If he was, it would never have happened in the first place.'

The door opens and Ravi makes quite the entrance. 'I am doing just fine, sir. Thank you for your concern. As for moving past Tabrez, it might be news to you that he is the man behind today's attack. They want you to think it's new, it's indigenous, everything you're probably thinking right now. Let's not fall into their trap, please.'

Anil laughs derisively. 'This is exactly what I'm talking about. I understand Tabrez getting away was the one blemish on your moment of glory with the train blasts investigation, and you're keen on closing the loop. But personal pride has turned it into an unhealthy obsession, and like I was saying, our best resources are being diverted towards tracking down a man in exile, who, as things stand, poses absolutely no threat to us. And the consequences of personal obsession are plain for us to see today. Anyway, I shall stop at that. But for the sake of the nation and this organization, I hope you will pull out a rabbit from your hat once again and save the day. I'm just going to bet on it.'

Ravi smiles. 'Thank you, sir. That's possibly the nicest thing you've ever said to me.'

Anil mutters under his breath as he makes a quick exit. Almost immediately after, Sarita asks Ravi, 'So, how did this happen? I thought you had Suleimani under constant surveillance.'

'We did, ma'am. But I have a feeling even Suleimani wasn't aware of this attack. We've followed every step of his ever since he entered India, and he was never even close to the sites that were attacked today, nor have we found him engaging in the patterns of activity that typically go into planning and executing strikes of this nature. He did survey some sensitive sites in Uttar Pradesh, and we significantly bolstered security cover at these locations. They weren't the ones attacked today.'

'So, you mean to say he knows we're onto him and has been able to outsmart us somehow? Does this have something to do with their new communications portal? How else did they manage to pull it off without us having even the slightest hint? I'm tempted to consider Anil's suggestion that this might be an entirely new organization we're dealing with here.'

'Does he know we're on to him? I'm quite sure he doesn't. But does this have something do with their new communications portal? Yes, it does. Is this a new organization? They certainly want us to think that way, and Anil fell right into that trap.'

Sarita is confused. 'I'm sorry, I don't quite follow. It feels like you're contradicting yourself.'

'What I mean to say is there is more than one Suleimani on the ground. There's Karim, who's still lodged in Kolkata Central Jail, and so it couldn't have been him. Our asset inside the prison tells us that Karim was sent to help set up a secure cash-and-arms route. Suleimani, on the other hand, seems to be more of an organizational chap, who's been tasked with setting up highly localized sleeper cells The point is, I think it's safe to assume after today's attack that there are several such dangerously capable individuals out there, all acting independent of each other's plans but ultimately working as part of the same mission. It's the communications portal that allows the people pulling strings from afar to coordinate all of this with the precision and stealth of a guerrilla unit. Because not a word of any of this is spilling over into the regular chatter.'

Sarita is left dumbfounded. It's a lot to take in, and she thinks aloud, 'But what I don't understand is, why would they target mosques? I mean, some within the IB have pursued this suspicion in the past, but we've never found conclusive evidence linking jihadi groups to attacks on Islamic places of worship. But of course, if Al-Brittani is involved this time around, I suppose it is to be expected. Something like attacking a mosque is quite consistent with the way his mind works. But what's the end game?'

'My gut feeling is that they have a definite political strategy that goes beyond merely inflicting terror on civilians. After the train blasts and the other attacks that happened last year, the entire nation—Muslims, Hindus, Sikhs, Christians—everybody came together and firmly aligned themselves against terrorism. Al-Brittani is a sharp one, and Tabrez is no fool either. They've learnt from their mistakes and are looking this time to destabilize the delicate fabric that holds our people together.'

'But more than Tabrez or Al-Brittani, what I see most clearly in all of this is the handiwork of the ISI. The fact that K2 has been kicked off in Uttar Pradesh of all states makes sense. They're looking to stir up the ghosts of Babri and unleash them throughout the country.'

Ravi concurs. 'It's also their only way. Their star bombmaker continues to languish in our jails, and we've secured all of the traditional supply routes. Which is why all they could manage were low-intensity blasts with hardly any casualties. We'll have to wait for forensics, but I think it is most likely that very low-tech improvised explosive devices (IEDs) were deployed today. Whatever it is that they have in mind for the next phase of K2, I think it's safe to assume there won't be more bomb blasts.'

Sarita shakes her head. 'You're right for the most part, but I think it is too early to safely assume anything. It would be very dangerous to do that. The fact that these were low-tech IEDs is what worries me the most. Suleimani, and . . . God knows who or how many others like him are going around the country putting into place a particularly rabid radicalization module. And they have a secret communications channel that we cannot break into, through which instructions for putting together these IEDs using domestic materials can be easily passed along to hundreds or thousands of these new recruits who can act as lone wolves and wreak havoc across the country. What do we do, Ravi? It seems completely hopeless to me. Even if we manage to track down the people who executed today's attacks, they'd probably have no clue about what lies in store. The enemy is going to be a step ahead no matter what we do.'

Ravi has never seen Sarita display her vulnerabilities and fears so openly. But he himself doesn't entirely share her pessimism.

'It's not entirely hopeless, ma'am. It's important to bear in mind that despite the novelty and complexity of this entire operation, it's still being centrally managed. You pull the plug at the top, and the entire network is dismantled in an instant. The fact that their new organizational structure is so diffuse and spread out, with everybody on the ground acting independent of one another, is not only their biggest strength but also their greatest vulnerability. If you remove the people coordinating from above, there's no organization left any longer. So, we need to double up on our efforts to get to Tabrez.'

Sarita counters him, 'Anil was right. You are indeed obsessed with Tabrez, and I can see why. But how on earth will we ever do that? We don't have much time, because if this pattern spirals out of control and spurs genuinely home-bred insurgencies across other minority groups as well, then it's over. Pakistan is not going to hand him over to us, or even acknowledge that he's on their soil. The ISI doesn't want to be seen as having anything to do with all of this. They know they can't risk armed conflict or international ostracization at this point. Their economy is in a shambles, and another war or more sanctions from the west will obliterate them.'

Ravi wears a sheepish grin on his face as he pulls out the sealed envelope from his pocket. Finally, the moment he was waiting for has arrived. He carefully tears open the flap, and reveals a set of pictures of Tabrez, 'These pictures were taken by our assets embedded in different locations inside Pakistan, including this one taken outside Islamabad International Airport, days after he fled India. If these pictures go public, it would be an international embarrassment for Pakistan. It still won't be enough to convince them to hand him over. He's integral to their plans in these early stages. But it might be enough to force them to smuggle him out of Pakistan. There are only so many places they can send him to. There's an Interpol red corner notice against him. My hunch is, Nepal or Bangladesh. Knowing Tabrez's overconfidence and his penchant for risk-taking, he might even attempt infiltrating the Indian border. It's hard to say. But the moment he is out of Pakistani soil, he will be forced to engage physically with his operatives already on the ground, and that's going to leave him vulnerable to detection by our assets. And even if that doesn't happen, if we continue infiltrating their network at various levels, as we have done so far, we might be able to zero in on his whereabouts. But it all depends on us getting him out of Pakistan.'

Sarita ponders over Ravi's plan for a few moments.

'It is a long-drawn strategy that may or may not work. But let's assume for now that it is our best shot. Even then, what do I tell the Prime Minister? And what is he going to tell the nation? He came to power on an anti-terrorism platform. This is a huge embarrassment after all these months of peace and rebuilding.'

Ravi smiles. 'The truth, ma'am. That this was a cheap attempt on Pakistan's part to sow internal discord. But they are not going to succeed. Our secular democracy is far too strong to be threatened by such low-brow attempts.'

Sarita chuckles. 'You should really consider becoming a politician after you retire, you know.'

'I'd rather be dead.'

* * *

At Kolkata Central Jail, a beaming Karim returns to his cell with a copy of the newspaper, which he discreetly flicked from the reading room during leisure hours. He flings it at Cyrus, who in the absence of any definite leads emerging from Karim after the initial breakthrough, and no assurance forthcoming from Ravi or Anjali on the matter of his release, has been growing slightly despondent these last few days.

Cyrus picks up the newspaper and looks at the front page headlines and sub-headlines screaming out in red and bold— 'UP in Smoke: Serial Low-Intensity Blasts Rock Uttar Pradesh', 'Holy Carnage: Gurudwaras and Mosques Targeted Simultaneously', 'Police and Intelligence Agencies Caught Napping, No Answers Forthcoming'.

'It has begun,' Karim declares proudly to Cyrus.

'What has begun?'

Karim peeks through the bars to ensure nobody's around. 'The war that will finish this country once and for all.'

Cyrus doesn't share Karim's excitement, 'These were low-intensity blasts. Hardly any casualties. How will this finish the country?'

'You're a well-educated person. Surely, you've studied some amount of history . . . and so you'd know that no war in human history can be reduced to one incident alone. They're long affairs, wars. Plenty of battles and skirmishes and politics and bloodshed and intrigue.'

'I'm assuming you're a part of this war, and that's what brought you to India,' Cyrus surmises.

'Yes. And since we're talking in terms of war, you can assume that I'm the commanding officer of an important regiment.'

'But you're in jail. And you haven't had a single visitor since the time I've been here. That doesn't seem like an ideal position for a commanding officer to be in.'

'I'm in jail because I chose to. Once the conditions outside are conducive to the pursuit of my mission objectives, I'll be out of here.'

'And when will that be?'

'Now. Yesterday's attack is the signal I've been waiting for.'

Karim looks away for a few moments, as he thinks of an idea that's been playing in his mind for the last few days.

'Fate works in strange ways, you know . . . Getting arrested for illegally crossing the border and then seeking asylum was intended merely as a way for me to bide my time and stay under the radar. That way, even if other units were to get exposed, I'd be completely safe. But then, quite unexpectedly, I also ended up meeting you. And I've been thinking that with your help the scope of my operation can widen exponentially.'

Cyrus is visibly excited. And he isn't faking it.

'So, all those things you told me the other day, you weren't just pulling a prank on me?'

Karim shakes his head with a mild grin on his face.

Cyrus presses further, 'So what is this plan, and how can I be a part of it?'

Karim raises his palm and gently rocks it back and forth, as if to signal patience.

Cyrus realizes he's being overly eager and decides to compensate.

'Don't take this the wrong way, but how can I even believe you? I mean, if you're actually serious and not just messing around with me, how can you so casually be revealing all these incriminating details? What if I were to reveal all of this to the prison guards?'

Karim is taken aback slightly. He quickly recovers and fires a rejoinder, 'I should be the one asking you this question. How can I believe you? Are you really the heir to a multimillion dollar conglomerate, or are you just a drug-addled liar who enjoys making up wild stories for fun?'

Cyrus bursts out laughing, and Karim joins in. It is irreverent banter of this sort that has brought them closer over the last few weeks. But this time, Cyrus can see clearly that Karim is headed somewhere with all of this, and so is eager to pursue the conversation to its logical conclusion.

'On a serious note, Karim Miyan, I am eager to do my bit if this is a real revolution we're talking about. Name it, and it shall be done.'

The smile disappears from Karim's face.

'I was being entirely serious. How can I believe you? You might be the son of a business tycoon, but if your father is anything like many others I've known of, then you as his heir would have about the same amount of spending freedom as an old wife in an Arab sheikh's harem. Essentially, nil.'

Cyrus dismisses Karim's concerns. 'Thankfully, I am not one of those. I have significant wealth at my disposal, completely independent of the assets overseen by my father. How can I prove it to you?'

Karim thinks for a few moments as he assesses the sincerity of Cyrus's expressions and body language.

'Two hundred thousand dollars. In cash.'

Cyrus must try very hard to keep his jaw from dropping. Keeping a straight face, he tells Karim confidently, 'It will be done. But in return, I will need to know exactly what the money is going to be used for.'

'Arrange the money, and then you'll be made privy to the details. In fact, you'll be part of the operation too. The money will have to be handed over, after all.'

Cyrus pushes his luck. 'Not even a hint?'

'Let's just say it has something to do with the question you asked earlier about how low-intensity blasts were going to destroy this country. You were right, they won't. But you can't make a high-intensity explosive device using household materials. You need military-grade supplies, or better still, military-grade explosive devices. And that doesn't come free. And even if one did have the money, it's not like you can walk into some store that sells these things. It has to come from across the border, and that's not easy either. Every single one of our established supply chains have either been neutralized, compromised or are under very close surveillance. And we cannot risk interdiction, no matter what. And so, it will have to be an entirely new route.'

'And how would you go about doing that?'

'I've said enough for now. You bring in the money, I'll make the exchange happen, and then we'll talk specifics.'

It's still technically leisure time at Kolkata Central Jail on a dry and dreary Monday afternoon, and Cyrus leaps on to his feet. 'Let me set up a meeting with my lawyer. The sooner I can get out of here, the sooner I can arrange for the funds, and the sooner I can finally do something righteous in my life.'

But Cyrus doesn't really have to set up a meeting with his lawyer. Ever since his arrest, Anjali has turned a guest house within the prison complex into a temporary field station turned residence. Except for the superintendent, who is a close confidante of additional commissioner Bose—Anjali's batchmate, who had put together this entire arrangement at her request—none of the prison staff is even aware of Cyrus's daily interactions with her. They assume that she is a senior officer conducting an elaborate audit of the jail's accounts. As for Cyrus, they know that he's a rich businessman—not in the least because of all the handsome tips he's been paying them for special privileges like smoking and the use of his mobile phone. And so, they assume that like most other white collar inmates, he's been permitted to use the secure video conferencing room inside the superintendent's office building, in order to attend to his business.

Anjali's already waiting for him inside. Cyrus's phone has been bugged to also serve as an uninterrupted audio recording device, and so she has been privy to every conversation he's had with Karim.

'This is good. Finally, something concrete,' she tells him as he walks through the door, which automatically seals itself shut to prevent unauthorized access.

'Is Ravi Sir aware?'

'He's aware, and as we speak, he's already working on putting together Karim's demand.'

'Great! So, will you get me out of here as soon as Karim gives me what information we need to figure out the exact logistics of this exchange or transshipment, or whatever modality he has in place.'

'We'll try our best.'

Cyrus is stumped.

'What do you mean?'

'What I mean is, we're going to hire a very expensive lawyer who will be able to build a strong case in favour of at least getting you bail. But there's no guarantee. You assaulted respectable senior citizens, and there are charges of attempted murder. No judge will be inclined to be lenient, and there is a significant possibility that it might take weeks, if not months. You knew all of this when you signed up, right?'

'Not really. Ravi Sir told me to go create a ruckus and get myself arrested. Although now that I think of it, there were so many other ways I could have got arrested, without coming across as a rich jerk who takes pleasure in terrorizing the old.'

'I'm not talking about this operation, but the organization itself. You can, in the course of your duties, skirt around the law if it is necessary to secure a strategic objective like in this case where it helped you establish a connection with a senior LeH commander. But you can't expect special treatment in the eyes of the law, if you are to get caught.'

'But ma'am, in this case, getting caught itself was the strategic objective.'

'Yes, but we can't go and reveal all of that in court, can we? Not unless you want the entire world to know about what we're doing here. And so, the law must take its own course.'

* * *

Not for the first time, and certainly not the last, Ravi turns up unannounced at Sarita's office. And as per her standing instructions, Sarita's secretary does nothing to prevent him from just walking in.

'Ravi, good you're here. I wanted to give you an update on this whole business of forcing Pakistan to kick Tabrez out. As you're aware, our relationship with Pakistan is on very shaky ground. They recently expelled our ambassador for no good reason, and so we're currently not even on talking terms. And the prime minister's not very keen on raking this up in the public domain without first taking this up at a diplomatic level. He's very particular that the government plays by the rule book, at least as far as diplomacy goes. And so, we'll have to wait for a few more days at least, for the relevant channels to be opened. For now, the prime minister has decided to take the bold and commendable step of owning up to our security failure, rather than conveniently blaming Pakistan.'

'For once, ma'am, I'm grateful for these bureaucratic technicalities I can never wrap my head around. The delay works for us. In fact, please do everything in your power to ensure that this conversation with Pakistan does not take off. Instead of the long-winded plan I suggested, I've come to you with a more straightforward one. If this new plan works out, then we can go to them with something far more explosive than just pictures of Tabrez at Islamabad Airport. I don't want to jinx it, but if this pans out the way I want it to, we might be able to force Pakistan to give us Tabrez's head on a platter.'

Sarita sighs. Knowing Ravi, she should have seen this coming—a complete reversal of advice, and the recommendation of a radically different plan with more ambitious objectives, all in less than twenty-four hours.

'And what is this plan?'

'I'm still trying to figure it out myself because my source doesn't yet have all the details. And he won't, unless we can meet some very specific demands.'

'And what are these demands?'

A poker-faced Ravi stares blankly at her. 'Two hundred thousand counterfeit US dollars. And to keep my source happy, I will also require the services of the best criminal lawyer in all of West Bengal.'

Mosale

Cyrus is a relieved man. Finally, he has been granted bail. But he still has unfinished business to attend to at Kolkata Central Jail and is desperate to bring it to completion. As things stand he still has only a vague picture about the procurement of arms that his fictitious persona, the prodigal heir of a millionaire, is going to fund. Karim has been non-committal about the details and has asked Cyrus to drop the money at a particular junction of two narrow alleys in Kolkata's Dharapara slum, in the dead of the night.

Although they could place the location under intensive surveillance, and then follow the money to its final destination, Cyrus knows from past experience that it is a huge risk. If the network of exchange from that point onwards is a fairly sophisticated one, as he fully expects it to be, then there is a good chance that they might lose the trail. And so, he is intent on handing over the money directly to the final source of the arms, a proposition Karim isn't very enthusiastic about signing off on.

But Cyrus has always been a persuasive one. And so, in the final moments of his incarceration, he is striking a hard bargain.

'It is non-negotiable,' he declares flatly to his perplexed cellmate. 'Unless I'm actively involved in the operation, I will not be comfortable committing the funds. Two lakh dollars is a huge sum, you do realize that, don't you?'

Karim makes a show of his disappointment, 'So you mean to say you don't trust me?'

Cyrus shakes his head. 'If I didn't trust you, we wouldn't even be having this conversation.'

Karim is flustered. 'Then why won't you let me handle it?'

'Because I want you to trust me, too. Just by funding this operation, I am not going to suddenly fill the void in my life. I need to get on the ground, get my hands dirty. You do understand, don't you? Besides, if you minimize the number of intermediaries involved, it would be safer on the whole, wouldn't it?'

'It's safer, but it's not in the best interests of the movement. To win a war it is essential that all your units are constantly engaged, and the chains of command and communication keep tugging along in the manner they're supposed to. And just like you, these men too want a piece of action. To bypass them would not be advisable.'

'But they're not the ones bringing in two lakh dollars, are they? And like I've told you already, this is just the beginning. I have considerably large resources at my disposal. Think it over. I'm out of here in less than ten minutes, and unless you agree, we will never see each other again. And so, good luck finding another source of funds.'

Karim throws his hands up in frustration. He has given in. Cyrus has left him no option.

'All right, but I need to know you're for real. There's a boy named Suhaim at Qureshi Pharmacy in Bhawanipur.

Seek him out and tell him I sent you. Give him a thousand dollars in hard cash and tell him that the money is for new mountaineering boots for the youngsters at the academy. But since I'm in jail, tell him that you'll be the one going out to buy the large order for the final K2 expedition. And so, you need to be put in direct contact with our main distributor.'

Cyrus is seized with a sense of déjà vu, and an overwhelming sense of everything falling in place. Outside Qureshi Pharmacy in Bhawanipur was where the false-flag operation to expose Mihir had been staged by the devious Rukhsana and her associates. It feels like things are coming back full circle.

'So, this distributor, I'm assuming he's an arms dealer, he'll hand me the arms if I give him the money? And who do I then hand over the arms to? Suhaim?'

Karim chuckles. 'Don't be foolish. This is precisely why I don't think it's such a good idea for you to be bypassing everybody else to get directly to our source. Like I told you already, it's not like you're going to a showroom and buying a new car. The exchange of arms will happen at sea. It's a tricky business and demands highly skilled sailing. There are specialized men for the job.'

'I am an expert sailor. My father owns multiple yachts.'

Karim laughs disdainfully. 'And do your leisurely sailing trips involve having to bypass the coast guard at every step of the way? This is not child's play. For God's sake, don't screw this up with your stubbornness. You pay the arms dealer, and he'll set up the exchange and arrange for a professional to execute the exchange. Handing over money directly to the dealer is as far as I can let you go. You'll be given proof of the arms having been handed over, but you'll play no further part. And even if you did, you wouldn't be handing it to Suhaim.

He's an insignificant player who won't even know who the dealer is. He himself will have to get in touch with someone else in order to get you the details you'll need. That's the beauty of our new operational set-up. It's as strong as it can get because nobody knows everything there is to know. And so even if somebody were to get caught, the others can carry on unimpeded.'

Cyrus wants to know more but feels a tinge of discomfort as he considers pushing Karim a little harder, well aware that it would be unwise to arouse suspicions. He has already let out the most crucial details Cyrus needs. But he will stay in prison for as long as C3 needs him to, with no way of getting his word out to his men outside, barring a prison break. And so, Cyrus has nothing to lose, and is determined to eke out as much information as he can. Even if Karim were to suddenly discover that Cyrus is in fact an Indian spy, there is nothing he can do to prevent Cyrus from activating the rest of the plan with the information he now has at his disposal.

'And who is this someone else who Suhaim will get it from?'

Karim is flustered. 'You're way too curious for your own good. I have good reasons to be suspicious, you know . . .'

Just then, two prison guards walk to the cell. One of the guards tells Cyrus that it is time to go, while the other informs Karim of the superintendent's decision to put him in solitary confinement. Even as Cyrus bids goodbye, an aghast Karim begins to protest, demanding to know the grounds on which he is being punished.

The guard laughs at him. 'For stealing newspapers from the common room.'

Cyrus chuckles secretly as he walks away swiftly. He completes the formalities and walks into a waiting car, with Anjali in the driver's seat. Cyrus asks his senior, 'I thought I was going to be in there for months. What changed, suddenly?'

'I hadn't taken into account the special affection you command in the hearts of those who matter.'

Cyrus is intrigued.

'Ravi sir called in a favour to get me released? That's impossible.'

'Of course he did not. I don't think he'd do that even if his own son were in prison. But what he did was, he engaged the most sought-after criminal lawyer in all of North-eastern India to fight your case and get you bail.'

'So, I have to come to court every time the case is listed?'

'No, not you. Do you know who got bail?'

'Saqib Khan.'

'What is your name?'

'Cyrus Bandookwala.'

Anjali and Cyrus have a hearty laugh.

* * *

'Let us welcome Mr Bacchus for his award-winning performance,' begins Ravi, addressing his key operatives who have assembled in the C3 board room for yet another brainstorming session. Such gatherings are organized whenever there is a need to solve jigsaw puzzles in espionage.

Coming to the agenda of the meeting, Ravi continues, 'Though we have got very crucial information that routes of weapon smuggling have changed from land to sea, the vastness of our coastline makes the task all the more daunting. I would like to pick your brains about the possible route of transshipment. Cyrus can enjoy his samosa and jalebi for his hard work.'

'Sir, since we got the information, we activated our assets among seafarer communities in Gujarat and Maharashtra as these coasts are close to the Pakistan maritime boundary. But there is nil report from them,' informs Anjali.

'It is fair to assume that the landing point would be on the western coast. But given the attention on Gujarat and Maharashtra coasts it is only natural that these may not be used for such a delicate operation.'

'Sir, may I . . .?'

'Carry on, Professor Cherian'

'Elementary, sir . . .'

'Oh, it seems that Jose Cherian has recently read a Sherlock Holmes novel,' says Ravi, chuckling.

'It is possible that the probable landing point would on be on the south-western coast. We may recall that LeH had its training location in the western ghats in Kerala, and sir, we had traced that the boat-shaped explosives used in blasts by the outfit were manufactured in a fishing village near Mangalore . . .'

'Thank you, Mr Holmes,' Ravi interrupts. 'Meeting is dismissed.'

* * *

In the afternoon, even as the sun beats down hard on the Konkan coast, the Ernakulam Express drops Mihir off at the Udupi Railway Station in Karnataka. Mihir's distinctly Kashmiri appearance marks him out for the overeager rickshaw drivers at the station as an out-of-towner who in all likelihood is a student at the neighbouring university town of Manipal. And so, they crowd around him, each quoting a lower fare than the other. Mihir doesn't respond, and as other passengers make their way through the platform, the crowd thins. The rickshaw drivers spread out and target other passengers. Mihir clarifies to the sole driver who remains that he is not a student but a filmmaker who is here to make a documentary on the lives of the local fishing communities. He asks to be taken to the fishing hamlet of Kodi Bengre, where the river meets the sea. The rickshaw driver is thrilled. Kodi Bengre is much farther away than Manipal, and so there is a lot more money to be made. To keep his cover intact, Mihir pulls out his bulky video camera and begins recording as soon as the rickshaw driver sets out from the railway station and captures every random sight on the forty-minute journey.

It is a hot weekday afternoon, and apart from a student couple bunking their lecture for a romantic rendezvous on the beach, the hamlet of Kodi Bengre seems virtually deserted when Mihir gets there. The sight of his camera doesn't quite grab the attention Mihir expects it to. And so, he finds a seat at a small toddy shop and orders some snacks as he figures out his next step. After an hour or so, with still no locals approaching him, Mihir decides that he needs to draw attention to himself and starts going around the village knocking at every door requesting an interview. Word spreads, and after several pointless interviews, a scrawny man with a deep scar on his collarbone approaches Mihir and asks to speak to him in private. The man is already drunk, and Mihir can smell it from a distance. He escorts Mihir back to the toddy shop, which continues to remain deserted. He orders a large pot of toddy and offers a glass to Mihir, who turns it down.

'I don't drink, thanks.'

The scrawny fisherman sizes him up.

'Documentary film, eh? Who's your producer?'

Mihir smiles. This is the man he is seeking.

'Ravi Kumar from Cine Creations Corporation, Delhi . . . C3.'

The scrawny fisherman, who goes by his nom de guerre Mosale, meaning crocodile in Kannada, also smiles.

'Tell that boss of yours to come up with a new tactic. Every other rich kid in Manipal has a video camera these days. I can't be going up to every one of them and checking if they're actually here to film crocodiles.'

Mihir hands Mosale his phone. 'Why don't you tell him yourself?'

* * *

Examiner paces up and down the large courtyard of the dilapidated haveli that has been his home for more than a month now. It is well past midnight, but sleep can wait, for he intends to corner Altaf who hasn't been around much these last few days. The times that he has been home—for thirty minutes a day at best, mostly for a quick meal and change of clothes—Altaf has tended to be evasive about his whereabouts, claiming that he has been busy with routine organizational duties. Examiner knows that this is not true, and something is brewing.

And so, as soon as Altaf arrives, riding pillion on a heavily modified Yamaha motorcycle that is loud enough to wake up the entire neighbourhood, Examiner waves affectionately. Altaf is surprised to find him still awake. Bidding a hasty goodbye to his compatriot, who is swift to speed away into the darkness, he tries to quietly weasel his way past his grand-uncle into his room.

But Examiner stops him. 'Your mother has been really concerned, you know? You're hardly around.'

'I know, Dadajaan, but I can't help it. When there's work, there's work. You know how it is.'

Examiner glares at Altaf. 'No, I don't know how it is. Why don't you tell me?'

Altaf is taken aback. 'It's, um . . . work, you know. I have to manage a lot of things. I've been selected as a youth community leader by the foreign dignitary who you listened to the other day.'

'And what exactly does your work as a youth community leader entail?'

'Multiple things, but mainly it is about mobilizing youngsters from our community and putting them on community service activities.'

Examiner puts his arm around Altaf's shoulder. 'Listen, kid, you can fool your mother, but you certainly can't fool me. We've spoken about this earlier, and you know that I do not have a problem with the path you are headed down. It's just that I do not want you to be misled or get carried away. You have to be careful . . . it's difficult as it is being a young Muslim in this country. If you run into trouble with the law . . .'

Altaf feels a stinging pang of anxiety at the mention of the law. Examiner notices and tries to put him at ease. 'I'm not saying you will necessarily get into trouble with the law. God forbid such a horrible fate, but if that happens you need to have somebody who can look out for you and get you out of trouble. Someone elderly and respectable, with both money and a reputation. Someone like me. And I can be there for you only if I know what's happening and what you're really up to.'

Altaf hesitates, as he lowers his tone sharply, 'I swear, I'm not up to any of what you're hinting at. Not directly, at least. And in any case, I'm not allowed to talk about it to anybody. If they find out, they'll kick me out.'

Examiner reassures him, 'I'm not a random anybody. I'm your Dadajaan. I'm here at home practically the entire day, except for when I'm at the mosque. With you gone most of the day, your mother's the only person I even speak to. And of course, I can't tell her these things. So, who else will I tell? They won't find out. You need not fear.'

Altaf thinks for a few moments.

'I really don't know exactly what it is I'm doing. I mean, I've been assigned specific tasks, but it is nothing out of the ordinary, and I don't really know who or what it's all for . . .'

Examiner knows that the boy isn't bluffing. For underneath Altaf's confusion and lack of clarity, Examiner can see the tell-tale signs of a highly diffused organizational network at work, with each worker carrying only a small piece of what might possibly be a gigantic jigsaw puzzle. It is consistent with everything he has gathered so far about Suleimani's modus operandi.

Examiner pushes further. 'And what are these tasks?'

'Well, all kinds of things. For example, these days, I've been hunting for houses that can be rented to accommodate visiting dignitaries and guests. They're very picky about the kind of houses they want—in quiet areas, conducive to prayer and meditation, and not too many people around. Where in Lucknow of all the cities in the world will I go finding houses like that? It's difficult, and that's why I've been out all the time for the last several days. And it's not just me. Because it's such a hard task, nearly everyone in my group has been assigned to look separately. I'm assuming they've finally found some houses that tick all their boxes, but I can't really be sure. All I know is that we've been asked to stop looking. But the point is, I'm doing nothing illegal, trust me.'

Examiner smiles reassuringly. 'I know, you have absolutely nothing to be worried about. Now, go inside and get some sleep. You need to stay healthy if you want to continue serving your community and your people. It's a long road ahead, I presume you're aware.'

Behind Examiner's reassuring exterior lies a mind bursting with intrigue and uncertainty. The fact that Suleimani's boys are on an intense house-hunting mission presents a vast range of operational possibilities—from bomb-making workshops to safe houses for cross-border terrorists.

* * *

Perched on a high mountain, from where he can see the Afghan valley in its majestic entirety, Ravi is drained of all energy. All around him are bodies—of his own men, of enemy soldiers, even of civilians. He sets his rifle down. It feels like the long war has finally ended. But as he gazes listlessly at the horizon, he can see the faint contours of the armies marching towards him. It's a war that might never end. Ravi picks up the rifle, but he doesn't take aim. Instead, he sets it upright and leans against it. He shuts his eyes, hoping to drift into an endless sleep.

The phone rings and Ravi's slumber comes to a swift and abrupt end. But when he opens his eyes, he finds himself not in Afghanistan but in his bedroom in Delhi. Before he can pick up the phone, it stops ringing. Ravi looks at the clock. It is 3 a.m. He gets up and almost instinctively reaches into his bedside drawer for cigarettes, only to be reminded of the fact that he has stopped smoking.

The phone rings again, and this time Ravi picks up immediately and carries the receiver to the balcony. He does not want to wake up Rita.

'Good evening . . . I mean, good morning, sir. This is Mahesh Dubey from the Lucknow desk. I am really sorry to be disturbing you at this hour, but something has come up, and you need to know.'

'Go on, I'm listening.'

'Sir, I've learnt from Baaz, who's a very credible asset, of an assassination plot that is at a very advanced stage and could be executed anytime.'

'Who's the target?'

'Targets, sir, not target. We do not have the exact names, but we have reason to believe that anywhere between ten to fifty important political figures might be on the list.'

Ravi is stunned.

'A serial assassination? Just when you think you've seen it all . . . Any idea what the motivation is, or who's behind it?'

'Could be anybody, sir. Although our inputs are credible, it's all very non-specific. We're getting it from assets embedded inside underground contract-killing networks. And you know better than me how these networks operate—client anonymity is paramount, and so they're used by a wide range of players . . . gangsters, businessmen, Naxals, even politicians themselves. I will let you know if I learn more, but at this point, my recommendation is that we immediately alert the DGP and request him to tighten security cover for all prominent political figures and recommend the cancellation of all publicly held political events until we get to the bottom of this.'

All that Ravi can think about is the information passed on by Examiner. He wonders if this plot is connected to whatever Suleimani is planning. 'And what about terrorists? Do you think this could be a terrorist conspiracy?'

Dubey goes silent for a few moments. It's a possibility he hadn't considered.

'Um . . . it's possible, sir. But isn't it unprecedented for terrorists to hire contract killers? They'd do it themselves.'

Ravi sighs. 'Until 9/11 seizing control of civilian aircrafts and crashing them into buildings was unprecedented. When you're dealing with terrorists, everything is unprecedented. Anything and anybody can be turned into a weapon. Get to the bottom of this as soon as you can. Take people into custody if you need to. I will call you in three hours for an update. I will in the meantime speak to the DGP, but it's quite a pointless exercise. What can the police really do with such little information? I mean, this is Uttar Pradesh. There are over 400 sitting MLAs and thousands of former legislators and ministers. It simply won't be possible to extend security to

every single one of them unless we can narrow down the list
of possible targets.'

* * *

Examiner is shaken out of his sleep by a visibly excited Altaf,
'Dadajaan, wake up. Something has happened.'

Examiner rubs his eyes as he struggles to shrug away his
sleep. 'What do you mean something has happened? Is your
mother all right?'

'Nothing to do with my mother. I think it's about what
we talked about two nights ago.'

The sleepiness evaporates in an instant and Examiner is up
on his feet. 'What happened? Are you in trouble?'

'I don't know . . . I mean, I don't even know what has
happened, but something big has happened or is going to
happen in the next few hours. They aren't spelling it out.
We've been asked to keep an eye out for the news and prepare
ourselves for possible communal violence on a scale never
witnessed before.'

Examiner feels dreadful as he wonders if it is already too
late. He needs to talk to Ravi immediately and reaches for
his phone, 'I need to call up some friends. Of course, I won't
mention anything but in case things go out of control, we will
need to get out of here to somewhere safer. At least for your
mother's sake, it's better to be prepared. I'll set it up. You keep
your eyes glued to the TV and let me know as soon as you
learn something.'

Altaf nods in agreement and returns to the living room,
where the television is tuned to a news channel, while

Examiner makes a quick exit. It's an emergency and there is no time for talking in riddles, and so complete privacy is a must. He walks to an abandoned textile mill complex at the end of the road. Getting in is no easy task, and he has to make his way past large patches of thorny shrubbery and rusted barbed wire. Paying little heed to the bloody scratches all over his arms and legs, Examiner pulls out his phone and dials Ravi.

Revenge

Ravi picks up a note that has just been faxed to the headquarters. As he begins to examine its poorly handwritten contents, its quality further diminished in the course of transmission, he realizes that he will need to use a magnifying glass, if not call in a handwriting expert. It's almost like whoever wrote it wants to frustrate him. But Ravi's frustrations have hit something of a saturation point, and it will take a lot more to get him as riled up as he had been twenty minutes ago, when the news had reached him. He'd been provided two highly credible leads, both pointing to the same event several hours in advance, but he simply hadn't been able to do anything to prevent it.

Banishing these unamenable feelings of helpless anguish to the recesses of his overworked brain, he leans closer to the note. Squinting his left eye, he places the right against his decades-old stainless steel-framed magnifying glass.

He reads aloud in his mind, as he moves from left to right, character by character, 'This is an act of revenge perpetrated by ordinary . . .'

Sarita barges in.

'How bad is it, Ravi?'

The note has his full attention at this point, and so Ravi doesn't look up as he responds, 'Depends on what you really mean by bad here. Something terrible has happened, no doubt, but if we can control the outflow of information, I think we can defuse the situation.'

Sarita doesn't always mind Ravi's distinctively convoluted manner of speaking. But sometimes she wishes he'd just get to the point. 'Just spell it out, Ravi. What is it?'

Ravi raises his head from the magnifying glass and looks at his wristwatch. 'It's about time. It should be all over the news now.'

Sarita turns on the TV.

* * *

In Lucknow, Altaf gets up with bated anticipation as the breakfast news bulletin is interrupted by the ominous swoosh of breaking news. Standing at a distance is Examiner, whose sombre expression is matched by that of the newsreader. 'Big breaking news just coming in from Lucknow. The former home minister of Uttar Pradesh, and textile baron Chandrakant Mathur, has been shot dead by unidentified assailants. For the latest updates on this sensational news this morning, we have our correspondent joining us from outside the Gautam Buddha Park in Lucknow.'

As the channel cuts to its correspondent, Sarita fields a seemingly unending stream of calls on her mobile phone. Ravi knows that everything from this point onwards depends on how the killing is reported.

The correspondent seems nearly out of breath as he reports, 'Right behind the barricades on the right of your screen, you can see the BMW in which the former home minister was found dead, his body riddled with bullets. It is believed that the killing took place several hours ago but was discovered only half an hour ago. Given Mathur's wide-ranging business interests, and long history of political involvement, the government is looking into all possible angles.'

Ravi heaves a sigh of relief, but it is a moment too soon, for the correspondent continues, 'But we've learnt independently from eyewitnesses that the assailants left behind a note claiming responsibility and describing their motives. But because this is a sensitive matter that is being investigated even as we speak, the government is being tight-lipped about the contents of this note, or who is behind this killing. But highly placed police sources have told our channel on the condition of anonymity that the murder was communally motivated. Viewers may recall that Mathur was widely believed to have played a key role in facilitating the illegal demolition of the Babri Masjid by Hindu mobs in 1992, and so this might be an act of retribution. Further, the note is believed to have warned of a series of such assassinations that will be carried out in quick succession against enemies of Islam. Sources have also told us that there is reason to suspect that today's assassination is linked to the recent blasts in the state. Although the government is yet to confirm this officially, this is bound to send the entire political establishment of Uttar Pradesh running for cover. More worryingly, and this is the biggest fear running across the security establishment: is this assassination inevitably bound to bring back the ghosts of Babri?'

Ravi can't help but let out his rage at the news. 'Why don't you just read out the entire bloody note? Brainless oafs being fed by even bigger buffoons. You yourself conjure ghosts, and then you say that ghosts are scary. Not even the slightest sense of responsibility or caution.' Sarita, who is just getting off the phone with the chief minister of Uttar Pradesh, is startled by Ravi's sudden outburst. And when she discovers why, she can't help but feel equally outraged.

But better sense prevails, and Ravi is quick to calm his frayed nerves as well as Sarita's, 'What's been said has been said. There's no way to unsay it, but we can refute it strongly, maybe even plant false evidence if that's what it takes. But we've got to quash this narrative, unless we want Uttar Pradesh to burn, which is exactly what the ISI is hoping for.'

'What exactly does this note say?'

'Exactly what you heard, plus a few other things. They're claiming that it is a spontaneous act of retribution carried out by a group of ordinary young Muslim revolutionaries and intended as a wake-up call for ordinary Muslims across the country to unite and join the fight to uphold their faith.'

Sarita is alarmed, 'Is it true? Was this really pulled off by one of Suleimani's chapters? But, how? And that too right under our noses?'

'He and his boys were definitely involved in laying the groundwork, but our undercover asset embedded in close proximity to these networks told me that they themselves had no clue. It is quite likely that a few of them, the more senior ones whose links with Tabrez and the ISI predate Suleimani's arrival, were actually at the crime scene.'

'We can't obviously say all of this to the public. It'll just seem like a very convenient explanation, blaming the ISI. Nobody's going to buy it at this point. What we can and must do is stress on the fact that the murder was carried out by a professional hitman. Leak a fabricated note, make it seem like a business deal got wrong. Do whatever it takes.'

'We're already on it, but it might only buy us time. People won't easily forget what these journalists are saying right now. It's going to spread, and when tensions are sufficiently high, these things work like self-fulfilling prophecies and facts cease to matter after a point. One more assassination is all it will take, and you'll see self-proclaimed revolutionaries, both Muslim and Hindu, springing up and carrying out spontaneous killings.'

Sarita is stunned. As the dots come together in her mind, she thinks aloud and puts into words what Ravi knows just as well, but is too afraid to articulate, 'If their plan succeeds, it isn't a riot we're staring at. This isn't being driven by some politician looking for petty electoral gains. This is an enemy state that is out to rip our country apart from inside.'

Sarita's voice trails off as she grapples with just how bad the situation is.

Ravi sums it up, 'We need to nab the killer and pray that he is the only one. It's either that, or we're headed towards civil war.'

* * *

Altaf looks through his phone, even as his heartbeat continues to pick up pace. The chatter is incessant, and messages are being exchanged at a dizzying speed. It is almost like they're preparing for war. At least, that's the impression Examiner gets from the tumultuous mix of emotions manifesting themselves in Altaf's unsteady body language. But he knows there is little time to waste, and impressions alone will be of little value. And so, he tries to prise information under the pretext of expressing concern. 'Altaf, what have you heard? What's going to happen next? Is it going to be safe for us here? Should we be prepared to leave Lucknow?'

Altaf has no clue himself. 'They aren't saying much. I mean, everybody's saying a lot of things, but I don't really know what the larger plan is. I'm not sure anybody does. For now, my unit has been asked to go to one of the new safe houses, and help with keeping our soldiers safe, until another unit arrives to transport them to the next battlefield.'

The casual use of war rhetoric has Examiner, both as sleuth and grand-uncle, worried. 'Are you sure it's safe? I understand your commitment to the cause, but to go out there, in this atmosphere . . .'

Altaf isn't entirely indifferent to Examiner's concerns, but he has made up his mind. 'Of course it's not safe. But if a storm's coming, then everybody is going to be swept away by it. I won't be an exception.'

Examiner knows Altaf has made up his mind, but for the sake of appearances, he decides to try dissuading him, 'But we can still get out of the storm's path, move elsewhere . . .'

'I know I can count on you to keep my mother safe. But I have to go. My people, our people, they need me. It would be a real disgrace if I were to chicken out now and flee at the time of reckoning. I cannot let them down.'

Examiner feels a lump in his throat as he nods in acknowledgement and gives Altaf a warm hug. This is the sort of moment from which there will be no going back for the lad, a descent down a dark tunnel with no light at the end of it. At a very visceral level, behind all the cloaks and daggers, it truly breaks his heart to see a bright young boy like Altaf—devout, caring and genuinely committed to working for his community—falling prey to a flawed vision of justice and revolution, manufactured by deranged individuals seeking power for themselves, in the name of a greater good. In all these decades, Examiner has seen hundreds like Altaf, and it always ends in tragedy.

But Examiner is far too attuned to the greyness of the world, its inescapable tragedies, and his own place in the larger scheme of things to let these private ruminations come in the way of his efficiency as an undercover operative. And as far as this operation is concerned, Altaf is nothing but an unwitting asset, who will lead them to their primary target. If, in the process, Altaf ends up on the wrong side of danger, he will ultimately have nobody but himself to blame.

And so, as soon as Altaf leaves, Examiner dials his boss's mobile number.

'There is good news. There is only one assassin unit on the loose from the looks of it, and they're going to be carrying out the next hits too. Follow the boy. He'll lead you to them, and you can nab them all at once.'

Ravi asks Examiner to stay on the line, even as he scrambles towards his office landline to issue the orders.

After a few minutes, he returns to his mobile phone. 'I've notified the police and our men on the ground. They're already in pursuit and have him in sight.'

'Do you want me to pull out of here, or should I hang around just in case the boy comes back? Either way, we will have to make arrangements for the boy's mother. She'll be left all alone after this.'

'Neither. What I want you to do is follow the boy too, but independent of the other teams. As for the mother, it goes without saying, we will take care . . .'

'But isn't it risky? What if he sees me, by some chance? If he gets suspicious, then the whole thing can blow up and we'll lose them.'

'That's the whole point. Hang around the safe house, wherever it is, and make sure you're seen by him. If a conversation ensues, then let it play out. Confess to him, tell him that you're not who he thinks you are, and the whole thing was a set-up. What sort of a set-up how and why, I leave all of that to you. You're a man of vivid imagination.'

That's all Examiner needs to hear. He has known Ravi long enough, and has been in this game for even longer, to know exactly what the crafty spymaster has in mind. But because there are no certainties in this game, he listens carefully as Ravi fleshes out the details of an ingenious strategy.

* * *

As soon as Altaf enters an isolated house located by the side of a highway on the arid outskirts of Lucknow, a lorry pulls up at a distance, and indistinguishably wedges itself between several other long-haul lorries parked by weary drivers looking for a few hours of shut-eye. Inside the fully enclosed lorry, an elite anti-terrorism squad is in position, helmets up, guns drawn. The driver, a plainclothes policeman, gets out of the lorry and starts stretching his arms and yawning, even as he watches Examiner parking his car closer to the safe house.

Examiner gets out and throws the slightest of glances in the policeman's direction. The policeman pulls out a bottle of water and starts washing his face. It's a sign that they're ready to go. Examiner bends down to tie his laces, a sign that he's ready to go too, before walking towards the house. There is no compound wall, but the thick overgrowth looming over the unpainted cement house serves the same purpose. If not for the fact that Altaf had gone in just moments ago, Examiner would have assumed that the house was an abandoned one.

Examiner looks towards the lorry one last time and sees the plainclothes policeman throw a heavy crowbar onto the ground. Carefully making his way through the heavy overgrowth, he perches himself under a large open window, mostly obscured by creepers except for a few tiny gaps through which he can catch glimpses of the inside. There are three men inside, of whom Examiner recognizes two. There's Altaf, and then there's Zia, the boy who had been suspicious of Examiner when he had turned up uninvited for Suleimani's lecture at the mosque and had even asked him to recite the Shahadah. The third looks completely unfamiliar and seems to be at least twenty years older than the other two. Presumably, this is the contract killer they're sheltering before he can be safely transported to the location of their next hit.

Zia catches Examiner spying on them through the window and immediately turns pale, terrible possibilities run through his mind. Altaf notices the sudden change in Zia's demeanour and turns around, as does the contract killer, who wastes no time in picking up his revolver. Altaf holds him back, 'That's my dadaji.'

Altaf cautiously makes his way to the window, followed closely by Zia who picks up his revolver just in case.

Altaf asks Examiner, 'What are you doing here? How did you even know I was here?'

Examiner assures him, 'I followed you here. It's my duty to watch over you.'

Altaf is conflicted, as Zia scoffs at Examiner, his revolver pointed at Examiner's head. 'It's a little hard to believe. Tell us the truth.' Then turning to Altaf, he continues, 'Are you even sure this man is your grand-uncle? I mean, isn't it convenient that he simply showed up at your house a day before. And it's clear you've been telling him things. You broke your vow of secrecy. Do you realize what you've done? You've potentially jeopardized the entire operation because you couldn't keep your bloody mouth shut.'

Examiner decides that he's heard enough.

'Relax, kid. There's no need to fight amongst ourselves. Nothing's been jeopardized. I'm not an Indian agent if that's what you're suggesting.'

Zia snaps back, 'That's exactly what an Indian agent would say. Tell me, are you really his uncle? Or else I'll pull the trigger. There's a silencer on it, not a sound will escape, and you'll never be found.'

Examiner realizes that Zia's a sharp one who is much wiser to the ways of the world than Altaf is. But he also seems like a highly volatile one, Examiner can tell from the aggression visibly simmering in his muscles, threatening to spill over into the finger resting tentatively on the trigger.

And so, he must be extremely deft in keeping the young terrorist's temper in control. He decides to cut straight to the chase, 'Okay, I admit it. I am not Altaf's uncle. But before you do something reckless, let me assure you. I am not an Indian agent either.'

A chill runs down Altaf's spine. 'Then who are you?'

'Imrul Kandhari. I work for the Sheikh. I've been sent to oversee things.'

Zia looks at Examiner with stinging distrust. 'Do you really take us for fools? Sure, Altaf is a gullible idiot who let you take him for a ride, but don't assume you can fool me. The Sheikh is in solidarity with us, I don't doubt that, but he has no direct interest or involvement in our struggle. Only a poorly informed imposter like you would try cooking up a story like this. It's a pity you didn't do your homework.'

Examiner begins to laugh derisively. 'You really think you know everything, don't you? Truth is, you know nothing. This thing you're a part of is much larger than your imagination can even comprehend. Know your place. To even claim to understand what the Sheikh is interested in, and what he is involved in, is to insult him.'

Altaf feels a little lost, and he turns to Zia. 'But who is this Sheikh?'

Zia stares at Altaf with disbelief, as if he's just asked him what colour the sky is.

'Osama Bin . . .'

Zia freezes midway, as heavily armed policemen swarm the house from all directions, leaving no time to even react, let alone escape. Altaf looks at Examiner desperately, hoping against hope that he's actually here to help them out. But Zia has no such illusions, and he stands vindicated as Examiner swiftly flees the premises.

It is all over in less than thirty seconds, as the policemen seize the weaponry, handcuff the trio and blindfold them before herding them into the back of a police van that pulls up right outside the door.

As soon as the van starts moving, Zia spits on Altaf, 'You have let yourself down, your people down, and your religion down. If I were you, I'd kill myself at the first chance I got, rather than live with the shame.'

Altaf doesn't respond. He's still coming to terms with the crushing realization that the sweet old gentleman who'd first claimed to be his grand-uncle, and moments ago, to be an associate of Bin Laden, is in all likelihood an Indian agent who had preyed on his naivete to foil the entire mission.

The contract killer isn't perturbed. Indeed, he's almost a little amused. The fear coursing through Altaf and Zia's veins is palpable despite their shared blindfolds.

He tries easing the tension. 'First time in jail? It's not that bad, you know. If you have decent money to spare, you can live like a king and get other inmates to be your servants to do all your work for you. And if you don't have money, then you can expect to be one of those servants. But don't worry. Since you're with me, you'll be treated well even if you don't have money. I'm a respected veteran, you see the first time I went in . . .'

The proud smile vanishes from the contract killer's face, as the van comes to a sudden grinding halt, swerving dangerously as it does. They can pick up bits and pieces of what appears to be some sort of a commotion that has erupted outside the van.

Sighing deeply, the contract killer announces to the others, 'Prepare yourself, young friends. Our time has come. Pray, sing, dance, do whatever you want to do, because it's the last time you'll ever do anything.'

'What do you mean?' Altaf is quick to ask. The fact that they can't see a thing makes it all the more confusing.

The contract killer shakes his head in dismay at Altaf's ignorance. 'You don't read the newspapers, boy? You've never heard of fake encounters? This is what's going to happen, now. They'll open the door from behind, tell us that there's a puncture and ask us to get down. If you're stupid, you'll try to escape, and they'll shoot you down immediately. And even if you don't, they'll still shoot you and tell the world that you were trying to escape. That's what you get for . . .'

His voice is drowned out by loud pounding on the door. After almost a minute of incessant pounding, the door is thrown open. Altaf's blindfold is the first to be removed, and he is shocked at what he finds—Examiner wielding a heavy crowbar, which he then uses to deftly break open Altaf's handcuffs.

'What about the police?' Altaf asks with incredulity as Examiner starts pounding at Zia's handcuffs.

'Temporarily incapacitated. I punctured the tyres, and then knocked them out with this. But we don't have much time. There's another police vehicle following at a distance of two kilometres, and they'll be here any moment now.'

The sound of a police siren breaks out at a distance, and Examiner goes into a tizzy. 'We've got to leave right away. Get into my van.'

The contract killer—who continues to be blindfolded—begs to be freed too, but Examiner pays him no heed. He rushes into his van and drives away with Zia and Altaf, just as the second police vehicle converges on the scene of the accident and secures the contract killer's custody.

Altaf and Zia are stunned by what has just happened.

'What about Zaheer? Shouldn't we go back for him?'

Examiner shakes his head as he takes in the duo's expressions through the rear-view mirror. 'He's expendable. Just a professional who was hired for a specific task. We'll find another one like him, it's not the end of the world.'

'So, it's true what you said. About being sent by the Sheikh to oversee this mission . . .'

Examiner nods. 'Well, not literally by the Sheikh himself. I mean, I do know him personally. I have, in fact, fought alongside him in the war against the Russians, which is when I got the name Kandhari. But anyway, the Sheikh doesn't involve himself in operational details any more, nor does he entertain too many people. He has a trusted inner circle that does everything for him. But when these men issue orders, it's in the name of the Sheikh and carries his explicit blessings. I was sent by one of them, a great man you might have heard of—Al-Brittani.'

Altaf's guilt begins to abate, while Zia feels embarrassment and shame. After much hesitation, he launches into an apology, 'Please forgive me, sir. I feel terrible for having doubted you. You were right, I should know my place. You risked your life and single-handedly took on so many policemen to get us out. I, on the other hand, truly am nobody. Just because I was given charge of leading this mission on the ground, I got carried away and led myself to believe that I'm important. Do you know, one of my most cherished dreams is to be able to kiss the Sheikh's hand? And to think that you actually fought alongside him long before I was even born. What would I really know about how his mind works and what he is interested in, apart from whatever I've read on the internet?'

Examiner smiles nonchalantly. They've bought into his wild yarn more easily than he'd expected them to. But it isn't yet time to rest easy. Although a grave danger has been averted, and Examiner now has control over Zia—an asset who clearly knows a lot more about the larger conspiracy than Altaf—Examiner knows that this is only the tip of the iceberg. And from where he stands right now, he can't really tell how deep into the ocean it goes.

Cobweb

Mihir feels a mix of joy and trepidation as he catches sight of Cyrus, who is making his way past the familiar crowd of rickshaw drivers at Udupi Railway Station. Cyrus can't help but feel similarly ambivalent. The last time they had seen each other things had taken a sharply bitter turn, and they had nearly come to blows. But so much has happened since then. Mihir is emerging from a sabbatical, while Cyrus is coming out of jail. Both events had been directly tied to the same operation that brings them together now. In many ways, the significance of this mission to them as individuals mirrors its significance to their organization. In choosing to tread the risky path of allowing a dangerous collusion of forces to put sinister designs into action, C3 has pushed itself into fraught terrain that might just crumble right under their feet at any point. But it's the only way, the bosses are convinced, of uncovering all the various moving parts of Pakistan's shadow war against India. But if they fail, the consequences could be apocalyptic, as they've already been shown terrifying glimpses of.

In Mihir and Cyrus's short and turbulent careers thus far, the stakes have never been this high. And so, they know that they must put away whatever bitterness lingers from the past as they come together to uncover a particularly crucial node in the entire network—the procurement of arms and explosives. A little over a year ago, they had played a key role in neutralizing the most prominent arms smuggling routes, and this had led to a marked abeyance in the attacking capabilities of terror outfits inside the country. But the ISI and its proxies had improvised and developed a clandestine maritime route between the south-western coast of India and Karachi, which Mihir and Cyrus are to now infiltrate.

But despite all their determination to move away from past tensions, it isn't all that easy. Until not so long ago, they had been best friends. And then suddenly, they'd stopped talking to each other. And Cyrus knows that the onus is on him. Apart from the fact that he perhaps holds a larger share of the blame than Mihir as far as the souring of their relationship is concerned, Cyrus is the one with a marked gift for reading the room. In almost any conceivable situation, he can somehow find a way of provoking conversation—trivial or profound— and then gently nudge it towards the elephant in the room. It is a skill that has made him the cultivator of choice in many of Ravi's experiments, including the most recent one in Kolkata Central Jail.

But given the vicious ferocity with which they had attacked each other the last time around, even Cyrus finds himself unable to get down to it right away. It is only after they've attained a certain distance from the chaos of the railway station that Cyrus finally punctures the uneasy silence. The rickety old van Mihir has commandeered for the purpose of this mission is ideal fodder. 'I'm amazed, you've spent some ten days here, and this is the best vehicle you could find. Quite jarring, considering I'm carrying two lakh dollars in cash. Actually, three. There's been a slight change in plan. But anyway, coming back to the van, it feels like I've stepped into a time machine.'

Mihir, of course, is no blockhead. Their friendship had in the first place sprung from a mutual admiration of each other's gifts for quick-footed banter. Cyrus is reminded of this as a straight-faced Mihir fires a repartee, 'It's the best I could do. C3 hardly has any money left in its reserves. They spent every last penny on getting you out of jail. Which is also why they could only afford to buy counterfeit dollars and not actual foreign exchange.'

Cyrus is thrilled to discover that Mihir has maintained his form. He quips encouragingly, 'Oh, that's why? My sources told me that it was all spent on putting you through a five-star rehab facility for your alcoholism.'

Mihir begins to laugh, and Cyrus joins along. The ice has been broken, as it necessarily must as the fire draws closer. The ride from the station to the Malpe shipyard, where Cyrus is to meet the arms smuggler, is supposed to take only twenty minutes, but the old van moves along at a frustratingly slow pace. The real reason why Mihir has commandeered such a rickety old van is of course completely unrelated to the facetious wisecracks they're throwing at each other in an attempt to restore the warmth in their relationship. Given the particular sensitivity of this cross-border operation, and its complete absence from the books, they cannot afford to leave behind a trail, however minute. If something were to go wrong, they would have to be able to get away without anything leading back to them. Mihir had purchased the van from a local car-thieving syndicate that had assured him that every single part, down to the chassis, had been manipulated in such a way that it would legitimately tie back on record to an entirely fictitious individual. Which is why it had in fact cost him a lot more than buying a new van.

But Mihir doesn't feel the need to explain all of this to Cyrus, who in turn doesn't feel compelled to ask. They've both come to acknowledge and accept the fact that they are condemned to regularly finding themselves on the wrong side of the law. Finally, they know what 'need to know' truly means.

* * *

Ravi shifts restlessly in his seat as Jose puts forth a hypothesis, 'I'm convinced more than ever before, sir, that the entire K2 network is running on a cobweb of digital communication platforms. How else do we explain the fact that Suleimani has been able to carry out all these plans completely evading the elaborate surveillance net we've thrown around him? We know where he's going, who he's meeting, even what exactly he is talking to them about. And yet, in all the intelligence we've gathered, we have only found the faintest of hints about what he has gone on to execute. This means information is being exchanged on a medium we have no access to. Which, from everything we know so far, is most likely an end-to-end encrypted digital apparatus.'

But the boss isn't convinced, despite Jose's unrelenting exhortations, and he shakes his head dismissively. As is quite often the case, Ravi's stubborn refusal to acknowledge an amply clear explanation frustrates Jose. And he isn't the sort to hold back, 'It's either that, or we assume that Suleimani has nothing to do with the assassinations, and it is a pure coincidence that Altaf and Zia have connections to the assassination as well as to Suleimani. Everything we have is entirely circumstantial.'

Ravi is partly amused by Jose's self-righteous exasperation, but it is hidden behind the frighteningly scornful look on his face, 'Don't be stupid. Of course, he's connected to the assassinations. And don't use words like circumstantial just because they sound cool and technical, if you don't really know what they mean. They make sense only when you have a very clearly defined crime and victim, but inconclusive evidence and a motive that could possibly be denied. For instance, imagine I were to be murdered at this moment. The police come around, find your fingerprints all around me, and they begin to suspect you. Now you might not have done it, and the real killer might have actually wiped out all traces of his presence. They don't even find a weapon, and they can't precisely demonstrate how you killed me, but they still suspect you. Why? Because they also ask around and find out that you've always nursed an extremely bitter grudge against me and have confided several times to your colleagues about your strong desire to see me dead. Based on that, and the fingerprints, if you were to be convicted, then you would be correct in saying that the evidence was all circumstantial. But with Suleimani, it's a meaningless term. This is a very murky affair we're dealing with here. You can't say it's either this or that, and nothing else could be a possibility. To begin with, the crime isn't a well-defined one, because it is an ongoing one.'

Ravi's voice trails off as his attention shifts to a train of thought that has just been set off in his mind. Jose is still grappling with the strangely vivid scenario playing out in his head, of being convicted in court for murdering his boss, and it takes him a few moments to realize that Ravi has zoned out as well. Although Ravi is an unpredictable man whose mind is inscrutable to most people, there are patterns that those closest to him learn to discern over time. Jose knows, for instance, that these abrupt retreats into contemplations are often followed by sudden bursts of insight and fresh direction.

Overcome with curiosity, Jose gently nudges Ravi towards letting him in on his speculations. 'You were saying, sir, about how this crime we're dealing with is an ongoing one.'

Ravi doesn't respond. It takes him a full minute to emerge from his private sanctuary.

'Actually, you were saying . . . about how you're convinced that either the operation is being coordinated entirely digitally, or we're got everything wrong and Suleimani has nothing to do with any of it.'

Jose isn't quite sure where this is headed. 'Yes, sir, and that is what I've been saying since the beginning. And the only way to infiltrate an entirely digital network that is encrypted end-to-end, is through a digital persona.'

'Tell me one thing, since you've been going on and on about end-to-end encryption, if it's so foolproof that you can coordinate an operation as complex as K2 entirely on it, why is it that we haven't adopted it ourselves? Why do we still rely significantly on non-electronic means in exchanging information?'

Jose searches for an intelligent answer but can't find any. In any case, he knows that Ravi doesn't really expect him to answer and is merely setting up the premises for his own hypothesis, whatever it may eventually turn out to be.

But clearly, Jose overestimates his understanding of how Ravi operates. He is sharply reminded of it when Ravi snaps at him sternly, 'I expect you to answer that. Why aren't our covert operations coordinated through entirely digital means?'

Jose continues to struggle for an answer.

'Let me phrase the question differently with a concrete example. Let's go back to the day this all began, the day we discovered the existence of this individual named Suleimani. How did that happen?'

Finally, something Jose can answer with some semblance of confidence, 'From the drafts folder of an email ID created by Takshak. Again, digital.'

'Rewind a little further. How did we even learn about this email ID?'

'Okay, from a physical postcard. But hypothetically, it could have been entirely digital. Instead of sending you that postcard, he could have sent it to you on an end-to-end encrypted platform, which our email servers essentially are.'

'But anybody could send me an email, claiming to be anybody, passing on any sort of information and send us on an unending false trail if they wanted to. Whereas this postcard was mailed to a particular post box number at a technically fictitious address, which I'd set up just before the last time I met Takshak. In its entirety, this address is known only to me, Takshak, and partially to Subramaniam. If a letter arrives there, then it necessarily is from him alone, and intended for my eyes only.'

Jose thinks for a moment. It still isn't a clincher for him. 'But even then, there's a direct digital equivalent to be drawn, which would be a lot simpler and more efficient than this convoluted system you're describing. I mean, you could have just created an email ID known only to the two of you, and he could have mailed stuff to that ID. Same thing, theoretically.'

Ravi smiles. 'My dear boy, the last time I met Takshak email was little more than a theoretical concept still being worked out by computer scientists.'

Jose is stumped, but still unwilling to concede. 'Sure, but email is now a fully realized idea. Everybody knows about it, everybody uses it. And K2 is happening today.'

'You're not getting the point. What's happening today is tied to everything that's already happened. It took an old hand like Takshak to alert us to Suleimani, who himself has been trained by a veteran. I'm not denying the fact that a large part of this K2 nonsense, particularly at the lower levels, is being coordinated digitally. But that can't work at the top. Because if that was true, we could have just kidnapped Suleimani at the very beginning, used his phone and infiltrated the platform to convey the impression to his handlers that everything was going smoothly. We're dealing ultimately with a professional intelligence agency just like ours, and they know just as well as we do that an ongoing operation of this nature with so many moving parts is highly vulnerable to infiltration, especially when it's such a diffused network that's being controlled from across the border. It is of course susceptible to infiltration at the lower levels, which is what we've achieved now with Altaf and Zia. But that won't bring the whole network down, because those boys know so little about the larger picture. To be sure that they're firmly in control, the ISI must have some way of physically confirming that Suleimani hasn't been captured or replaced by one of us. It's highly unlikely that they have him under constant physical surveillance on Indian soil because our teams would have picked up on it by now. But how else? We know what he is doing every minute of the day. We're clearly missing something.'

* * *

Shahzad Chacha, Sulemani's housekeeper in Delhi's Defence Colony, runs a popular canteen right outside the Jama Masjid. On any given day of the week, the devout and not-so-devout, the rich and the poor, tourists as well as locals, all flock to his tiny eatery in equal measure to get their fill of the finest Awadhi fare in all of Old Delhi. The strategic location of his establishment, and the sheer diversity of the crowd that it attracts, gives Shahzad Chacha access to an unusually vast canvas of information. And because he has the memory of an elephant and the sharpness of a hawk, even at the ripe old age of seventy-five, hardly anything ever escapes his attention. Old-timers often quip that even a fly cannot whizz past Chandni Chowk without Chacha learning about it somehow and continuing to remember it even ten years down the line.

All of this makes him an invaluable asset for anybody invested in the business of information. And there is arguably nobody in the country as deeply invested in this business as the spymaster at the helm of C3. It was a match made in heaven. Ravi has been a lifelong admirer of the old man's culinary skills, while Chacha understands and deeply respects the significance of Ravi's work, having survived the horrors of Partition.

But even the otherwise infallibly sharp Chacha has been unable to discern anything amiss in Suleimani's activities. Every single day he has spent in Delhi, Suleimani has unfailingly visited the Jama Masjid. And all throughout Chacha has kept a close watch; particularly on Fridays when the crowds swell up and allow even a closely monitored target like Suleimani the possibility of communicating discreetly with a third party. But at no point has Suleimani seemed to interact with anybody.

Ravi is convinced nevertheless that there is more to Suleimani's daily visits to the Jama Masjid than compulsions of piety and worship. He has asked Chacha to double up on his efforts and pay attention to every action. And so, when Suleimani next arrives in the area—on a Friday noon— Chacha immediately sets off in pursuit. Every few metres or so, somebody or the other recognizes him, and he is forced to acknowledge all the salutations and greetings that come his way. And although this slows him down a little, it suits him perfectly for it gives him sufficient distance from Suleimani and an alibi as well, just in case the vultures are also tracking the Pakistani agent.

Suleimani doesn't look around much, and quickly heads straight to the entrance of the mosque and stops at a footwear stand—one of many lining both sides of the street, run by different individuals. Just then, Chacha walks up to a footwear stand opposite the one Suleimani used. The attendant is busy stifling a yawn with one hand, and fanning himself using the morning newspaper with the other, when Chacha looks at him with a hint of mischief. 'Heavy lunch?'

The footwear attendant, mildly embarrassed at having been caught in the act, smiles awkwardly. 'No, Chacha. I haven't yet eaten.'

As they get talking, Chacha's attention remains fixated on Suleimani, who seems lost in thought as he stands in front of a rusted metal stand, on which over a hundred pairs of footwear are lined up on multiple levels. Suleimani seems to be deliberating on where exactly he should place his footwear.

The young footwear attendant notices too, and chuckles as he points out to Chacha, 'Usually, only thieves spend so much time looking at other people's footwear. But this man is no thief, although I had my doubts at first.'

Chacha's curiosity is piqued. 'So, what is it all about, then?'

'Who knows, Chacha? Rich people have strange habits, especially these foreigners. Remember that rich kid who got arrested for lifting slippers? He was doing it just for the kick of it. But this man isn't into all that. He's into shoes, I think. You should see the flashy blue leather shoes he wears every Friday. You see a lot of flaunting on Fridays around here.'

Chacha laughs, making a note of what he's just discovered, even as he continues paying careful attention to Suleimani, who finally seems to have made up his mind on where to place his shoes. But after a few moments, just after he's placed them on the stand, Suleimani reaches into his pocket, pulls something out and extends his hand towards a dark brown leather shoe resting right next to his before walking off to the mosque. Chacha notices a small, crumpled chit fall from his hand into the leather shoe. Or at least that is what it seems like. Chacha can't entirely be sure if he should trust his ageing eyesight. And Suleimani's actions are so quick and carefully concealed that the young footwear attendant doesn't even notice.

Chacha excuses himself and walks over to the side, where he pulls out his phone from his pocket and dials Ravi.

'I think your kid dropped a toy when he came to the restaurant earlier. Should I pick it up and keep it with me?'

'No. Leave it where it is. Wait and see if somebody else comes and collects it. I don't know if my relatives have already sent someone else. You know how it is with joint families.'

Chacha hangs up and returns to the footwear stand.

'Listen, kid, you haven't eaten lunch yet. Why don't you go over to my canteen? Tell Faizan that I sent you. He'll feed you.'

The footwear attendant hesitates. 'That's kind of you Chacha, but I can't leave the stand unattended. I'm on duty for a few more hours.'

'I'll stick around for a while, you go eat. I'll hand out tokens and keep a watch. Don't worry, go.'

* * *

At the headquarters, Anjali scribbles on a whiteboard, as Jose rattles out the facts, 'A penchant for flashy blue shoes on Fridays and . . . what else?'

Ravi adds, 'Also, a penchant for dropping chits into brown leather shoes.'

The phone rings, and he walks away. It's Chacha calling for the second time in an hour.

'A man came and picked up the toy. Don't really know who he is, though. Nobody does. I mean, some have seen him in the area once or twice, but nobody really remembers. He was wearing sunglasses and an expensive blazer to go with those expensive shoes.'

Ravi is disappointed. 'You know how large my family is . . . those non-specific details don't help at all. How will I find out who's taken my child's toy?'

But it is a moment too soon, for Chacha hasn't completed, 'I followed him as he hurried to the end of the road. He was quick and he got into his car immediately, so I couldn't follow him any further. But I did get the registration number. It was a black Sedan.'

Ravi sighs. 'Let's just hope it wasn't a taxi. Even if it was, we still have something to go by.'

'Impossible,' Chacha replies. 'That was no taxi, I saw the number plate.'

'A lot of taxis have white number plates.'

'But no taxi has blue number plates, and no taxi can have the registration number this one has.'

Ravi hangs up and turns to the others. 'Can you actually believe this?'

Anjali and Jose look at him perplexed, as Ravi stares into the distance for almost an entire minute, alternating between shaking his head and scratching it.

Jose finally asks, 'Believe what, sir?'

'A diplomat, travelling in a car with blue coloured number plates, which is allotted to an official diplomatic vehicle, is the man at the other end of a dead letter box. It's one thing for an undercover asset to clear dead letter boxes. Even if you knew, there's little you could do because there's never any proof of linkages. But an officially accredited diplomat? This right here, this is the motherlode. A case of miscalculation that his visit to Jama Masjid on a Friday would pass off as a normal call.'

Bon Voyage

Although his hands and legs are uncomfortably bound by thick rope and tied to a chair placed at the centre of his own boatyard in Malpe, Noor Mohammed cuts a calm figure. It is late at night, and the only sound that can be heard is that of the waves lashing against the harbour. He hasn't been gagged, and if he wants to, he can raise an alarm and alert his men. But the hefty boat builder-turned-smuggler has been involved in this line of work long enough to sense that the two men holding him captive aren't to be messed around with.

They aren't thugs from a rival operation, or enforcers hired by the loan sharks who are perennially after him.

Nor are they policemen, as he'd first assumed when they'd raided the boatyard an hour ago, quickly secured his custody and started asking questions about his arms smuggling operation. If they were policemen, they would have formally arrested him or demanded money, as Noor had come to expect from his previous run-ins with the law.

These men are of a more powerful breed.

Instead of demanding money, they're offering it to him.

'It's simple . . . you either give us your vessel and tell us the exchange protocol, or you go to jail. If you give us what we want, and the exchange comes through smoothly, not only will you stay out of jail, but we will also reward you. We'll pay you double of what you would have made otherwise. Think about it.'

Noor realizes that these men, whoever they are, are desperate for the information only he can provide. And he is desperate to stay out of jail. He takes the deal with little hesitation. Cyrus, who's the one doing all the talking, looks at Mihir and smiles in quiet triumph. The smuggler is blindfolded and cannot see any of this. He begins describing the specifics of the rendezvous near Karachi waters. At a slight distance away, in an unlit corner of the workshop, local fisherman asset Mosale sits in silence, committing every detail to memory. It will be his task now to sail to Karachi in Noor's place.

In ordinary circumstances, sailing in a normal fishing vessel, it would have taken Mosale up to four days to sail from Mangalore to Karachi. But Noor, the arms-smuggler who now is in Cyrus and Mihir's custody, has outfitted the boat with special engines to make the journey in less than three days. It's the only way he could compete with smugglers from Mumbai and Gujarat.

Even though it is a relatively short journey, it's a precarious one and Mosale is mindful of staying inside Indian waters for as long as he possibly can. Noor has assured him that he can venture out in full confidence as long as he sticks to protocol at every step of the way. But Mosale is nonetheless very cautious as he closes in on the point of exit from Indian territory. From here on, he keeps a low profile and navigates to the designated point of exchange at Churna, an uninhabited island off the Karachi coast. While often frequented by tourists for scuba diving and snorkelling, the island's primary function is as a firing range for the Pakistani navy.

And so, as soon as Mosale begins to approach Churna, the Pakistani coast guard takes notice and surrounds his vessel. Dawn is just about to break, and Mosale can see flashlights of the Pakistani coast guard. No noise can be heard except for the repeated warnings coming from them, 'Please declare your intentions, and drop your weapons.' Mosale does not panic. As per Noor's instructions, he reaches into the hold and pulls out two flags. He lifts up both hands and starts waving at them. It seems to temporarily put the coast guard at ease. Convinced that they have understood his intentions, Mosale proceeds to move his arms around and contort them into specific patterns and positions that correspond to individual characters in the alphabet. But halfway through the designated message in flag semaphore—I-N-Q-U-I-L-A-B Z-I-N-D-A-B-A-D—the coast guard appear to grow suspicious and begin moving in on him. Desperate to convince them that he is there on designated business, Mosale continues waving his flag around, but they sternly rebuke him, 'Please drop your flags and keep your hands up in the air. We are coming over to search your vessel.'

Mosale wonders what the problem might be, and as he drops the flags, he gets his answer. He realizes that in his hurry, he'd picked out orange flags from the hold, and not red flags as he should have. He curses his fate and musters his courage. All he can do is hope.

* * *

Suleimani's arrival in the Jama Masjid area, on a Friday just before prayer time, triggers a chain of events being directed from C3's headquarters several kilometres away. The prospect of catching an accredited Pakistani diplomat in the act, conspiring with a deadly terrorist through an ingenious dead letter box arrangement, is exciting enough to draw even Sarita into the command room. She watches with full attention, along with Ravi and Anjali, as a projector beams live CCTV feed from several cameras, both public as well as private, placed all around the area. The footage is of variable quality, and it is only around the footwear stands—where a covert C3 unit led by Jose has installed multiple high-resolution cameras over the last few days—that they can see sharply focused visuals. And that is all they need if they've made the right inferences about the workings of the dead letter box arrangement.

Just as they expect, Suleimani is wearing a pair of bright blue shoes. He spends little more than a second at the footwear stand and disappears into the mosque. Ten minutes later, the Pakistani diplomat arrives.

'Zoom in,' Ravi orders Jose, before turning to Sarita and explaining, 'So, whose turn it is to stare at shoes depends on whose turn it is to send the messages. Today, it is our dear diplomat's turn. Which is why it is up to him to scan the footwear stand and spot Suleimani's shoes so he can drop his message.'

Sarita wonders, 'But the idea doesn't seem as great as you've made it sound. I mean, so many people might own the same pair of shoes as Suleimani, and at a place like Jama Masjid, what are the odds? You could drop a chit in someone else's pair.'

Ravi is focused on the screen and instructs Jose, 'Capture as many frames and angles as you can of the embassy man as well as Suleimani. This here is the equivalent of gold dust.'

He then turns to Sarita, belatedly responding to her doubts, 'That's what I had assumed. Especially with this diplomat fellow. Unlike Suleimani's flashy blue ones, his shoes are dark brown and made of leather. So generic-looking that you'd be more likely to make a mistake than leave a message in the right shoe. And that's when we decided to take a closer look, and there is this large logo at the back of the shoe, where you've got the heel cap. It's the logo of a shoe brand called Banalio. We looked it up, and as it turns out there's no such brand anywhere in the world. There's only one other pair, at least that we've come across. That bright blue pair Suleimani just left behind, the one into which the diplomat just dropped a little piece of paper. We now have exactly fifteen minutes before Suleimani returns.'

Ravi moves aside and gets on the phone. Less than a minute later, Chacha appears on the screen. He surreptitiously reaches into the shoe and fishes out the chit, before quickly walking away. After another minute or so, Ravi's phone rings again. It is Chacha. 'There's a message on this, a very short one, written in Urdu. It says, "They have picked up on parts of the plan. Before they get to you, disappear."'

'The paper, is there anything special about it?'

'No, it's ordinary paper.'

'Excellent. Which means, you have similar paper lying around? Cut out a scrap of the same size and write on it in Urdu—"Keep it up. Things are going very well."'

Ravi hangs up and returns to looking at the screen. After a couple of minutes, Chacha reappears around the footwear stand and drops a chit into one of Suleimani's shoes before walking away. It takes a full ten minutes before Suleimani emerges from the mosque and collects his shoes.

A jittery Anjali articulates the fear that is slowly beginning to gnaw at her bosses' minds too, 'This isn't good news at all. They know we're onto them. Something or somebody has been compromised. Unless we can find out, we're just grazing on minefields. Things can go horribly wrong from here on.'

Ravi shares the anxiety, but not her sense of doom. He tries to strike a reassuring note, 'It was only inevitable that they found out. It's a necessary risk of the route we've taken. Not only have we infiltrated so many loose ends, we have also left them hanging. We're dealing with a formidable adversary here . . . a foreign intelligence agency, and not a ragtag band of insurrectionists operating from caves. But even so, it's not all lost. Things don't necessarily have to go horribly wrong. In fact, this might work to our benefit ultimately if we play it right. Either way, brace yourself for some very taxing mental gymnastics in the days to come. It's possibly the most exciting scenario in the world of birdwatching. We found out what they were up to, and they went on to find out that we know what they're up to. And now, we've found out that they know that we've found out what they're up to. But do they know this? Will they find out?'

Anjali begins to chuckle, and Ravi joins in. He is glad his deputy can see the lighter side of things, even in circumstances as despairing as these.

* * *

Examiner turns the stove off, and carefully pours out three cups of steaming hot tea. In the time that has passed since they were heroically rescued by Examiner, Zia and Altaf haven't grown any wiser about his real identity or motives. They're at a C3 safe house and for all practical purposes in firm custody of the Indian security establishment. But the young militants do not have the slightest idea as they sip noisily from their clay *kulhars,* looking at Examiner with much anticipation. In the one week that they've been here, Examiner has tended to serve his tea with a peppering of exciting anecdotes— about militant camps in Pakistan, underground explosive factories in Sudan and perilous encounters with Russian forces in Afghanistan. Altaf laps it all up without question and sometimes without even knowing what is being talked about, while the worldly-wise Zia wears a hint of scepticism at times and raises pertinent doubts. But Examiner always has an answer. There's a reason he'd been given this nom de guerre in the first place.

Examiner himself, however, is beginning to grow a little tired of this ruse. It has become evident to him that Zia and Altaf by themselves are next to worthless and have little to no understanding of what they're really a part of. And so, there is none of the excitement and intrigue that Examiner has come to expect from undercover assignments as deep as this one. But all the same, he has strict orders from the spymaster. He must bide his time and keep them entertained for as long as it takes for them to receive concrete instructions from their handler.

Examiner checks for an update. 'Any messages at all, from above?'

Zia puts his kulhar on the ground, 'Yes, sir . . . the same thing, to remain in hiding while we await further instructions. It is a receiver set, we cannot transmit or ask questions.'

Examiner lets his frustration out, 'Don't they realize that the longer you camp out here, the greater your chances of getting nabbed? The police are still actively looking for you. They'll get here if we give them enough time, mark my words. And if I get caught in the process, all hell will break loose. This is very poor leadership, whoever is handling you. They can't leave you hanging like this.'

Altaf wonders, 'But why haven't you got in touch and found out? Why is it that you don't even have a phone?'

In his mind, Examiner can't help but chuckle at the irony of the question. It is precisely because he doesn't have a phone that he's even here, babysitting them. What is particularly frustrating for him is that he barely understands why he needs to. If their phones are the sole link to the larger LeH network, and that is the primary objective of keeping these men safe, why not simply take the phones away? When Examiner had posed the question, just before the staged rescue operation, Ravi had laughed, 'Sir, if you were a junior, I would have hidden my ignorance under the guise of need-to-know. But I have no shame in admitting to you that I myself have only a faint understanding of why we can't simply take the phones away. And since your understanding of digital technology is even more rudimentary than mine, explaining what little I know would be an utterly futile exercise, a case of the blind leading the blind. What the far-sighted insomniac seers say, us blind fort-dwellers must follow without question . . .'

Examiner snaps back into focus after Zia repeats the question, 'In all seriousness, why don't you have a phone like ours? Why is a senior commander like you dependent on foot-soldiers like us for instructions?'

Examiner downs the last of his tea in one long sip, before getting up. Patting Zia on his back with feigned affection, he asks, 'Have you ever wondered how the Sheikh has managed to evade capture, even after all these years? Think about it. The US and its allies have poured more than a trillion dollars into finding him, and they haven't been able to.'

The two scratch their heads.

Altaf speculates, 'Has he changed his appearance?'

Then, Zia proffers his hypothesis, 'Has he escaped to Indonesia? Or . . . there's this one theory I'd read about online, that he is actually hiding in America itself because that is the last place they would look for him.'

Examiner laughs. 'Very creative theories, but very far-fetched too.'

'Then what is it?'

'It's a combination of several things, to be sure. A fiercely loyal inner circle, active dissemination of false leads . . . but it ultimately comes down to one simple thing. The Sheikh doesn't have a phone. He depends on a network of human couriers, most of whom do not themselves know what they are a part of. Like the two of you are, within our organization.'

There is awestruck silence as Altaf and Zia relish their daily dose of insight into the Sheikh's enigmatic mind. So blind is their admiration of Osama Bin Laden and their faith in Examiner's authority on the subject that if he were to tell them that the Sheikh eats camel dung to counteract the effects of ageing, it's likely they would believe it.

* * *

Jose clocks in for his late evening shift and heads down the dimly lit hallway that leads into Insomnia, sipping from a large steel bottle filled to the brim with cold filter coffee. The only noises that can be heard inside the caffeine-fuelled dungeon that houses the country's best cyber-sleuths are all electronic— the mechanical pitter-patter of keyboards being thumped away on, the low whirring noise of high-speed fans running round the clock to keep the machines cool, and the oddly pleasing screeching of a dot matrix printer churning out transcripts of an intercepted phone call. Within this environment, Jose feels truly at home.

He sinks into his chair and turns on his computer. And as he does at the beginning of every shift, he opens up multiple browser windows and logs into a series of email IDs. There are fifteen in total, and all of them serve as electronic dead letter boxes for assets to securely pass on information. It is usually the least exciting part of the day, but he is required to monitor them regularly lest something comes up and nobody sees it. He stifles a yawn as he scrolls through the inboxes one by one. There are no new messages, except in the last one on his list, the dead letter box the agency shares with Takshak. A heady brew of trepidation, fear and excitement travels up his spine as he suspends his cursor over the unread message. Takshak is the sort of asset who gets in touch only rarely, but when he does, it is usually to pass on highly critical information. The last time

he'd done so, after a gap of nearly two decades, it had been to
alert C3 to the K2 conspiracy and then to Suleimani's plans.

A few moments of hesitation later, Jose finally opens the
message. After taking a quick glance, he dials Ravi, who is still
in office well past his official working hours.

'Cherian, calling to gloat about having uncovered the
identity of the Pakistani diplomat? Don't bother. This isn't
the sort of stuff to waste computing power on. It's all on file
already. I know who he is. Anything else, or can I get back to
using my time productively?'

Jose cuts straight to the point, 'There's a message, from
Takshak.'

'Go on, read it out.'

'Indian trawler caught lurking around Karachi. Strong
buzz on the inside: this was a counter-intel plot gone wrong,
fisherman an Indian agent trying to smuggle explosives into
Pakistan. True or not doesn't matter. It will be made to
seem like it, either way. Prep for major offensive on global
diplomatic front being made. Backchannel resolution can
happen, but stakes must be matched. Odds are heavily against
you at the moment, reach out when ready to gamble . . . End
of message.'

'So, this is how they know. They tried alerting Suleimani
two days ago, which means they've had this fisherman in
custody for at least three days. Of course, we're going to
gamble. Not just match the stakes but raise them. Perhaps get
them to chase out some overstaying guests as well . . . it's all
possible from here on.'

Jose feels a little lost, 'I'm sorry, sir, but I don't follow
entirely . . . this fisherman, he's one of us? Or an actual

fisherman? And gambling? Are we talking about a trade here? Is that even legal?'

'If you don't follow, that's because you don't have to. And we are not talking about anything. It's need-to-know, and in this case, you don't need to at all. In fact, nobody needs to. Don't put this message down in your logs, ensure there is no record of it whatsoever. Not even Jyotirmoy can see this. And you can stop checking Takshak's messages after this. I will do it myself.'

Checkmate

Ravi is almost sprinting by the time he gets to Sarita's office. Even by his standards, this is unusual behaviour. But it is only to be expected, given the unusual circumstances that he confronts. There is little time to waste, his health be damned!

After catching his breath and getting a glass of water from the cooler, he tries to walk in, only to find that the office is locked. The light in her secretary's cubicle is still on.

Ravi knocks on it. 'Ratna?'

Startled, Ratna—a kindly lady, the same age as Subramaniam—who'd been busy knitting, looks up.

'Sir, you.'

'The chief, I'm unable to reach her. Mobile, residence, I tried everything. Is everything okay?'

Ratna smiles. 'Yes, sir. Didn't she tell you? Her daughter-in-law gave birth yesterday. She was tied up and couldn't travel immediately, but she is on her way to Trivandrum now to welcome her grandson into the world.'

Holding up the sweater she's been knitting, she points out, 'I'm knitting this for the baby.'

Ravi flashes a sardonic grin. 'What a thoughtful present! The baby would be thrilled, I'm sure.'

Ratna is no stranger to Ravi's sarcasm. She gets the hint and drops the sweater. Reaching into her drawer, she pulls out a copy of Sarita's ticket. 'She is boarding Air India flight AI801, Delhi to Trivandrum direct. The flight is scheduled to take off in forty minutes and should land in about three and a half hours. I will let her know as soon as she does to get in touch with you. Is there a particular message you'd like me to deliver?'

Ravi stares at his wristwatch.

'There's no point in alerting a doctor after the patient is dead. I need to reach her immediately.'

The tension gets to Ratna, and she tries desperately to help, 'Are there some files in her office or on her computer that you'd like to access, sir? She has authorized me to permit you in case of an emergency.'

Ravi shakes his head and begins to pace around anxiously. An idea strikes him.

'What you can do, Ratna is to get me the phone number of the director of the Delhi airport.'

* * *

Sitting at the front of the economy section onboard Flight AI801, Sarita gazes through her window. Nobody on the flight knows that the modestly dressed, soft-spoken lady is in fact the chief of the IB, and by virtue of that, one of the most powerful individuals in the country. But Sarita makes no effort to brandish her credentials, as many bureaucrats of her stature perhaps might have. Indeed, they wouldn't even be flying on an economy class ticket to begin with.

As she looks straight ahead, her mind's eye filled with images of the newborn she will soon hold in her arms, an announcement by the flight purser rings through the intercom, 'Ms Sarita Sanyal, seat 8A, could you please step out of the aircraft to identify your luggage next to the cargo hold?'

Sarita sighs as she turns away from the window and unfastens her seat belt. She knows that the curious announcement can mean only one thing. In the thirty minutes or so that she's been away, a crisis has erupted requiring her immediate attention. She will have to wait longer to see her grandchild.

Sure enough, as soon as she gets out of the aircraft, and climbs down a step ladder onto the tarmac, Ravi is waiting for her.

'I'm terribly sorry, ma'am. You know I wouldn't have done this unless it . . .'

Sarita waves away his apology, 'Please, Ravi. Do not embarrass me by apologizing.'

Ravi takes in a deep breath, before rattling off, 'Mosale has been captured. This happened a few days ago, but the Pakistan government has not uttered as much as a single word. This means the ISI is determined to milk the situation to the fullest by making it known to the entire world that India is sponsoring cross-border terrorism. And this isn't just a hunch, I have very concrete information that they are indeed working on this. Utter rubbish, of course, but trust the ISI to come up with a watertight case. They'll plant explosives, secure a confession under duress, the usual . . . We need to defuse this immediately.'

'Before they do that, can't we announce that one of our fishermen is missing? That way, their campaign will naturally lose steam. After all, it was a rudimentary trawler with no modern navigation equipment, correct?'

Ravi sighs. 'We could have done that. But which fisherman veers hundreds of miles off course? Mangalore is nowhere close to Karachi.'

'So, we disown him? It's a terrible thing to do to one of our own, but I suppose there's no other way. It's a professional hazard, after all.'

'In ordinary circumstances, perhaps that would have been the best way to move forward. But we cannot afford to do that in this case, because I fear it will wreck everything we've been working towards, as far as neutralizing Lashkar-e-Hind and nabbing Tabrez is concerned. We must attempt to secure his release. My source has told me that the ISI might be open to backchannel negotiations.'

'And what do we offer in return? They know they've stumbled on a goldmine here and I'm assuming they certainly aren't going to yield unless we can offer something equally valuable.'

'I can't help but wonder . . . what if this is actually a godsent opportunity to put the brakes on this K2 nonsense and LeH once and for all?'

Sarita has known Ravi long enough to tell when he is beating around the bush.

'Go on, Ravi. What's the outrageous idea you have in mind this time?'

'It's not exactly outrageous, ma'am. Far from it. What I've been thinking about is a swap. Spy for spy, straight out of the Cold War playbook.'

'That isn't such a bad idea. But do you think that will really interest them? We do have close to a hundred Pakistani spies languishing in our jails, but the ISI disowned them a long time ago. They aren't going to backtrack on that suddenly. In any case, they're all worthless to Pakistan right now because we've extracted every last piece of information. And even if they do agree, how is that going to help us with neutralizing LeH and K2?'

'I wasn't considering the spies in our jails. I was thinking about the man we've deliberately allowed free rein over the minds of our impressionable youngsters.'

'Suleimani?'

Ravi nods, a sly smile playing on his lips as he pulls out a dossier, 'Or, as he is better known within the higher echelons of the Pakistani security establishment—Colonel Tajuddin Hussaini. They'll be spooked beyond their wildest imagination when they find out that we've known all along. Although the ISI can be very careless and overconfident, as they've been with Suleimani, they're also masters of abundant caution. K2 is a conspiracy of unprecedented scale, amounting to nothing short of a direct assault on our sovereignty and internal stability . . . an act of war, so to speak. Once they realize that we know, they're going to make every effort to do away with every last link, starting of course with our old nemesis, Tabrez. Of course, they can't admit they've been sheltering him, and so they'll either kill him or politely ask him to get out of Pakistan. My money is on the latter. He's a formidable ally and far too precious to kill. There are only so many places outside of Pakistan he can possibly escape to, and we have eyes and ears in every single one of those.'

Sarita is left dumfounded by the farsighted ingenuity of the plan.

'There's little to debate here, Ravi. You have my approval. But the home secretary will have to be briefed, and he will update the PM. I have to go see my grandchild, so I hope you can take care of this for me. Is there anything else you need?'

Ravi nods gratefully, 'For now, just that, ma'am, your approval. I will set the wheels in motion straight away.'

* * *

The corridors of power inside the ISI headquarters in Islamabad are wracked with tension and paranoia. In particular, Brigadier Ifthikar—who to external assets like Tabrez is known by the nom de guerre Karbala—can't help but feel like doomsday is upon him and his organization. It is a dramatic reversal of fortunes. Only a few days ago, he had felt an overwhelming sense of triumph. His confidence had led him to go as far as to send word to the prime minister's office, promising sensational evidence against India.

But his Indian counterparts have given him, not for the first time in his long and distinguished career, a stunning surprise of Himalayan proportions. The fact that his protégé, Hussaini, is in Indian custody is only the tip of the iceberg. More worryingly, they also have a large trove of irrefutable visual and material evidence directly tying not just the ISI, but the Pakistan government itself to a sinister plot to tear India apart from inside.

As he walks towards a conference room, where his anxious subordinates await him, he knows that the only thing he can possibly do at this point is controlling the damage. Nevertheless, he feels the need to vent his frustration. And so, as soon as he walks in, he unleashes his rage in dramatic fashion, flinging into the air the facsimile copies of evidence sent in by Rikabdaar, their asset who had facilitated the infiltration of Colonel Hussaini. Little does Ifthikar know that Rikabdaar is in fact the man who had led the Indian agencies to K2 and Suleimani. Or that he also goes by another nom de guerre, Takshak.

Ifthikar's subordinates rush to pick up the papers as he begins to yell, 'It's finished. Everything we've worked towards is all over. I was a fool to have trusted you nincompoops to handle this with any degree of competence. I can't even blame the officer in Delhi. He is a career diplomat with little understanding of espionage. But you buffoons, couldn't you have at least inculcated the basics . . . Who the hell travels to a dead letter box in an embassy vehicle?'

Desperate to save face, a junior officer ventures forth, 'B-but sir, we still have their agent in our custody. Can't we salvage the situation by speeding up our campaign?'

Ifthikar curses his fate.

'Don't talk garbage. What do we have? Nothing except evidence we ourselves have planted.'

There is stunned silence as Ifthikar struggles to regain his composure.

'Anyway, there's no point crying over spilt milk. We need to limit the extent of their knowledge to Suleimani and his radicalization module. Under no circumstances can they know that Tabrez is in Pakistan. I mean, it's fair to assume they already do, but we can't let him hang around for a moment longer. The fact that they discovered Suleimani means we have snakes in our midst. There's no guaranteeing that they won't find concrete evidence of this too. As it is, half our energies are spent in denying Osama's presence on Pakistani territory. Get in touch with Tabrez and tell him to leave straight away. We'll continue to support him like we used to earlier, but we can't harbour him on our soil any longer.'

* * *

As he has been doing every day, Examiner wakes up at 4 a.m., several hours before Altaf and Zia typically do. He steps out of the house, carefully locks both doors and makes his way down the pothole-ridden road that connects the house to the highway. The road is mostly deserted, and except for a bicycle-mounted chaiwallah at the end, catering to workers heading out from the neighbouring villages into the city.

Examiner wishes the chaiwallah a good morning, and he in turn responds by handing out a hot cup of tea. Examiner accepts gratefully and sips on it in silence, waiting for the other customers to clear out. As soon as they're gone, he flings his empty clay cup into the designated basket and looks at the chaiwallah in expectation. He shakes his head, a sign that there are no messages from the headquarters. After paying for the tea, Examiner makes his way back to the house, and commences his chores for the day.

He is in the bathroom, after having cooked breakfast, when Zia impatiently begins banging on the door, 'Miyan, instructions are here. They want us to go to Nepal, where we'll be reunited with all our brothers.'

Quickly finishing his business, Examiner excitedly steps out to find a highly charged Zia pacing up and down the room.

'Where in Nepal?'

'Birgunj, on the border. It's only about ten hours from here. We can set out immediately. Once we're there, the Indian police can't lay as much as a finger on us. We won't have to live this wretched life of self-imposed imprisonment.'

Examiner is pleased.

'Where exactly in Birgunj?'

'No idea. The message only said to get to Birgunj. Then they'll let us know.'

Examiner looks around and finds Altaf sitting quietly in a corner.

'What's the matter, kid?'

Altaf shakes his head, 'Nothing.'

But Examiner can clearly see that Altaf is not nearly as enthused about the prospect of fleeing the country. He moves closer and sits down next to him.

'It's all right, son, you can tell me what it is. There's no need to be dishonest to your conscience. It is God who speaks through the conscience. And so, never be ashamed of how you truly feel, in any situation, around anybody.'

Reassured by Examiner's encouraging words, Altaf sets forth his thoughts, 'I'm not sure if I want to leave.'

Zia lets out a sarcastic laugh. 'I knew it. You're a coward, always have been.'

Examiner looks sternly in Zia's direction. 'That's enough. Let the boy speak.'

Altaf continues, 'I am all my mother has. If I leave the country now, it's possible I might never return. The heartbreak alone would kill her. I'm not sure.'

Altaf's voice trails off, and he begins to sob. 'I'm not sure if I really want to do this. What are we really fighting for? And against who? This is our own country, there's nothing that can change that fact.'

Zia voices his consternation, 'Our own country? I can't believe what I'm hearing, this is sheer blasphemy. Why did you even join our ranks? As for your mother, do you think I don't have a family that I might never see again? Wasn't it made sufficiently clear to you that you'd have to leave it all behind in service of the greater good?'

Examiner finds himself in a fix. On the one hand, he is delighted that Altaf—a kid he has begun to develop a strange sense of affection for—has of his own accord come to recognize the futility of his actions and see through the vitriol he has been fed by unscrupulous elements who have never had his best interests at heart. But at the same time, allowing Altaf to take his newfound scepticism to its logical conclusion might jeopardize the plausible ending of this operation. It truly is a catch-22 situation, the resolution of which will require dispassionate decision-making. Examiner knows that he cannot trust himself to make that decision. Only Ravi can.

Seeking to buy some time, Examiner proposes a compromise, 'Zia, you should back off. The boy is entitled to his doubts. If he doesn't want to join us, he can leave and return to his mother. Better now than later, because ultimately, it is our mission that will be adversely affected by his reluctance. You get ready to leave. Altaf, you make up your mind on what you want to do. Just remember, if you choose to leave now, there will be no coming back. In the meantime, I will immediately make arrangements for our travel.'

Locking the door from outside, Examiner sets out once again down the pothole-ridden road that leads to the highway. A steady stream of customers flock to the chaiwallah, but Examiner doesn't have time to wait. And so he goes up to him and asks, 'Brother, I need to make a phone call, but I've lost my phone. Can you please lend me your phone?' The chaiwallah nods, and hands over his mobile.

Moving away from the crowd, Examiner dials a number that has been hard-coded into his memory.

'Birgunj, Nepal. That's where our friends will be reunited with their brothers.'

At the other end of the line, Ravi is pleased. 'Just as I'd expected. Keep the boys engaged for a few hours. I will arrange for a vehicle that can safely ferry them all the way to their rendezvous point, after which we'll swoop in.'

'There's a small problem, boss. One of them, the kid whose house I'd infiltrated, has developed cold feet. I don't have the heart to persuade him to stay on this godforsaken path.'

'And the other one?'

'He's hardened beyond redemption.'

'One is all we need. Let's rehabilitate the one who wants to stay back. He hasn't done anything, in any case. Just been hanging around the wrong people. This is an encouraging development . . . if only more of his clique could see reason.'

'But he's not a fool either, the hardened one. If I encourage the other one to stay back, things might get complicated . . .'

It is now Ravi's turn to grapple with the perplexing dilemma presented by Altaf's change of heart.

'I think we can afford to lose him, if in return, we're able to rescue a young boy from the clutches of extremism. We have assets in Birgunj, and I'll also send in one of our men from the headquarters. It's a small town. Shouldn't be all that difficult to identify their hideout.'

Ravi hangs up. Examiner hands over the phone to the chaiwallah and makes his way back to the house, where a stunning surprise awaits him. The lock has been broken. Filled with dread, he peeps in. Altaf is still there, but the other one is nowhere to be seen.

'Where's Zia?'

'There was a call from Iqbal bhai. I don't know what he said, but Zia grew very impatient after that. He wanted to leave immediately. I told him to wait for you, but he said that you'd be able to find your way. He broke the door open and fled.'

* * *

Ravi and Mihir walk out of the briefing room after a marathon brainstorming session in which they have fleshed out every little detail of the precarious plan of swapping Suleimani for Mosale. Mihir doesn't share Ravi's barely concealed enthusiasm for the operation, 'Are you sure you want to go through with this, sir? We have the upper hand here. They have no real evidence while we are sitting on a goldmine of evidence. We can get Mosale without necessarily having to give away Suleimani.'

'And what will you do with Suleimani? Mission K2 is exposed. We've got everything we needed from him. In fact, a little more than expected. I just received word a short while ago that our old nemesis Tabrez is on his way to Birgunj, Nepal. It's a direct outcome of all our efforts over the last several months.'

Mihir throws his arms up in the air. 'Exactly, sir. We're getting what we wanted, independent of whether we let go of Suleimani or not. If he is in fact a senior ISI operative, there's so much information we could extract from him.'

'Why do you think we let him roam around freely, instead of taking him into custody at the very beginning?'

Mihir doesn't respond, knowing full well that Ravi doesn't expect an answer.

'He's a hardened operative, Mihir. Holding on to him could be dangerously counterproductive. Assuming we pack him off to prison and interrogate him, if and when he does open his mouth, I am willing to bet my last shirt that he will send us off on all kinds of false trails. Don't make the mistake of viewing him in the same mould as any of the other individuals you've had the chance of interrogating so far. Tell me this, if you were to be captured by the enemy, would you give out a single piece of valuable information?'

'I don't think so, sir. I wouldn't budge, no matter what.'

Ravi smiles. 'Precisely my point. Suleimani is essentially a version of you, except that he works for Pakistan and is a lot more devious and experienced than you are.'

'I get all that, sir, but it still seems a little unfair that we have to give him away in exchange for Mosale, who unlike Suleimani, wasn't crossing over into their territory to incite civil war and break the country from inside. There must be some way that we hold Suleimani to account and get him to pay for his deeds. Can't we, for instance, inject a slow-acting poison into his veins, which would kick in after he's been handed over? The bastard doesn't deserve to live.'

Ravi laughs. 'Has Jose been lending you his spy novels? Technically, of course we could. But you see, that's the difference between us and the ISI. We're rooted in a culture that stresses on conciliation and not vengeance. The most treasured texts from our heritage all teach us the same thing. Even during the bloodiest of wars, we've treated enemy soldiers with dignity. A deal has been struck, and we must honour it, no matter what.'

As they walk down the stairs to the exit, where Ravi's car awaits, a thin sliver of dissatisfaction continues to hang over Mihir's chest. Asking Gurmail to wait, Ravi puts his arm around his protégé's shoulder. 'Look, I understand you're still upset about Mosale's capture. This was your first mission after coming back from suspension, and you're desperate for your moment of redemption. How about this? Why don't you travel to Birgunj and track down the fellow who started this all? A solo mission. For all you know, you might even bump into that old flame of yours—Spa Maid. You'll have redemption, vengeance . . . everything you're seeking.'

The weight of the task falls at once on Mihir's shoulders, and he feels suddenly overwhelmed. He takes a few moments to regain his composure.

'Are you sure I'm up to it, sir? I mean, do you genuinely trust me to do it?'

Ravi smiles. 'The more important question is, do you trust yourself?'

'I do, sir.'

'Very well, then.'

'But sir, as much as I am grateful for this opportunity, I can't help but wonder, what if this is a mistake? It's possible they took pictures during that false flag operation in Kolkata, and so they know what I look like. And if Spa Maid is going to be there . . .'

Ravi brushes away Mihir's concerns. 'It's nothing that a touch of makeup and prosthetics can't take care of. In any case, the last thing they'd expect is for us to send you, a disgraced spy.'

A tinge of guilt and embarrassment dawns on Mihir's face, and Ravi is quick to reassure him, 'Relax, I'm only pulling your leg. But on a serious note, think of it this way . . . the obvious strategic choice in a case like this would be to send in someone else. Your cover's already been blown wide open, and the expectation would be that you've been relegated to desk duties if not fired. But that's precisely the sort of expectation we're going to subvert. If you're careful enough, as I fully expect you to be, you'll catch them napping with their eyes wide open. If there are any other lingering doubts, please take it up with Anjali. If you'll excuse me now, I have a date with an old nemesis.'

Rahab

In the living room of his rented bungalow in Delhi's posh Defence Colony, Suleimani is in a relaxed mood as he walks towards the bar cabinet.

'The perks of being in India,' he tells Madan Singh, as he pulls out a bottle of expensive scotch whisky, 'something I will truly miss when I'm back home. That's why I like France. My family in Pakistan is very conservative, you know, as are most of my friends and colleagues. They'd be scandalized if they knew I drink. With a Sikh, that too!'

Madan Singh takes the bottle from Suleimani and pours out two large measures. 'You don't particularly care for religion, do you?'

Suleimani chuckles. 'Of course I care for religion, when I need to. Like back home for instance. If I didn't care for religion there, I'd be ostracized, possibly killed even. But do I believe? That's a different matter altogether. To tell you the truth, I think it's all a grand lie invented by human beings, just to give some sort of sanctity to the dirty political games they play. It all comes down to power, ultimately. That's what drives us all, in varying degrees. The quicker one learns to cut through these games and see it all for what it is, the way the British did when they gradually tore apart this country into two, the better.'

A strange voice calls out from the unlit dining hall, 'But you couldn't see through our games, could you?'

A startled Suleimani feels a chill run down his spine. And as the source of the voice creeps out from the shadows and comes into the light, the glass nearly drops from Suleimani's trembling hands. The man looks a little different from the old pictures Suleimani has seen, but it's hard to make a mistake. This cannot be anybody but Ravi Kumar, the enigmatic spymaster who's been a constant thorn in the path of Suleimani and his organization.

Suleimani's immediate instinct is to flee, but only a moment later, he sees the futility of even trying.

'Relax, Colonel Hussaini. Take a seat,' Ravi tells the bewildered French–Pakistani sleuth. 'I don't know what they taught you in Rawalpindi, or what Brigadier Ifthikar has but we sincerely believe that there is such a thing as honour among spies. You're our guest, a distinguished one. So, please sit down and finish your drink. I'm glad to hear there's at least something about India that you don't abhor.'

But Suleimani is hardly at ease.

'When did you find out?'

Ravi steals a quick glance at Madan Singh before winking, 'Weeks before you even set foot on Indian soil. We watched every step of yours, as you went about plotting the destruction of our motherland. You did outwit us at times, and that led to the unfortunate loss of many innocent lives, but I'd like to think we've squared our accounts in the long run. I'm sorry to be the bearer of bad news, but you can employ all your might, all your guile, but you'll never be able to break us. We're too strong to be torn apart by your petty schemes. Like you rightly pointed out, the British did that to us, not so long ago. But we've learnt our lessons.'

Suleimani shakes his head in disbelief. 'So, what next? Prison? Is that how this all ends? You must know, I'm not going to utter a single word. You can torture me all you want.'

Ravi flashes a wry all-knowing smile, further unsettling an utterly zapped Suleimani, who wonders aloud as he takes a large gulp from his glass. 'The gallows? A fake encounter?'

Ravi gets up, and begins to hum Bismil Azimabadi's poem,

Waqt aane de bata denge tujhe e aasma
Hum abhi se kya batayein kya hamare dil me hai . . .

(When the right moment arrives, I shall reveal to you
Why should I tell you now, what's going on in my heart?)

Suleimani can't help but laugh, 'Brigadier Ifthikar always described you as a *gorakhdanda,* an enigma. Now I know what he meant.'

* * *

As he alights from his bus, Mihir has little information at hand other than the fact that Tabrez is in hiding somewhere in and around Birgunj. This is apart from everything else that the Indian intelligence establishment has on file about Tabrez. In particular, it is Tabrez's closely guarded fondness for the pleasures of the flesh that forms much of Mihir's plan. At the headquarters, a team of psychological profilers in close consultation with Anjali—who has been tasked with overseeing this mission—have determined that the best way to get to Tabrez would be to cultivate assets within the town's flesh trade networks. With his wife's whereabouts unknown and having spent close to a year under the ISI's thumb in Pakistan, they are convinced that he will be desperately looking to satiate his carnal desires. But it is a plan that is at least partly grounded in speculation, and neither Mihir nor his bosses can be sure that it will pan out the way they want it to.

But if there is one thing that Mihir knows for sure, it is that even his closest friends would struggle to recognize him in his current appearance. It's not just his head that's been shaven clean, even his eyebrows have been fully plucked away. Barefoot and clad in faded saffron robes, he has nothing by way of possessions except for a tattered cloth bag worn over his shoulder, containing a spare set of robes, a bundle of currency notes and a piece of paper with the address for a ramshackle lodge located bang in the middle of a small red-light area. After careful vetting, the headquarters had picked it as a safe and convenient location for Mihir to base his scouting mission.

The cover of a travelling monk had itself been picked after much deliberation. Although it had been decided at first that Mihir would assume the identity of a middle-aged aluminium trader, the uncertainty over just how long this mission might last and the consequent challenge of consistently maintaining complex prosthetic makeup on his own had led to the idea being overruled in favour of this cover. This, of course, came with it its own set of challenges and risks—most prominently, the conspicuous dissonance of a monk trying to cultivate prostitutes.

But Mihir has it all rehearsed. And as if his current avatar isn't already convincing enough, Mihir walks with a pronounced limp in his left leg. It is an excruciating detail to maintain, but one that is worth it given the additional distance it confers from his real identity. As he gets into a rickshaw and asks to be taken to the address scribbled on the piece of paper he's carrying, the rickshaw driver pays him a puzzled look. 'Are you sure you want to go there? It's not a place meant for saints, you know. If it's money you're worried about, I can take you to a dharamshala where you can stay for free. You'll have more of your kind for company, you know, other monks and holy men. But this address you're headed to, I don't know where you got it from. It's a very small area, but the worst one in the entire district where crooks and lowlifes hangout. It's where men go to satiate their vilest desires.'

Mihir flashes a calm smile. 'In today's world, is there really a difference between holy men and crooks? In any case, after one has renounced the ordinary ways of seeing, everything is the same, and it becomes clear that everybody is made of the same essence. Noble desires, vile desires, whatever . . . ultimately, they are desires, and they only serve to steer one away from the union with the divine. This is why I make it a point to spend most of my time around the people you would normally call lowlifes. Even they can be redeemed and shown the futility of the material world. That is the mission my guru sent me on before he left his mortal body.'

The rickshaw driver is impressed. 'Such words of wisdom, Swamiji. You are absolutely right. If only all saints were like you, religion wouldn't have such a bad reputation in today's world. The rich have cornered it for themselves with their convenient high moral ground, leaving people like me to lose faith in all things holy.'

All through the twenty-minute ride, passing through the dusty by lanes of the main commercial area, the rickshaw driver keeps his holy passenger engaged with spiritual queries. And Mihir has an answer to everything. By the time they finally arrive at the lodge—an ugly, dilapidated structure that looks like it hasn't been painted or repaired since the time of its construction—the rickshaw driver is convinced that Mihir is the holiest man he has ever met in his life.

And so, when Mihir pulls out money from his bag and hands it to the rickshaw driver, he flatly refuses. 'Please, it is my real fortune to have met a pure soul like you.' Bending down in obeisance, he seeks Mihir's blessings. Mihir complies gracefully before limping into the lodge.

The man at the front desk, who owns and manages the lodge, is busy talking to a conspicuously dressed dwarf with false teeth and flashy jewellery. They're talking about the price of ivory in the grey market.

The dwarf, a sharp man, is the first to notice the monk. He nudges the lodge owner who immediately tries to chase him away. 'Swamiji, I've already given away my share of alms for the day. There's no food either. Go away, I have nothing to offer.'

Mihir flashes the same calm, rehearsed smile at the man. 'I'm not here to beg, son.'

The lodge owner is at least two decades older than Mihir, but monkhood confers him the right to address him in this manner. Sizing Mihir up, head to toe, the lodge owner asks, 'What do you want, then?'

'I would like a room to stay and I'm prepared to pay for it.'

The lodge owner grows a little suspicious. 'Really? Do you have any ID?'

Mihir shakes his head. 'ID? Do monks have such things?'

The dwarf turns to the lodge owner. 'And since when did you care about IDs?'

The lodge owner laughs. 'Of course, I don't. I was just asking to see if he is who he claims to be. Not that I care about that either.'

Turning to Mihir, he continues, 'But you have money, right? That's one thing I do care about. And you'll have to pay in advance. It's Rs 150 a night if you're staying for only a few days. Hundred if you plan on staying for longer than a week.'

Mihir pulls out his bundle, and carefully counts out the notes. 'Here's 1500. I intend to stay for fifteen days for now. I might extend it later on.'

The lodge owner looks at the dwarf with pleasant surprise. 'Looks like a loaded monk, this one. Anyway, who am I to complain? It's the off season and all money is welcome. Why don't you wait here, while I show him to his room?'

The dwarf nods and takes a seat, while the lodge owner takes Mihir up a paan-stained staircase to a cramped, dingy room. 'This is your room. There is an attached bathroom, but no running water. People usually rent out rooms here by the hour if you know what I mean. But for those who stay longer, we expect them to come down and fill their buckets by themselves. But out of reverence, and also since you've paid in advance for fifteen days at a dry time, I'll do it for you. If you want food, that will be Rs 100 extra per day, all three meals included. Anything else, you can always find me downstairs.'

Mihir surveys the uninhabitable conditions with a feigned look of contentment, before turning to the lodge owner. 'What did you say your name was?'

'I didn't. It's Chowdhury.'

'So, listen Chowdhury. There's something I need your help with. I would like to meet prostitutes.'

Chowdhury shakes his head, a wicked smile playing on his face. 'I should have known. This is why I asked for an ID. A monk coming into this area with so much money. What crimes are you running away from in this disguise? Murder? Rape? Dacoity?'

Mihir shakes his head. 'You misunderstand. I am interested in meeting them not to derive pleasure, but to partake in their sorrows.'

Chowdhury chuckles. 'Partake in their sorrows? I've heard all kinds of cover-up stories, but this one takes the cake!'

Mihir doesn't laugh, and wears a stoic look on his face. 'It's not a cover-up story, son. I mean what I say. I am merely following in the footsteps of my forebearers. My guru always used to say—any fool in saffron can captivate those who are comfortably placed in life and respected in society. But the real test of divinity lies in being able to live and teach amongst the fallen, the downtrodden. It starts with the greatest teacher, the Buddha himself.'

Chowdhury can't stop laughing. 'You're a strange monk, I must tell you. I mean, I have seen missionaries going around saying these things, but a monk . . . Anyway, like I said, I don't really care as long as you're paying. If it's the prostitutes you're interested in meeting, I can arrange that too. But you've picked the wrong time of the year if that really is your purpose of visiting Birgunj. This is the tourist season, not the trading season. Not much tourism here, as you can probably see. During this time of the year, all the girls move up to Kathmandu, and all the brothels are temporarily shut. There is only one that functions through the year, some ten girls or so in total, so not much choice. Anyway, since you claim that you're here for other reasons, I assume you don't care for choice.'

'You're right. It is not my place to choose who is to receive divine light.'

Chowdhury has heard enough. 'Honestly, I'm already sick of your preaching. You're not going to convince me to renounce, try all you want. If it's the prostitutes you want, I'll give you the address of the brothel. You can go lecture them all you want.'

Mihir smiles. 'There is a minor problem. You see, I can't visit the brothel. From my experience in other places, as soon as the pimps find out what my purpose is, they tend to drive me away. And so, I was wondering if you could arrange for these women to visit me in my room, one at a time, and keep it a secret?'

'Of course, I could. What do you think this lodge is meant for? But it will cost you a lot more. The pimp will want extra, for out call service, and I'll want extra . . . for keeping it a secret'

'Money is not a problem.'

'All right, then. When do you want the first girl coming in?'

'Right now.'

* * *

As the AN-32 propeller aircraft ferrying them hovers over Srinagar airport, a few hours past midnight, Ravi goes over the plan one last time, 'As I've stressed a hundred times already, we cannot take anything lightly. We might be honouring the deal from our end, no dirty tricks whatsoever, but we can't count on the ISI to do the same. Let me remind you once again, this is a clandestine operation that is completely off the books. And they know this, and we can expect them to try and take advantage of the fact.'

The small, handpicked team that is to carry out the operation—Jose, Cyrus, Dr Himwal and Swaminathan, his trusted compounder of several decades—nod solemnly, as the plane begins to make its descent. Ravi continues, 'But as long as we execute our respective tasks with military precision, we should be able to thwart whatever trickery they might have up their sleeve . . . explosives, poison, pathogens, anything conceivable in an operation of this nature. I know I can count on all of you to make absolutely no mistake. Now, put on your seatbelts and get ready.'

The plane lands right next to a black SUV and an ambulance, their engines already running although they remain unmanned. Except for the blinking navigational aids on the runway and the headlights on the vehicles, the airport is enveloped by darkness. Suleimani is quickly herded into the ambulance, a large, retrofitted truck that in its interior resemblance is closer to a small hospital than an ambulance— replete with advanced diagnostic equipment and a portable x-ray machine. While Dr Himwal gets into the ambulance, to be driven by Swaminathan, the others get into the SUV, which Cyrus is to drive.

'All teams copy. We're ready to go,' Cyrus announces through his walkie-talkie, and both vehicles immediately set out.

* * *

'Do you enjoy your work?' Mihir asks the befuddled call girl sitting opposite him. She's the seventh girl Mihir is meeting since setting himself up in this dingy room in Birgunj, but he hasn't yet been able to extract any clinching leads.

The call girl, who has been given the biblical nom de guerre Rahab, shakes her head, still a little sceptical of the saffron-robed monk's intentions, 'Of course I don't enjoy it. That's why it's called work. I do it for money. And it's not like I had a choice. My own father sold me off when I was still a young girl.'

'You still are very young, and there always is a choice, child.'

Rahab scoffs. 'You're a man, that's why you can say this. You can do as you please. Today, you can roam around in a monk's robes and tomorrow you can choose to become a shopkeeper or a driver or anything you want. But me? I can't dream of even becoming a dishwasher.'

Mihir feels real compassion. 'I understand your plight. And you are right, it is an unfair world. But you must know this. In god's eyes, there are no men, no women, no shopkeepers, no dishwashers. Everything is one.'

Rahab finds Mihir's words comforting, but she's too hardened by the realities of life to respond with anything short of bitter cynicism, 'Easy for you to say, when you're not the one getting whipped almost every day . . . when you're not the one expected to comply with the strange desires of strange men.'

Rahab's voice trails off. She is repulsed by the traumatic memories that pop up in her mind. After a few moments, she continues, 'It's strange, you know. Although it is painful just to think about it, talking to you about all this feels strangely comforting.'

'Please feel free to speak your heart, child. I am here to partake in your sorrows.'

'I mostly try to forget. It's the only way to cope. But the most recent events stay fresh in your mind. And the last week has been particularly strange.'

Mihir waits patiently, as her voice trails off again. After a few moments, she regains her composure and continues, 'There is a group of men, who've come from outside the country, staying in a rented house not too far from here. I don't know what they're here for. But every few days my owner has been sending a girl to that house . . . to stay there, for as long as the boss of the household pleases. The others wouldn't even look a woman in the eye, they seemed like very religious people. But the boss has an insatiable appetite for women. This week, it was my turn. I was there for four days, and he . . . he's unlike any man I've ever met. Extremely handsome, like a film actor almost. He'd be extremely nice and polite, and then suddenly transform into a monster. I've had to deal with all kinds of men, but I've never met anybody like him. To tell you the truth, I'm still a little scared of you because he was behaving exactly like you. Most men, they just want to do their business and leave. But he would talk to me, sometimes for hours. And then suddenly, he'd become unimaginably violent.'

Mihir can't help but get the feeling that he knows exactly who she's talking about. On the pretext of finding a book on peace of mind, Mihir deliberately drops the newspaper clipping of a look out notice for Tabrez. Rahab's jaw drops to the floor. 'H–He is the man!'

Mihir flashes his calm, monk-like smile. 'I am a sage, young one. You can call it divine revelation.'

At once, Rahab falls at his feet, weeping miserably. 'Please save me, swamiji. God has finally listened to my prayers. Only you can rescue me from this wretched existence. I am willing to become a nun if you will take me with you.'

A little embarrassed, Mihir nudges her to get up, before consoling her with a glass of water.

'I meant what I said at the beginning. I am here to help you. But you have to help me, first. Show me the house where he lives, and I promise, you will forever be freed from the clutches of your owner. Whatever you want to do, study, work, whatever it is . . . I will make it happen.'

Regaining her composure, Rahab nods, 'It's on the way to the brothel, and I can take you till the very edge of the road on which the house is, but no further than that. They are very bad people, and I do not want to risk running into them. But you'll be able to find it easily from that point. It's a blue house with a tall compound wall.'

As Mihir follows Rahab down the staircase, Chowdhury gives them an inquisitive look. Since his arrival, this is the first time Mihir is stepping out of his room.

'What's the matter, swamiji? Finally felt like you could do with some sunshine?'

Mihir merely smiles as he limps along. Chowdhury's attention turns next to Rahab, whose demeanour bears the distinct stamp of a newfound tranquillity. He says, 'What, girl? Swamiji gave you moksha?' Rahab too decides against responding and follows Mihir out through the exit. Chowdhury shakes his head, muttering under his breath.

On the other side of the narrow street, the dwarf watches from his small pawnbroker's store. He waits a few moments before shuttering his shop and decides to follow from a distance. As Mihir and Rahab make their way through a junction that leads out to the main commercial street, Rahab's calm exterior seems to crumble, and she is overcome with worry.

'A lot of people know me here. What if they tell my boss?'

Mihir reassures her, 'Don't worry. You told me that this house is on the way to the brothel, is it not?'

'It is, but I'm walking with you, talking to you. I'm not supposed to interact with anybody. I could get punished.'

'But I am a holy man. Just say that you were seeking my blessings.'

Rahab shakes her head, the discomfort growing as more people begin noticing her. Some pass lewd comments.

'You don't know my owner. I once tried helping a young boy who had got separated from his father and was roaming helplessly on the streets. Just for doing that, I was . . .'

Her voice trails off, just as they're about cross the road.

'Don't look, but that man at the paan shop on your left . . . the tall man wearing a white kurta, he is one of the men living in that house. He's the one their "nice" boss would summon to have me beaten up.'

Mihir, who has mastered the art of looking without being noticed, steals a quick glance nevertheless. He turns to Rahab and notices that her face has turned completely pale. Realizing that her fear might jeopardize the mission, but also wanting to spare her the risk of whatever it is he might be getting into, he asks her to leave. But not before making a promise. 'I am a man of my word. No matter what happens, I will have you rescued. Either I or someone else will come to get you in the next few days. You have to trust me, and you have to remain strong.'

Rahab nods and beats a hasty retreat, while Mihir walks over to the paan shop and buys a packet of biscuits. The tall man in the white kurta scoffs, 'What sort of a monk are you, paying money for food? Aren't you supposed to be begging?'

Mihir feels a shiver run down his spine, as he realizes that he is standing less than a metre away from a man who in all likelihood is a high-ranking member of the most dreaded terror outfit in the subcontinent, and by virtue of that, one of its most wanted men. But not wanting to arouse any suspicion, Mihir puts on a calm smile and turns towards the man, also using the opportunity to take a good, long look at him, 'You are right, my child. But this money was given to me as alms, by somebody who had no food to offer.'

The tall man laughs dismissively before spitting paan on the ground and walking away. Mihir puts the packet of biscuits in his bag and starts following. And unbeknownst to Mihir, he too is being followed from a measured distance.

Vamana

The convoy transporting Suleimani comes to a stop just outside the heavily barricaded zone that marks the entry to Kaman bridge in Uri—a particularly sensitive node on the Line of Control. Cyrus pushes the talk button on his walkie-talkie, 'This is Charlie, Charlie, Charlie, confirming arrival at point E1. Requesting clearance to proceed to point E2.'

'Roger. Requesting visual confirmation,' comes the response from the other end.

Cyrus fiddles with the headlight dimmer. In quick succession, a long burst followed by a short flash, then another long burst, followed by a short flash. The sequence is repeated thrice—morse code for Charlie, Charlie, Charlie, or C3.

'Roger, you may proceed to point E2. All units have fallen back, as requested. But a crack squad is on standby for SOS,' comes the response from the other side. The barricades are moved, and the convoy drives on for a few kilometres until they reach the bridge that separates the two countries. Two parallel pairs of headlights flash at them from the other side of the border. Cyrus takes a deep breath as he pulls a mosquito net mask over his face, before stepping out. Positioning himself in front of the SUV's headlights, he begins waving a large white flag. A masked man on the other side steps out of his vehicle and mimics Cyrus.

'All right, this is it. Start jamming,' Ravi tells Jose.

Jose furiously begins thumping away at his keyboard.

Ravi speaks into his walkie, 'Unit 2, can you come in? Unit 2.'

Dr Himwal responds at the other end, 'Roger, sir. Everything is in place. Awaiting go-ahead.'

Jose flashes his thumb at Ravi. 'Jammer in place, sir. We may proceed.'

Ravi nods, before confirming to Dr Himwal, 'You may proceed with the disembarkment. Safeguards against explosives are in place.'

The rear door of the ambulance is thrown open by a masked Swaminathan, who then stretchers Suleimani out, stopping just before the bridge. Almost in perfect synchronization, the same set of actions play out on the other side of the border. Continuing to wave his flag, Cyrus moves closer to the point of exchange. A masked ISI man uncuffs Mosale and shines a torch against his face, while Swaminathan does the same with Suleimani. Cyrus takes a close look, before confirming through his walkie-talkie, 'Identity confirmed, sir. They have our man.'

Ravi responds, 'Roger. Proceed with exchange.'

Swaminathan looks at Cyrus, who nods in confirmation.

'Walk on straight ahead. Do not look back,' Swaminathan instructs Suleimani, as he uncuffs him.

As soon as Mosale crosses the bridge, Swaminathan pushes him onto the stretcher and runs towards the ambulance. Once inside, Dr Himwal takes charge immediately, drawing multiple blood samples even as he places Mosale under the portable X-ray machine. As the black-and-white images pop up on his screen, Dr Himwal pushes the talk button on his walkie, 'No trace of explosives. I repeat, no trace of explosives. Request ten minutes for pathological report.'

Ravi heaves a sigh of relief. 'Roger. All units return to point E1 and exit into mainland.'

The convoy makes a U-turn and drives through the barricades back onto the treacherous stretch of mud roads that connects Kaman bridge to the highway. The tense silence is finally pierced ten minutes later, by a crackling on the wireless. It is Dr Himwal, who has shed all code and technicalese, 'The pathology report is in, and I had a closer look at the x-ray. There is good news, and there's bad news.'

The tension returns, and Ravi braces himself for the worst.

'Good news is, no pathogens in the blood. Mosale is conscious and perfectly stable. But the bad news is, there is little blood in Mosale's veins.'

'What do you mean? How's that even possible? You just said he's conscious and perfectly stable!'

'What I mean is his veins are overrun with alcohol. Which explains the absence of pathogens . . . no virus or bacteria can possibly survive in such a highly sanitized bloodstream.'

Ravi laughs. It isn't often that he can be outwitted.

Eager to entertain, Ravi asks, 'And the x-ray?'

'Cirrhosis of the liver. Early stage, can still be treated . . . But only if the patient allows his blood to be de-sanitized!'

* * *

Still reeling from the adrenaline rush of the clandestine exchange at the border, Ravi decides to forgo his sleep and heads straight back to work after arriving in Delhi. Anjali is in his office, restlessly awaiting his return. But much to his surprise, she does not share his anticipation of imminent triumph.

'What's the matter? Are you gloomy because we soon might find ourselves out of thrilling things to do?'

She isn't quite sure how to break it to him and continues to sit around awkwardly, not responding to his typically cheerful jibe.

Ravi chuckles, 'Trust me, something or the other will soon come up. Do you really think the enemy is going to sit back and do nothing? Sure, nothing as thrilling as a spy swap is likely to happen anytime soon, but . . .'

Anjali sighs. 'Vamana has reported that Mihir has been captured.'

'That dwarf roving agent? His information is usually correct.'

It takes a few moments for the news to fully sink in. It's bad enough that he's learning that another of their operatives has been captured, mere hours after having secured the release of another captured asset, but the fact that the operative in question is Mihir is too much to take in, even for the battle-hardened veteran who has seen many of his finest men lay their lives down in the line of duty.

'How did this happen?'

Anjali briefs him, 'He located Tabrez's safe house yesterday afternoon, before which he was even spotted having an interaction with a man on the street whose description matches that of Iqbal. He reported back to me soon after. He wanted to return to the hideout, to try and get visual confirmation of Tabrez's presence, but I asked him to hold off until your return. But he was apprehensive of losing Tabrez this time too and was confident that his cover was foolproof. Besides, from what he'd learnt from the source he cultivated, there's only three of them. Tabrez, Iqbal and Zia. Vamana, who's been keeping tabs on him all along, saw him late at night entering the hideout, apparently under the pretext of begging for alms. He hasn't been spotted since then.'

Ravi shakes his head in anguish, before knocking hard at his temple with a tightly clenched fist. 'It's all my fault. I should have never sent him alone, that poor boy. What's most upsetting is that it's not about his abilities or temperament . . . he's undoubtedly among the finest we've had in a long time. It's just his rotten fate. No matter where he goes, what he does, tragedy tends to seek him out.'

Never the sort to sit around moping while a crisis awaits resolution, Ravi immediately springs to his feet. 'There's a not a moment to waste. I'm assuming you've already started working on something in my absence, and I'm assuming you've come to the same conclusions that I can deduce, based on all that you've told me. We can't take the risk of involving local police or even notifying the Nepalese government at any level.'

Anjali concurs. 'It is a risk, yes. Getting involved would mean acknowledging that Tabrez was able to find refuge in Nepal, and that would be embarrassing for them.'

Ravi starts pacing around the room, thinking aloud, 'But if it was just that, we could have still found a workaround . . .

have them all arrested, and just put out a statement that they were arrested near the border or something along those lines. But we must bear in mind, going by past experience, that the ISI might catch a whiff of any planned operation. They've always maintained a very strong covert presence in Nepal.'

Anjali doesn't fully agree. 'Even if they do catch a whiff, the chances of them facilitating an escape are slim. This is Nepal, sir, not Pakistan. Besides, we now have the house under close surveillance. If they try to run, we'll know.'

'It's not just about that. If they uncover Mihir's true identity, there's a lot they can do with that information. Perhaps they can't use it as leverage of the same degree as Mosale, given that this is Nepal, but you never know . . . just out of spite, they might kill him.'

'You're worried he'll cave in to torture?'

Ravi doesn't respond. The thought of Mihir being tortured, a near certainty given what they know of Tabrez's penchant for visceral brutality, disturbs him.

Anjali pierces the tense silence. 'Even if he doesn't succumb to the torture, and manages to keep his identity a secret, the possibility remains that they may have pictures of him, from Kolkata. And there's the fact that Tabrez's wife has seen him from an intimate distance. Sure, his disguise is very convincing, but . . .'

Anjali lets out a brief, bitter laugh, taking her boss by surprise.

Ravi is perplexed. 'What?'

Anjali shakes her head, straightening out the smirk on her face. 'No, it's just, I was just going to say . . . although Mihir in his current disguise would be almost completely

unrecognizable to the human eye, a fairly sophisticated
algorithm can immediately put two and two together. And the
irony of it all is what's upsettingly funny. I mean, it's thanks to
the Americans and their war on terror that the ISI has access
to the most powerful face recognition software in the world.
Anyway, my point is, we need to act immediately before it
even comes to any of that.'

She continues, 'I think it's best that we send in a
plainclothes Indian police team immediately. The Nepalese
government doesn't even have to know.'

Ravi considers the idea for a few moments, before
rejecting it vigorously. 'That might be disastrous. To begin
with, you've probably heard about what happened last time
around. I'm not saying that's going to happen again, but you
never know. There's a strong anti-India sentiment simmering
in those parts. A lot could go wrong. Besides, an armed
operation might be uncalled for. Apart from the risk it would
pose to Mihir's life, there's reason to suspect that Tabrez and
gang have weapons in their possession. They are smart enough
to know that movement of weapons will immediately trigger
red flags. In any case, much like the others who've come
before him, Tabrez can't shoot straight to save his own life.
He's a rabble-rouser, a man of ideas.'

Jose barges into the room, gasping for breath. He holds
up a phone in one hand, and a sheaf of transcripts in another.
Ravi looks at him quizzically.

'Sir, if I'd managed this earlier, things wouldn't have got
to this stage, and Mihir most certainly wouldn't have had to
put himself at risk, but . . .'

'What is it, Jose?'

'I've done it. I've got in. From the phone that we recovered from Altaf, and then also from Suleimani, I was finally able to work out a vulnerability and get into the portal. Before they could shut off access, I managed to create an alias for our digital asset, Varuna, and he has managed to stumble upon chatter between Tabrez and Al-Brittani.'

Ravi starts muttering under his breath, '*Dvau samnishadya yan mantrayete raja tad veda varuna tritiyaha.*'

Jose is left befuddled. It's a strange language he's never heard before. He stares at Anjali, who's just as clueless, before turning again to Ravi. 'Are you okay, sir?'

'I quoted from Atharva Veda—Wherever two men plot in whispers, King Varuna is there, a third.'

Jose isn't quite sure how to react, but Ravi spares him the trouble, snapping out of his sudden rumination to snatch the transcript out of Jose's hands. Jose points at a highlighted section:

Tabrez: We've captured an Indian spy. Bastard was trying to enquire about us. But he is a hardened one, won't admit to anything. He needs military-grade treatment. Please speak to Karbala and do the needful.

Al-Brittany: Well done. A local ISI asset named Zahoor will be there in 48 hours with the equipment that can get anybody to open up.

Ravi takes a few moments to process what he's just read. He announces, 'As the wise optimists of the world say, better late than never. We have no more time to waste. Before Zahoor gets there, we must. Time to launch Mission Entebbe. What I'm proposing is that we go in ourselves. I will lead the operation personally. It will be a very small unit. Cyrus and Anjali will come with me. We'll fly out to the border, and then drive to Birgunj. We'll be in and out in no time.'

'Are we being too optimistic, sir?' questions Anjali. 'I'm afraid we might be taking too many things for granted. Sure, an armed police operation might unfold horribly. But what if they do have weapons? That would be a disaster of an unimaginable level . . . we'd be putting too much on the line.'

Ravi shrugs his shoulders, 'Who says we won't be carrying weapons? Of course, I'm not talking about carrying real weapons. Have you seen the ones they use in the movies? They look, sound, and feel just like the real thing, and the audience just can't tell the difference. As long as we take Tabrez by surprise, those are all we need. And unlike the men who die on his command, he is at the end of the day a coward who cares dearly about staying alive. I'm confident he'll give in without a fight.'

Ravi pauses, then picks up the intercom. 'Subramanium, connect me to Pandey, our in-charge at Raxaul post.'

After few moments the intercom buzzes. 'Pandey on the line, sir'

'Anjali, Cyrus and I are planning to chill out in Kathmandu. We will travel by road and possibly cross over to Birgunj at night so that we are able to reach Kathmandu by sunrise and go to the casino as soon as it opens. Will you please notify your friend about our programme?', Ravi requests Pandey.

Neeraj Pandey had been part of Ravi's team during his posting in Patna. He had participated in many raids led by

Ravi on hideouts of Naxalites in Bihar and inside Nepal. Pandey understood when Ravi wanted to chill out and have a game at the casino. Police of both the countries had developed an understanding regarding informal visits in each other's jurisdiction for investigation of crime.

* * *

Tabrez watches with a look of deep and perverse satisfaction on his face as Zia places a piece of black cloth on Mihir's face, as he lies against a slanted desk. Iqbal brings in a bucket of water from the bathroom. He fills up a mug and is about to pour it over the cloth on Mihir's face, when Tabrez raises his hand, 'Stop!'

Iqbal backs off, as Tabrez moves closer to Mihir and pulls away the cloth, before pulling him up by his neck.

'Do you really want us to do this all over again? Or do you just want to put an end to it by telling us who you are? It's all in your hands. Just tell us, and the torture will stop.'

Mihir, bruised and battered all over, is only barely conscious, but he manages to muster a feeble response, 'I'm telling you again . . . I am a monk, I came here to beg.'

Tabrez lets go of Mihir and spits on his face, 'Suit yourself. But you should know you won't be able to resist for much longer. A veteran interrogator is on his way, with a far more sophisticated torture inventory. Electric shocks, barbed whips, rectal rehydration kit . . . forms of torture you can't even imagine. It doesn't have to be that way. That fake limp of yours, it'll soon be real. Just tell us, it's still not too late.'

Mihir shakes his head meekly. 'You can torture me all you want, but it won't change the fact that I'm a monk. And you should know, I have nothing but compassion for you. It is still not too late for you either, to give up your demonic ways. Tell me what ails your heart. There is always a way out.'

Tabrez is infuriated at Mihir's defiance. He yells at Iqbal, 'Drown the bastard one more time!'

Iqbal's hands tremble slightly. He and Zia are almost convinced by now that the man they're about to waterboard for the umpteenth time in the last fifteen hours is in fact a monk, and not an Indian agent as they'd originally suspected. Nobody would stand their ground in the face of such relentless torture. But orders are orders, and Mihir struggles violently, as water is steadily poured over the porous cloth on his face.

Tabrez, who seems to be in a state of manic frenzy, screams, 'Again . . .'

* * *

There is pitch darkness all around as the C3 convoy starts moving towards Birgunj. It suits them perfectly, but the heavy downpour lashing down on them makes for a far from ideal scenario.

Anjali points out, 'It appears God is not with us. In this weather, I'm not sure if we should risk it. Perhaps we should wait for it to clear up?'

Ravi quips, 'On the contrary, God is certainly with us. Look all around you. There is not a soul on the streets, not even policemen or night gorkhas. Even if the terrorists put up a struggle, the thunder and rain will prevent the noise from escaping the compound. Fortune indeed favours the brave.'

Pandey's liaison has made it easy for the group to pass the check point smoothly.

* * *

Despite the heavy downpour outside, Tabrez's razor-sharp instincts pick up the sound of footsteps. 'Quiet,' he tells the others as he steps out of the room to check. Zia gags Mihir, while Iqbal mutters a silent prayer asking God for forgiveness. The relentless torture might not have broken the monk, but it surely has done that to Iqbal.

'Who is it?' Tabrez calls out.

'It's me, Zahoor. Karbala sent me. I'm here with the kit.'

'Tell that fake monk that his time is up, once and for all,' Tabrez gleefully yells in the direction of Iqbal and Zia before opening the door, 'Zahoor Bhai . . .'

Tabrez freezes at the sight that confronts. Gun pointing towards him. Pointing it is none other than the head of C3 himself. Before Tabrez can respond, Cyrus charges at him and pins him to the floor, before cuffing him—both hands and legs, thus preventing any chance of escape. Iqbal runs inside, Anjali follows him. As Iqbal tries to open the door of an almirah, a powerful flying kick crashes his head against the wall completely incapacitating him. Anjali cuffs Iqbal, tying his hands behind back. Mortified, Zia is sitting in the corner. Tears running down his cheeks, he waves crying, 'Don't beat me, don't beat me.'

Ravi runs inside to check on Mihir, who's drifting in and out of consciousness. He struggles for almost a minute, just to open his eyes.

'Mihir, are you all right?'

A thin smile plays on Mihir's worn-out face, 'Mihir? Who's that? I'm Swami Abhigyananda.'

Anjali searches the house and collects weapons and phones. Outside, Cyrus replaces the India number plates with Nepali ones.

'*Rok* (stop),' shouts the sentry at the check post without stepping out due to the rain.

'*Ramro cha* (all is well),' replies Ravi in chaste Nepali.

'*Januhose* (go).'

All three of C3 take a deep breath seeing Pandey on the Indian side. A burst of huge cathartic laughter breaks inside the van as it crosses over to India.

* * *

Through a double-sided mirror, Ravi and Subramaniam watch Dr Himwal as he checks on Mihir who lies fast asleep on a standard-issue hospital bed in a solitary ward a few floors below ground level at the headquarters. After a few moments, Dr Himwal walks in, his face carrying palpable dissatisfaction over his patient's progress.

'It's not just the torture inflicted by his captors, sir. My feeling is that he has been torturing himself.'

Ravi is puzzled. 'What do you mean?'

'He has an alarming level of nutritional deficiency, a sharp drop in body weight and high creatinine from the time of his last medical assessment which was just a month ago. Looks like he's been taking his cover a little too seriously and eating very sparingly.'

Ravi shakes his head in dismay. 'He's always been a little too idealistic for his own good. At least he's alive, thank God for that. But what's the prognosis looking like? When do you think he'll be up on his feet?'

Dr Himwal looks unsure. 'It's hard to say, sir. He's regained consciousness, and his vitals are more or less stable. But it's not just his body that needs to heal, his mind and spirit are also broken, I would imagine.'

Ravi nods sympathetically. 'It doesn't get any more traumatic than waterboarding. I asked my officers to perform it on me once just to see what it felt like, to see if it was something we could use in extraordinary circumstances. My life flashed in front of my eyes, and I was certain I was going to die. That was from one instance. It was so terrible, I realized I wouldn't want to inflict it even on my worst enemies. Imagine poor Mihir . . . who knows how many times they did it to him? Fifty, sixty . . . I suppose it will take at least a few weeks before he can feel anything like himself. Why don't you recommend that in writing, doctor? At least a month of complete rest, at home. We can have somebody check on him daily.'

'Well, sir, since he has regained consciousness, he will have to first clear the standard tests before I can make any post-discharge recommendations.'

'Narcoanalysis? You really shouldn't bother. The kid's been through enough, and he's confirmed to me that he did not reveal anything. I trust his word, and you have my authorization to waive it.'

Dr Himwal sighs. 'I mean no disrespect whatsoever, sir, but you do not have the authority to sanction a waiver. A new SOP came into force a few months ago. It's mandatory for all captured spies to undergo narco-analysis and lie-detection tests, apart from a whole bunch of psychometric assessments as a preliminary condition for any further rehabilitation. Which is why we had to do it with Mosale as well, whilst you were away on this mission.'

'Surely, somebody must have the authority to waive the requirement. If the chief signed off, would that work?'

Subramaniam shakes his head, 'Unfortunately no, sir. It's a bit of a bureaucratic nightmare now, especially when it involves capture by non-state actors.'

'You mind describing this nightmare, Subramaniam?'

'Sorry sir, of course. After you put in a recommendation clearly stating the reasons for seeking a waiver, a committee will be instituted. The chief, Anil sir, and the NSA or a deputy recommended by him, are ex-officio a part of the committee. The fourth member is the highest-ranking officer of the particular sub-agency that the captured spy is attached to. In Mihir's case, that would be you. But since it is you who will be putting forward the request for waiver, you will have to recuse yourself, and Anjali madam will be . . .'

'That just sounds depressingly laborious. But basically, there is a way?'

Subramaniam nods.

'Well, then get started right away.'

Subramaniam hesitates as he gently pulls Ravi to the side, out of Dr Himwal's earshot. 'A–are you sure, sir? I mean, there's already a lot of talk going around about . . . you know, favouritism, and how you're always . . .'

'If sparing Mihir the plight of narco-analysis makes me guilty of favouritism, so be it.'

Subramaniam nods, 'Understood, sir. Sorry for bringing it up. I just thought you should know.'

Ravi's phone rings, and he steps aside to take it.

'Cyrus. Everything checks out?'

As he listens, his ears perk up, and a faint smile dawns on his face, 'Excellent. Anjali will set it up. Coordinate with her and call me when it's all done. We'll hold off on announcing Tabrez and Sandhu's arrest until then. In the meantime, I think it's only fair that you do something for your bird friend. He has earned his return.'

* * *

At the Indira Gandhi International Airport in Delhi, a tall, slender woman wearing a stylish burqa and large sunglasses that block out nearly half her face confidently wheels her suitcase as she cuts her way through the crowd to get to the front of the line at the immigration counter. She stifles a yawn as she places her passport on the desk.

Sanjay Pateria, a veteran immigration officer, cross-checks the picture on the passport and other details, before keying in her specifics into his computer.

'Where were you born,' he asks, summoning all the Malayalam he had picked up in the decade or so he had served at Cochin International Airport.

The woman is taken aback

'Palluruthy in Kochi district. It is mentioned in the passport.'

Pateria keeps a poker face as he probes further, 'I see . . . And where did you study?'

'Kochi itself. I was born and brought up there.'

Although Pateria's own command over Malayalam is limited, he can tell at once that the woman's Malayalam is even poorer than his own. Apart from glaring grammatical mistakes, there is an unmistakable Bundeli touch to her accent. He is convinced that this is the woman he has been alerted about and discreetly pushes a button under his desk.

His silence unsettles the woman, and she asks, 'Is there a problem, officer?'

Pateria smiles. 'Not at all, ma'am. Just routine procedure that needs to be followed. Just a few more . . .'

He is interrupted by a group of armed security personnel who swoop in and usher her away. The woman is perplexed and demands to know where she is being taken but the guards do not acknowledge her and take her to a brightly lit holding room where a burly security officer takes over and escorts her down a long hallway, finally culminating in a series of offices. The woman isn't one to give in easily and starts protesting, 'You have no right to drag me in like this without telling me why!'

The security officer doesn't respond either, merely sizing her up in a typical policeman-like manner. She feels as if he is staring into her soul, and her knees begin to tremble as she continues to protest, 'This is a violation of my rights. Get me my lawyer!'

The security officer smiles, as they stop outside one of the offices. 'Well, of course you're well within your rights. In fact, you will definitely need your lawyer. But first, somebody is very keen on speaking to you.'

The woman shouts, a last-ditch attempt at getting out of the conundrum, 'But . . . I don't want to. Why should I?'

He opens the door for her and stands aside. 'It was an order, madam. Not a question. Please, go inside.'

She backs away from the door, hesitation in her step. The security officer smirks. 'I hope you don't actually believe you can run away from here, madam. You are inside the most secure area of one of the most secure airports in the world.'

With a heavy heart, the woman walks in, and the door thuds to a close behind her. Anjali and Cyrus are waiting.

Cyrus takes a good long look at her, and hums, '*Rukh se zara nakab hata do, mere huzoor* (Please remove the veil from your face, dear).'

'Cyrus,' Anjali shouts sternly, in the same manner as someone commandeering a horse galloping out of control.

Cyrus mouths a weak apology. The burqa-clad woman is perplexed all the more. 'I'm sorry, officer. I don't understand. What is this about? You have no business confining me like this. I am an Indian citizen. I will take this up at the highest levels of the government if that's what it takes.'

Anjali finds her persistent defiance amusing. 'Oh, don't worry, madam. The highest levels of the government will certainly hear about this. Indeed, the whole country will soon hear all about you. And not just you, but also your husband.'

Sweat trickles down the woman's face, and she continues trying to wage a losing battle, 'But officer, I am not married. You're probably looking for someone else.'

Anjali laughs.

'Not at all, madam. How can we be mistaken when it is your husband himself who led us to you? So, tell me, Miss . . .

Rukmini? Rukhsana? Or is it something else altogether? Do you want to come away quietly, or do you want to sit around pretending like you have no clue what I'm talking about. Either way I'm fine. I'm quite curious, actually, to see exactly how it is that you managed to con Mr Talreja.'

* * *

Ravi wears an ashen look on his face as he sits opposite Sarita.

'So, there's nothing that can be done, ma'am?'

'I'm sorry, Ravi. There's nothing to be done. Mihir is undergoing the tests even as we speak. As you know, the PM is yet to appoint an NSA, so that was one abstinence, leaving it at two votes against one. I suppose the grounds for seeking waiver weren't strong enough, not to mention the fact that Mihir doesn't exactly have a spotless record. Nobody's questioning his integrity, but the kind of torture he was subjected to, anybody . . .'

Ravi is curious. 'If only three votes were counted, that would be two votes against one in favour of the waiver. Anil surely voted against. Which means . . . wait, you voted against, too?'

Sarita glares at him. 'You really think I'd overrule your judgement on something like this?'

'No ma'am. It just seems more likely than the alternative, which is that Anjali voted against.'

Sarita smiles. It was Anjali.

For a few moments, Ravi is too stunned to respond. He exclaims, 'That's quite extraordinary. I didn't think she had it in her.'

The smile on Sarita's face gives way to a scowl. 'Had what in her, Ravi? I can't believe you're making this personal. It's not like she betrayed you or . . .'

Ravi shakes his head. 'No, no, not at all, ma'am. What I meant is . . .'

His voice trails off as his eyes dart towards the clock on the wall.

'I'll tell you what I meant, ma'am, in due time. But it most certainly is not what you think. For now, if you'll excuse me, I'd like to go do what I should have done ten minutes ago—check on Mihir and make sure he's doing okay.'

Ravi darts out of the office and gets into the elevator, which takes him ten floors down. He rushes towards the ward where Dr Himwal and a team of independent experts are packing up their equipment. Mihir is nowhere to be seen.

'Dr Himwal, where's Mihir?'

Dr Himwal shrugs. 'How should I know? As of twenty minutes ago, he was relieved from my care and taken away.'

'Taken away where, Dr Himwal? Don't tell me he . . .'

'Of course not, sir. He passed with flying colours. I have to tell you, in all my years of service in the military, and later here at the bureau, I've never met a single soldier or spy who's managed to hold out in the face of such brutal torture. Even the most battle-hardened at least end up revealing their names. It's only natural. Pushed to the limit, the body wants to preserve itself and all artificial defences crumble. But Mihir didn't even tell them his name, can you believe it? It's a miracle, truly.'

Ravi doesn't seem very interested. He already knows all this, which is why he had pushed so hard for the requirement to be waived. He is more eager to know where Mihir is, 'So, he went home?'

'I suppose so, sir. But I can't be sure. He left without saying a word.'

Ravi pulls out his phone and dials Mihir's number.

'The number you have dialled does not exist.'

Epilogue

Inside the opulent, high-ceilinged study at his residence in Chanakyapuri, Ravi is in high spirits, as he entertains his team. On his desk are the morning's papers, all plastered with bold headlines on their front pages: 'India's Osama Nabbed in Sensational Operation'; 'Massive ISI Conspiracy Unearthed: Dreaded Khalsa Tigers Terrorist Arrested After 20 Years Spills the Beans on Chilling Plan to Destroy India'; 'Families of Victims Celebrate as Mastermind of Mumbai Serial Blasts Lands in Counterterrorism Net'.

Ravi raises his glass to toast. 'We're of course celebrating belatedly. It took us a month to tie everything together before we could announce to the world, but that doesn't make this any less deserved. To get here you have all gone well beyond the line of duty and you have put your lives on the line . . . except Jose of course, who did absolutely nothing. But nevertheless, cheers, gentlemen!'

As Madan Singh, Examiner, Jose and Cyrus raise their glasses, Anjali glares at Ravi, who bites his tongue in apology, 'I'm terribly, sorry. What I meant to say was . . . cheers, lady and gentlemen! Please, drink up! Nobody's working tomorrow, and that's an order. But since I've mentioned work, there's one last thing before I forget . . . Cyrus, have you done the needful with your old avian friend?'

Cyrus nods. 'He has found his way back to Kashmir under the pretext of helping resolve a bitter feud between two warring factions of the Kashmiri militancy. He'll know if K2 ever gets reactivated again. And his family's been rehabilitated as well. We've helped his brother-in-law set up a carpet business, and we've also arranged for his asthmatic wife to get the best possible treatment right here in Delhi.'

'Well, that's that then. Drink up!'

Although they're all happy to be celebrating the fruits of nearly three years of relentless labour, an unacknowledged sense of dread looms over the room. And it is only after a few drinks that they're all sufficiently uninhibited to address the elephant in the room. Cyrus is the first to bring it up. 'I know you would have told us if you'd heard anything. But I'd still like to ask, sir . . . where on earth is Mihir? I don't know about you all, but I feel guilty about the fact that we're even celebrating. If not for Mihir, we wouldn't be here.'

Ravi, to strike a reassuring tone, says, 'I understand your anguish. I feel just as terrible.'

Jose downs his drink and pours himself another. His tone drops to an ominous register, 'What if he's . . . what if he's dead, sir?'

Anjali browses through a bookshelf, even as Ravi puts his arm around Jose comfortingly. 'If there's one thing I know for sure, it is that Mihir is still alive. Trust me, I've spared no effort in trying to track him down. If he was dead, we'd have known by now.'

Jose voices his doubts, 'Then why haven't we been able to find him, sir? Isn't it embarrassing that with all the resources at our disposal, we have no clue where he is?'

Ravi smiles. 'On the contrary, it is something to be proud of. The only reason we haven't been able to find him is because he doesn't want to be found. Goes to show just how skilled Mihir is. And so, we really shouldn't be worried. If he needs his space, let us give him that. He's endured unimaginable pain, so it's only natural . . .'

Ravi's attention wanders in Anjali's direction. She seems frozen as she stares blankly at a bookshelf in the corner. Sensing something amiss, he walks up to her, 'You've been looking at the same shelf for the last five minutes and haven't picked up a single book. What's the matter?'

Anjali is caught off guard. Her voice quivers. 'It's just . . . I feel terribly guilty sir. It's all my fault. If only I'd voted in favour of waiving the SOP, perhaps Mihir would have been here with us.'

Ravi shakes his head. 'Not at all, Anjali. When sixty rounds of waterboarding couldn't break him, you really think a narco test performed by his own people would? He would have left anyway. In fact, I'm glad that the test happened, and he cleared it. Otherwise, we'd technically have been left with no option but to consider him a rogue agent. And that would have been a really messy situation. So, I'm actually very glad that you voted against the waiver.'

'But I'm still very sorry, sir for second-guessing and being critical of your judgement. I'm sure you didn't expect that from me. In that moment, it seemed like the right thing to do.'

'And that is precisely what you were hired to do. To assess my judgement at all times. If I just wanted a yes–man or a yes–woman, there are plenty of them in the department already. But since we're having this discussion, I won't lie, I didn't see it coming and was genuinely stunned to discover that you voted against my motion. But not because I felt betrayed, but because I didn't think you had it in you to . . . you know, the courage to say and do the right thing, and be okay with being seen as indifferent or insensitive or even insubordinate. I was emotionally tangled up in Mihir's case, wasn't thinking straight. But you saw through it, and when you had the chance to put the brakes on an unreasonable demand I was making, you stepped up to do the right thing. Most people build their careers in bureaucracy through loyalty to individuals, and not the organization they serve. You are of a rarer breed, Anjali. The country is in dire need of more like you. The decision isn't up to me, and so I obviously can't promise anything, but I expect you to succeed me as . . .'

All eyes in the room turn towards Cyrus, who is leaping up in excitement, waving his phone for all to see. 'It's her. It's her. Gehna! She wants to give it another shot! She's coming tomorrow.'

Ravi raises his glass. 'Another toast! To Cyrus and Gehna.'

Madan Singh, who's now sufficiently tipsy, raises his glass. 'To second chances.'

Ravi's phone rings.

'Chief . . .'

'I'm given to understand you've applied for leave tomorrow, Ravi?'

'Yes, ma'am. I'm treating the team to drinks, like I'd mentioned to you. I expect all of us to be fairly hungover in the morning.'

'Well, sounds like you're having a wonderful time. But you might want to stop drinking and go to bed. The prime minister has invited the two of us to his residence tomorrow, to join him for . . .'

'Dinner, I hope? That should leave me enough time to make myself presentable.'

'Breakfast. I'll see you at 7 a.m. sharp.'

Ravi grumbles aloud as he hangs up, 'Looks like I have a date of my own.'

* * *

As they see Prime Minister Jadhav walking towards them, Sarita and Ravi strike an attentive pose on the well-manicured lawns of the prime minister's residence. As he smiles warmly at them, good mornings are voiced. First, Sarita. A moment later, Ravi. It's one of the peculiar and abiding customs of Indian bureaucracy. Even greetings are tendered in order of seniority.

The PM shakes their hands firmly, before pointing towards the gazebo, even as a peacock passes by. 'Please, let us walk.'

Sarita remarks, 'In all the years that I've come here, sir, I only had discussions on the lawn.'

'You might want to get used to it, Sarita. Ideally, this is where all national security meetings should happen. There's an anecdote from the Mahabharata that I've held close to my heart all through my political career—apparently, in the course of teaching young Yudhishthira the ways of statecraft,

Bhishma observed that secrets are best shared in the open, as opposed to a confined space.'

As they take their seats around the well laid-out table, the PM speaks up, 'So, I'm sure you're wondering why I've summoned you on this beautiful autumn morning. There's something that has been playing on my mind for the last few weeks, and I'd like to hear what you think, Ravi. Thanks to your unrelenting efforts, LeH has been neutralized, One K of K2 has been foiled and the other exposed. But the moment we put an end to one threat, another one springs up. It feels like we're constantly playing whack-a-mole. You clobber one, another pops up. The question I'm asking is . . . how do we usher in a terrorism-free India?'

Ravi, stoic-faced, looks at the prime minister with a hint of hesitation. 'Sir, I must tell you at the very outset that I do not have a solution. But what I can give you is a clearer description of the problem at hand. And since you mentioned the Mahabharata, I hope you will not mind if I play Vidur. I'd like to speak straight and get to the bottom of it.'

The PM chuckles. 'By all means, go ahead. I need Vidurs as my advisers. And I believe sincerely that a clear description of the problem at hand is already half the solution. So, please . . .'

'Thank you, sir. I believe that the problem comes down, at the most primal human level, to one thing: anxiety.'

The PM is curious, 'Anxiety? That's not what I expected to hear. I'm all ears, please go on . . .'

'Anxiety, in its rawest form, is not a bad thing. Indeed, it is the most potent force in the world. It is raw anxiety that has led to the greatest revolutions in the history of the world. Our freedom struggle, for that matter, was powered by the raw anxiety of the impoverished masses. At the same time, the most destructive endeavours undertaken by mankind have also been fuelled by raw anxiety. As you're very well aware sir, ours is a country united in its extraordinarily vast diversity. Linguistic, geographical, religious . . . there are a hundred different categories in which we can boast of genuinely rich diversity. And it is our greatest strength, there is no doubt. But diversity inevitably leads to feelings of superiority and inferiority, of majority and minority. Each identity and each group carry their own anxieties. It is human nature, after all. The majority is anxious about its place being usurped by the minority, the minority is fearful about being oppressed by the majority, I could just go on. But this is only natural, it's hardwired into us by evolution. But at the same time, we're also endowed with a capacity for being accommodating of the anxieties of others. Which is why although our anxieties are in constant collision with each other, we manage to get along just fine. The problem arises when these anxieties are deliberately fanned. Aided by technology, the warfare is constantly evolving. This has caused a change in the battlefield from physical spaces to cognitive domains. The internet has taken the battleground to our living rooms. Our enemies, in coming up with a plan like K2, have demonstrated that they've come to understand this very well. They don't need guns, and they don't need bombs. For there is no explosive that is nearly as destructive as raw anxiety.'

Ravi's voice trails off. Jadhav prods him, 'Go on, Ravi. Forget I'm even here. Speak your mind.'

'It's frightening, sir, every time I come to think of it. Our enemies have learnt all this from us. The way politics

has shaped up in our country since Independence is such that
the seeds of hatred and division seem to be the fundamental
ingredient of electoral victory. The enemy is not just outside,
but also within. Unless this changes, we're headed on a
very dangerous course. Unless our collective anxieties are
channelled into an anxiety for the future of this country
and the suffering of its people, a new Tabrez is going to
be born every day. I can think of no better example than
my own team, of how such a channelling can play out. A
Muslim, a Hindu, a Sikh, a Parsi, and a Christian . . . men,
women . . . unmindful of these identities, worked together,
and channelled all their anxieties to work for the safety and
well-being of their fellow citizens. And the results are for
all to see. Our enemies want to break us apart, but we must
remind them, and remind those within our own country
who buy into their lies, that there is something above and
beyond our divisions that continues to hold us together.
Like Allama Iqbal wrote, and we all sang throughout our
schooldays, "*Kuch baat hai ki hasti mit ti nahi hamari /Sadiyon
raha hai dushman daure jahan hamara* (Such is our existence
that it cannot be erased / Even though, for centuries, the
cycle of time has been our enemy)."'

The prime minister looks at Ravi with admiration. 'I
thought you said you don't have a solution . . .'

* * *

Ravi is in his office, looking into long-pending administrative
matters when the secure line rings.

'Hello. Ravi here.'

A strange yet typically bureaucratic voice greets him at the other end, 'The prime minister would like to speak to you. Please stay on the line.'

Ravi expresses his surprise. 'Are you sure you aren't mistaken? Perhaps it's the chief of the IB he wants to speak to?'

The PM's secretary laughs. 'This is the prime minister's office, Mr Kumar. We don't make mistakes. He wants to speak to you.'

The prime minister comes on the line a moment later. 'I'll get straight to it, Ravi. Sarita is superannuating in three weeks. There's no way I'm going to let her enjoy retirement so soon, and I've decided to appoint her as the National Security Advisor, a post that, as you know, has remained vacant for the last six months.'

Ravi is delighted. 'That is wonderful news, sir.'

'So, naturally, the Intelligence Bureau needs a new chief. And I'd like that to be you.'

Ravi is taken aback. Just then, Subramaniam rushes into Ravi's office with childlike excitement. Ravi signals to him to wait.

'As honoured as I am, I will have to most respectfully decline your offer, sir. This great institution is built on fairness and a well-established hierarchy and order of precedence. The chief of the IB, as you surely know, is de-facto the senior-most officer of the Indian Police Service. Such a massive promotion for someone like me who has over five years of service left would have a demoralizing effect on seniors and juniors alike. Nobody down the line will be sure of their career trajectories, and that uncertainty will have a detrimental impact on the efficiency of the organization as a whole. To use that word again, it will give rise to anxieties . . .'

The prime minister chuckles. 'I was told to expect this, and have already picked someone. I just want to check for myself. Anyway, the real reason I am calling you is to talk to you about a new agency that I'd like to institute. NCTO— National Counterterrorism Organisation. Fully autonomous, reporting directly to the PMO. And I'd like you to be its founding director.'

'I'm honoured, sir. But if I may ask, just to help me decide, how will NCTO be different from C3?'

'I'm not sure if you heard me clearly, Ravi. I'd like you to be its founding director, which means you get to decide. This can be your opportunity to put in place a more holistic approach to tackling terrorism. For the entirety of my term in office, you have complete freedom to set it up and structure it in alignment with the vision you described during our meeting. And you must know, it's a vision I wholeheartedly endorse.'

Ravi is overwhelmed. A few moments of silence pass before he finally responds, 'I'd be honoured to accept. Thank you, sir.'

'Thank you, Ravi.'

As soon as Ravi hangs up, Subramaniam rushes up to him, still reeling from childlike excitement. Ravi chuckles, 'What's the matter, Subramaniam? Don't tell me another grandchild?'

Subramaniam places a postcard on the desk. 'It's him, sir. It's him. Mihir. He has got in touch.' It is Ravi's turn to be filled with childlike excitement. He nearly jumps out of his seat, as he picks up the postcard and examines its neatly handwritten contents:

To my teacher,

I hope you will forgive me for leaving without a word. But I had to because you would have never let me go otherwise. I have embraced my final cover in all sincerity, and this is how I intend to live my life henceforth. I hope I have your blessings. But this does not mean that I am cutting off ties with you, or with the hallowed institution that I had the privilege of serving for the last three years. One thing will never change, no matter where I am or what I'm doing—Jananijanambhumishchswargadapigariyasi

PS: Please stop trying to track me down. You won't be able to because I learnt from the very best. But if you need to talk to me, or if I can ever be of service in any way, leave a message in the draft folder of the mail.

Yours,
Abhigyananda

Ravi can't stop smiling as he puts the postcard down. Subramaniam has an innocent question, 'But sir, where's the email ID and password?'

Ravi wears a cryptic look on his face as he gazes at a distant point. 'It's abhigyananda@cmail.com, and the password is a long one, Subramaniam: *Janani janambhumishch swargadapi gariyasi*. It means: Mother and motherland are greater than heaven.'